THE LOST WORLD

Novels by Edwin McDowell

THE LOST WORLD

TO KEEP OUR HONOR CLEAN

THREE CHEERS AND A TIGER

EDWIN McDoWELL

THE LOST
WoRLD

ST. MARTIN'S PRESS ▬ New York

Design by Judy Stagnitto

Library of Congress Cataloging-in-Publication Data

McDowell, Edwin.
    The lost world.

    "A Thomas Dunne book.
    I. Title.
PS3563.A2922L6   1988   813'.54   88-18222
ISBN 0-312-02301-4

First Edition

10 9 8 7 6 5 4 3 2 1

For
Sathie, Susan, Amy, and Eddie
Tsuruko Akimoto and Marguerite Foss
And to the memory of my brother,
John Joseph McDowell

The light turned red when I was halfway across Forty-third Street, forcing me to mark time on the traffic island separating Broadway and Seventh Avenue. While I waited for an opening in the stream of southbound taxicabs and delivery trucks, I saw him in front of the savings bank, laughing and jiving with the tall, muscular street photographer who was decked out in his familiar black Stetson hat, cowboy boots hand made of black leather, and a wide black belt studded with more rows of spikes than a fakir's bed.

Black Bart, as I called the coal black photographer when out of earshot, was a conspicuous target for the drug dealers, muggers, prostitutes, psychopaths, transvestites, and assorted other lowlifes who milled about the street corner he had staked out as his studio. That is, he would have been a target, except that his size discouraged any but the most reckless or the most deranged of the army of vagrants and psychotics who inhabited Times Square. When one of them made the mistake one night of trying to tear the camera strap from Black Bart's neck, the photographer flattened him with a single punch and stuffed him like the letter V into a wire trash container. Only when the crowd went from taunting the howling derelict to pelting him with trash and bottles did the photographer finally set him free.

This morning, though, I was less interested in Black Bart than his youthful companion, and as soon as the traffic light turned green I stepped into the street. But during the few seconds' wait, while impatient taxi drivers bullied me into surrendering the right of way, the youngster had spotted me and bolted toward Forty-second Street.

Had he run in the opposite direction, or even west on Forty-third, I would have given chase. But he must have sensed as much, which is why he lit out in the direction he did. Bounding like a frightened hare past the electronic games arcade, around a tourist snapping photos of his wife against a backdrop of giant billboards advertising Japanese cameras and film, and past a shop that specializes in king-size dildos and assorted other sexual implements, he scurried around the corner at New York's busiest intersection. There he could easily lose himself among the sightseers, the drug peddlers, and the merchant princes from Senegal who displayed watches and trinkets atop cardboard boxes. Or he could duck into the Times Square subway station, where eight lines converge and the labyrinth of grimy, spray-painted passageways makes pursuit virtually impossible.

So I abandoned the chase after only a few halfhearted steps and turned back to Black Bart, who among other adornments wore a large gold earring in his larger left lobe. "Mind telling me that young kid's name?" I asked, although I was reasonably sure he did mind. When he didn't reply I said, "Can you tell me how I can get hold of him?" I handed him my business card, which identified me as a reporter for the *New York Free Press*.

He looked me slowly up and down, studied my card for a few seconds, then tucked it into the black band around his hat, along with a half-dozen other business cards. "I didn't see no young kid," he said in a manner suggesting that the conversation was over.

I decided it was too early in the day to argue, even

though it was almost ten-thirty, and resumed my journey across Forty-third Street. Halfway down the block, on the sidewalk outside the Southland Hotel, where the city housed dozens of welfare families, a half-dozen black girls nine or ten years old were jumping rope and chanting a ribald couplet in that singsong cadence familiar to all kids.

None of the several other passersby paid any attention, nor did the children themselves appear to have any idea what they were saying. After listening to another chorus, I too continued on my way.

The *Free Press* was on Forty-fourth between Eighth and Ninth, but my usual first stop after emerging from the subway each morning was the coffee and doughnut shop on the northwest corner of Forty-third and Eighth—a shop heavily patronized by a coterie of bejeweled pimps, half of them outfitted in the white suits and floppy hats with purple feathers that were the uniform of the procurer's trade. They assembled at mid-morning, presumably after having tallied the take from the night before.

The shop was an anomaly in that sleazy neighborhood, where cocaine and crack far outsold coffee and crullers. But its steaming brew and warm doughnuts, especially its warm cinnamon rolls and apple fritters, beckoned me to Forty-third Street each morning, rather than the several delis or take-out shops along cleaner and safer Forty-fourth. But several of my *Free Press* colleagues, endowed with the skepticism that flows liberally through the veins of journalists, theorized that my commuting habits were dictated by an addiction to the stench of urine, which reeked from the walls and sidewalk along that entire glass-strewn block, or by the pleasure I derived from mingling with the street's bountiful population of perverts and male and female hookers.

Even Diane, my former roommate, was never entirely convinced that hunger alone steered me past the *Times*, which dominated the north side of Forty-third. "That's absurd," I declared. "I've never even noticed its gray stone exterior, its revolving doors, its blue and white company flag, and its fifteen exterior light globes with the word TIMES painted on them."

Seated at my desk this morning in the half-deserted newsroom, I flipped rapidly through the front section of the paper, fearful that my story had been pulled at the last minute. Then I breathed a sign of relief—it made it in. Only then did I sip from the coffee container, to fortify myself against whatever felonious assaults the copy-editors had inflicted on my prose. But before I could even begin this masochistic exercise, the affably overweight Irwin Haines shuffled over to my desk in his flatfooted walk, which reminded me of half the deli waiters along Seventh Avenue. He was wearing his omnipresent bedroom slippers and a grin that, anywhere but in a newspaper office, would have gotten him committed.

"I come bearing tidings of great joy," declared the city editor, snapping his trademark red suspenders.

"Let me guess." I placed the coffee cup on the desk with feigned weariness. "You have a moving human interest story for me: 'New Jersey Minister Robbed After Liaison With Transvestite.' 'Boy Scout Leader Propositions Undercover Cop.' 'Conservative Legislator, Foe of Porno Industry, Unmasked as Chicken-Hawk.' You're too late—they were all in the *Post* last week."

"You really are getting cynical," Haines chided. "Maybe we should switch you to another beat."

"Oh, please don't do that, Br'er Haines," I pleaded, rolling my eyes wildly. "Do anything else you want, throw me in that briar patch even, but don't take me out of Times Square."

Haines laughed appreciatively, the sound originating just behind his bow tie and playing itself out as a grin on his florid face. "Soon, Alex, as soon as I can," he assured me, as he had assured me since the very first week I was assigned to cover Times Square. "Meanwhile, I'm still trying to get you combat pay."

I couldn't help but smile. Haines was a decent person and a quite good editor, working for an undistinguished and financially precarious "all day" daily newspaper—"all day" meaning that our first edition came out just late enough in the morning so that we could publish imaginative rewrites of the *Times* and *Daily News*. My banishment to the Times Square beat had been decreed by Kenneth Parks, the managing editor, who from his glass-paneled sanctum at the far end of the newsroom laid down the law at "the *Freep*" (as employees referred to the *Free Press*), with no less authority than Roy Bean had laid down the law west of the Pecos.

"I have tidings for you also," I said. "You show me yours first and I'll show you mine."

"Be careful, Irwin, Shaw's making indecent suggestions again," warned Jill Leigh, our best general assignment reporter. Having just arrived at her desk, she was busy unpacking what looked like enough food for a picnic.

"Expecting visitors?" Haines asked, although he was well aware of her legendary appetite.

Jill, an Audrey Hepburn look-alike in size and weight, merely smiled at his cattiness, then bit appreciatively into a bagel piled high with cream cheese and lox, all the while thumbing hurriedly through the newspaper with her free hand.

"Oh, before I give you the good news, this came in the morning mail," Haines said, handing me a press release.

I read it with the same mixture of amusement and amazement that, in my early days as a reporter out West, I reserved for letters and editorials about gun laws and coyote control. "I'll hang on to it," I said finally, "in case things get slow on my beat."

Jill interrupted her banquet long enough to ask,

"What's so amusing?" I handed her the announcement and in a moment she too was grinning. The handbill declared:

FREAK SHOW COMING TO BIG APPLE

Sterling Brothers' World Famous Freak Show, acclaimed throughout Europe, Asia, and Latin America, will open a week-long engagement in historic Times Square on Sept. 5.

A two-hour live spectacular of the fascinating and grotesque, the XXX-rated show features sights never seen even in adult theaters or home videos. No optical illusions or trickery.

The show comes direct from sellout performances in London, Paris, and Berlin to its first appearance ever in the Big Apple. Many of the individual exhibits are themselves worth the price of admission, including:

• Roy and Rita, 30-year-old Siamese Twins who make love to different partners at the same time.

• Little Richard, the five-foot-four-inch marvel with the longest sex organ on record.

• Dorothy Love, the curvaceous 20-year-old who is the victim of one of nature's cruelest jokes.

• Glenda Gulp, the most unusual sword swallower ever to play Broadway.

All performances at the King Theater, 43rd Street between Seventh and Eighth Avenues, in the heart of New York's famous Great White Way. Show time 9 P.M., matinees Sunday and Wednesday at 2 P.M. Tickets, $20 and $25, can be purchased at any Tickets International or at the door.

"Just what Times Square needs, another class act," Jill said, pouring another cup of decaffeinated coffee from a large thermos.

"What I can't figure out is why anybody would pay to see in a theater what they can see for free on any street in Times Square," Haines said, shaking his head and shuffling his slippered feet.

"Don't tell me you aren't curious to get a peek at Little Richard," I kidded Jill.

"I'm dying of curiosity," she replied, unwrapping Brie cheese to eat with her Granny Smith apple. "But I doubt if any of my boyfriends will take me—they're all the jealous type. Either that or sore losers. So I guess I'll have to hear all about it from you."

I shook my head. "With any luck, I'll be back on a real beat by then, not playing Livingstone or Margaret Meade in Times Square."

"That's what I wanted to tell you," Haines said. "Your story about getting jumped by that pack of kids brought in so many letters that Parks ordered a full page of them to run on Sunday."

"I didn't know that many of our readers knew how to write," Jill said sweetly, piling the cheese high on the section of apple.

I feigned indifference, but I was secretly pleased. I had hoped my story would elicit some sort of response, especially from Parks. When he condemned me to my journalistic Elba, he assured me he considered it an important beat—important far beyond Times Square proper, that triangular wedge at the junction of Forty-second Street where Broadway crosses Seventh Avenue. It was important, he said, because the Times Square "core area"—between Fortieth and Fiftieth Streets, Seventh to Ninth

Avenues—encompassed the world famous Broadway theater district. It was important because the porn shops and so-called massage parlors were finally being zoned out of existence and the area upgraded to make way for hotels, office buildings, and restaurants. And it was important because here was a chance to upstage the *Times* on its very own turf.

"They cover it well when they cover it," Parks grudgingly acknowledged, "but they don't go in for a lot of crime stories and muggings and—"

"Depravity?"

The managing editor, who chain-smoked unlit cigarettes, looked to see if I was mocking him, but my face was expressionless. Apparently satisfied, he took a deep drag and replied, "I suppose you could say depravity. Why not? But not only that. We couldn't outsensationalize the *Post* even if we wanted to."

He walked slowly over to the large detailed map of mid-Manhattan, which shared the wall with an equally large oil painting of our publisher, Martha Liston, and he riveted his attention on Times Square. "What we can do is give readers a sense of movement, activity, excitement about the area," he said, with what for him passed for evangelic fervor. "I want you to write about every sensational crime in the area and most of the routine ones also.

"I want you to write about honest clerks and conscientious waitresses who *bust* their asses for two or three hundred dollars a week, while people right outside their door make more than that in half an hour *selling* their asses." He was getting wound up, and as he did his voice rose by several notes.

"I want you to talk to cops on the beat, find out how working this high-crime area affects their attitudes toward people, their marriages, and their off-duty relationships. Talk to the dudes who are really undercover cops and the 'bag ladies' who are really policewomen.

"Talk to the psychiatrists, psychologists, and mental health workers, find out why Times Square has become one gigantic outpatient ward for schizophrenics, psychotics, catatonics, paranoids, and alcoholics."

His eyes fairly glowed as he spoke, the way Hearst's must have glowed almost a century earlier when he dispatched Remington to Cuba. But Parks didn't want another Spanish-American war, unless maybe it was with the Hispanics in New York, whose presence made him uneasy. Nor did he care much about putting out a newspaper to impress out-of-towners, who bought pitifully few copies of the *Free Press.* No! What obsessed him was the possibility of upstaging the *Times,* from which he had abruptly departed a half-dozen years before for reasons that, depending on what *Free Press* veteran you talked to, had become increasingly vague with each passing year.

I might have fared worse—for example, by being assigned to cover the third-rate social events to which the *Free Press* was invited after the other papers turned them down. And I have no doubt that Parks wanted a veteran reporter to handle the Times Square beat. But his decision to assign me was not without its ironic aspects: in mid-January, at the height of the Broadway season, he had unceremoniously ousted me as *Free Press* drama critic after less than six months on the job—and in the very week I first got my name on a marquee, hailing the merits of a musical comedy. There, sharing the bill with a pithy remark from a television critic who never met a play he didn't like, it read: "SPIRITED"—SHAW, FREE PRESS. What I actually wrote was, "Even if the songs and dances had been twice as spirited, it wouldn't salvage this disaster."

I was still debating whether to protest the deception or to continue enjoying my brief fame when Parks had called me into his office and figuratively ripped the critic's chevrons from my sleeve.

I was "too cynical," he had said. But the real reason, I

subsequently learned from Bessie Gath, his secretary, was that the principal financial backer of the last show I panned was Lester Kable, a close friend of Martha Liston.

When I heard that, I had an urge to cross out the word FREE on the front of the building, but in our graffiti-scrawled neighborhood no one would have noticed. I can imagine the satisfaction it gave Parks when I swapped my two center-front seats on Broadway for a ringside one at Times Square. A month after my dethronement, Diane moved out on me and in with a guy who had something to do with *Playbill*, the theater magazine.

"Now you show me yours," I heard Haines say, his words snapping me out of my mid-morning reverie.

"Oh, that," I said, remembering. "I saw him this morning—my 'assailant.'"

"That little squirt? Where? Why didn't you kick his ass and drag him into the station house?"

"Because he saw me first," I replied, explaining how he took off running.

Jill stopped noshing long enough to offer solace. "It's only a matter of time before the cops get him and his buddies, thanks to your article."

"I hope so, but don't bet on it. You can't believe how many tunnels there are down there. Any street-smart kid could hide out in them for months, maybe years."

Seeing Haines's eyebrows arch upward toward his jug ears, I added, "Yes, Irwin, it *would* make a good story, and it just so happens I'm working on it."

"If you ever catch that little son of a bitch," the city editor said, "make sure you get lots of photos before you break his butt."

"Where would you suggest I take him? Randall Justin's?" I asked, mentioning a fashionable photographer on the Upper East Side.

"Hire a street photographer," Jill said. "Some of them

would photograph their mother being strangled, if the price was right."

"You mean there are some who wouldn't?" Haines remarked, padding off in his flatfooted gait.

I settled back to finish the newspaper, reading it the way serious journalists do—turning first not to stories about war, or Congress, or malfeasance, but to their own stories, seeing what page they are displayed on and at what length.

I tried to concentrate on reading but my attention was constantly drawn to Jill's cornucopia. Within minutes a tin of smoked salmon emerged, followed by miniature Scandinavian toasts and assorted wursts—all of it presumably intended to keep hunger at bay. Seeing me staring, she sighed. "It's a terrible curse," she said finally, in a voice laden with pity, "being afflicted with anorexia nervosa."

I still did not know the name of "that little squirt," but I was determined to find out. First, though, I wanted to retrieve my credit cards and driver's license, if they hadn't been sold or destroyed, and then I would see about having him and his delinquent friends arrested.

At the time it happened I had been on the Times Square beat only about a month, churning out stories often enough to keep Parks off my back. Returning from a jam session in the Village late one Saturday night, I decided to stop by Forty-second Street, at the height of its nocturnal debauchery.

"When I know you better I might follow you into Hell," said my date, one of the many free-lance writers who cluster around newspapers, "but there's no way I'll go with you to Times Square at night—especially Saturday night."

I didn't blame her, but since my curiosity overcame my concupiscence I dropped her off at her apartment and had the taxi driver take me to Forty-second and Sixth. I wanted to approach Broadway gradually, rather than be plunked into the middle of it by taxicab. Besides, I was not particularly anxious to haul out my wallet at midnight in Times Square, even within the relatively safe confines of a cab.

By the time I walked over to Seventh Avenue, past one store after another whose windows were covered by heavy metal gates or grills, I had traveled in less than fifteen minutes from the affluent Upper East Side to Manhattan's neon netherworld of vice. Vice! The word had an old-fashioned ring to it, like a word from a police report. Yet how else to describe a neighborhood overrun by hookers young and old, transvestites big and small, and soft-eyed Hispanic boys barely in their teens, who from the shadows of a dozen doorways offered to sell their bodies?

Young toughs, in muscle shirts or naked to the waist, offered a pharmacopeia of drugs for sale, under the marquees of movie theaters where XXX-rated flicks vied with martial arts films from the Orient. A half-dozen undernourished children from nearby welfare hotels darted playfully in and out among the drug dealers. Dudes staggering under the weight of "blaster boxes" perched on their shoulders sauntered by at intervals, all at ear-shattering volume.

Like the peddlers, the majority of strollers were blacks or Hispanics, and they included many young couples and families who found the remaining legitimate Times Square movie theaters an inexpensive, air-conditioned diversion. But the most determined strollers were middle-class whites—high school and college-age kids who made most of the drug purchases, and middle-aged men who after brief, whispered conversations followed the whores or young boys to sleazy "hot sheet" hotels in side streets nearby.

A sidewalk preacher in a clerical collar and an ill-fitting suit shouted warnings through a bullhorn, inveighing against Sodom and Gomorrah while occasionally dropping to one knee and thumping his open Bible against the other. During the brief time I watched his performance, the preacher attracted arguments and insults, but no converts and few donations. By contrast, the three white-robed black "ministers" in front of the subway entrance managed, through a deft combination of salesmanship and the hint of intimidation, to raise considerable money for what their poster said was a school for handicapped children in Harlem.

After viewing the passing parade for several minutes, and recalling Dostoyevsky's description of the slums of old St. Petersburg, where "no figure, however queer, would have caused surprise," I started toward Eighth Avenue. I thought about walking over to the Port Authority Bus Terminal to gather material for a possible article about the hustlers who for a "tip" directed bewildered or frightened passengers to waiting taxis. But I hadn't gone twenty yards when I was knocked down and my wallet was torn from my hip pocket as I hurtled toward the sidewalk.

Scrambling angrily to my feet, I saw a young Hispanic kid duck into the crowd. I started to pursue him when suddenly I found myself surrounded by a half-dozen ragged and dirty kids who, except for their color and the "felony sneakers" they all wore, looked like they might have stepped from the pages of a Dickens novel.

"Get out of here," I threatened, pushing them away as they inquired after my health and tried to brush off my clothes.

"What'sa matter, man, you don't want no help?" said a voice that was at once youthful and threatening. Its owner was a small, wiry Hispanic kid, no more than fifteen. His eyes were as wild as they were dark, and his shock of jet black hair looked as if it had not been cut or shampooed in years. His companions, a melange of Hispanics and blacks, were equally unkempt.

"No, I don't want help," I replied, trying to push him aside. As small as he was, though, I could not maneuver him out of my way. As I grabbed his thin wrist, intending to twist his arm behind his back until he got the message, he quickly emitted a sharp whistle—and again I found myself sprawled in the middle of the sidewalk, listening to the muffled footsteps as my assailants dashed off.

That was the last I saw of the gang that night, but for an hour or more afterwards they rampaged through Times Square, stealing pocketbooks, snatching chains from necks, and swarming over the few people who tried to resist. But I didn't learn all that until I stopped by the Midtown South Precinct on Monday morning, because by the time I had picked myself up a second time I realized I was not only bruised but broke—stranded in Times Square without a cent.

I decided to see if any of my friends were at the *Free Press* at this hour. Passing the *Times* en route, I fantasized about going through one of the revolving doors, flashing my press card at the security guard in the lobby, and asking to borrow ten bucks. When I remembered my press card was in my missing wallet, I modified the fantasy to dropping by my favorite coffee shop to put the touch on whatever pimp might still be about.

The *Times* loading platforms were aswarm with their nightly activity, and a half-dozen truck motors were noisily revving up while awaiting the final edition. Printers, including two wearing hats fashioned out of a page of newspaper, leaned against the building, leisurely watching the parade of drunks and derelicts. Despite the late hour, a bunch of dirty-faced kids were frolicking outside the Midtown Arms, the other hotel on Forty-third that housed families on welfare—if "housed" is the proper word for hotels that rented rooms to prostitutes and pushers and where security guards not infrequently sold drugs to the kids.

The *Free Press* was almost deserted, although I half hoped to find Jill Leigh finishing up a late dinner or early breakfast. Her journalistic talent, genial nature, and good looks, highlighted by sparkling hazel eyes and matching shoulder-length hair, made her a pleasure to work with. Those qualities were especially endearing at the *Free Press*, whose antiseptic newsroom lacked the practiced disorder and confusion that made most newspapers such enjoyable places to work, and made newsrooms in New York blood relations of newsrooms everywhere.

Fortunately, Gilbert Shipley, my successor as drama critic, was still hanging around an hour or more after having finished a review of a new musical, so I borrowed cab fare from him.

"Hope it wasn't a cynical review," I said, pocketing the ten dollars.

He smirked. He knew what had happened to me, and he understood how to prevent its happening to him. He was a veteran of a hundred journalistic wars—wars in which he had won unconditional victories, or sometimes surrendered without firing a shot, or sometimes prudently sought a truce. His only serious wound had been self-inflicted, when as a columnist early in his career he had plagiarized several passages from an obscure novelist active three decades earlier. He survived, but the stigma remained with him like a birthmark that eventually fades but never quite disappears.

"The word 'cynical' isn't even in my vocabulary,"

Shipley replied. "In fact," he said, reaching into his desk drawer and withdrawing a well-thumbed thesaurus, "neither are bad, stinko, lousy, terrible, awful, or any other words that might land me back on night rewrite."

I laughed, thanked him again for the loan, commented on how empty the newsroom was this time of night, and started to leave. "By the way," he said, "I don't think I ever told you, but you were a damn good critic." I looked for a glimmer of irony and was pleased there was none.

"A remark like that deserves a drink," I said, withdrawing his money from my pocket and waggling it between my thumb and index finger. "I can make it home on half of this, and with the other half we can have a blowout at Gus's."

Gus's was the atmospheric (i.e., inexpensive) bar directly across the street that catered to the *Free Press* crowd, to many of the financially strapped actors and artists who lived at Manhattan Plaza on Ninth Avenue and Forty-third, and to some of the upscale residents who had been buying and renovating the neighborhood brownstones. It had little of the clubby atmosphere that distinguished Bleecks, that home-away-from-home for reporters and editors of the late *Herald-Tribune*. On the East Side, Gus's would have been considered shabby but delightfully proletarian. On the West Side, though, it was considered proletarian but appropriately shabby. Its principal attraction, aside from its proximity to the *Freep* and its tolerable degree of sanitation, was that it served what may have been Manhattan's only forty-five-cent glass of draught beer, along with unlimited bowls of popcorn.

"I'd love it," Shipley replied without hesitation. "I can see the picture caption in my scrapbook now: 'Drama critic unwinds at Gus's while aspiring starlets line up at the newsstand, awaiting his verdict with bated breath.'" He paused, "You know, there's one thing I've always wondered."

"What's that?"

He switched off his word processor. "Just what in the name of God is 'bated breath'?"

A few weeks after I was mugged, I provided Kenneth Parks with some of the most enjoyable moments of his journalistic career—first, when I asked if the *Free Press* would reimburse me for the forty-one dollars I lost in the attack and second, when I turned out a succession of articles he said would annoy the editors of the *Times*.

I never heard whether they had that effect, but it was obvious that Parks was obsessed by the Newspaper of Record. Whenever he mentioned it, I listened for the thump of a peg leg on the bare newsroom floor, and many a time I stifled an impulse to reply, "Aye, aye, Captain Ahab."

Neither rich nor famous, the woefully understaffed *Free Press* was forced to make a virtue of necessity by stressing feature articles over hard news. Although the best of our reporters strived for a blend of style and substance, the worst used our breezy style to vent spleen, grind axes, and settle scores. The *Columbia Journalism Review* and other keepers of the journalistic flame periodically deplored the worst examples of the journalism practiced by the *Free Press*, but to my satisfaction, they had never singled out anything I had written.

However, Parks, and I suppose Martha Liston, considered our soft-news approach essential in an age when most people get their news from television, with its high excitement quotient and the short attention span of its audiences. Since we printed three editions between six A.M. and four P.M., we needed a formula that conveyed the illusion of competition with the established morning and afternoon dailies. And in the absence of a Sunday magazine or the weekend opinion section that on many papers allowed a departure from the usual journalistic forms, our unorthodox formula often worked to our advantage.

For example, my first-person account of my ordeal at the hands of the youth gang elicited a fan letter from none other than Lester Kable, the very impresario whose complaints to the publisher resulted in my ouster as drama critic. Regrettably, however, my account was not sufficiently compelling to move Liston or Parks to restore me to my critic's easy chair.

The next day, after interviewing Times Square merchants, I wrote a story saying that the youth gang (which in both stories Parks changed to "wolf pack") usually struck shortly after midnight. I quoted several victims, including a sixty-one-year-old Hispanic charwoman, who described how various gangs rampaged through side streets with clubs and chains, or swooped down on subway platforms before terrified passengers knew what hit them.

A few days later I turned my attention to the mobsters who controlled the bulk of Times Square's illegal activities, often using minors as prostitutes and drug couriers. "Immune from prosecution as adults," I wrote, "hundreds of thirteen- or fourteen-year-old boys and girls—kids who should be getting ready for summer camp, or the seashore, or Little League baseball—are pitiful pawns of adult criminals. Some of the youthful hustlers make more money in a week than they could earn in six months of honest work. But for the great majority, the payoff is a steady descent into the depths of one of the nation's most sordid and most brutal neighborhoods."

I also wrote that for years it was believed that if a visitor stood long enough at Forty-second Street between Broadway and Seventh, the unofficial "Crossroads of the World," he would eventually see every living acquaintance. By the same token, I continued, if that same person marked time by reading even a fraction of the reports and studies that had been churned out by blue-ribbon panels about the architecture, redevelopment, and crime problems of Times Square, he would have been exposed to almost every zany proposal the human mind can conceive. I then proceeded to cite a number of actual recommendations, everything from turning the area into a dirigible base to making it into a detention center for illegal aliens.

My stories may not have measured up to the reportorial standard set by the late Meyer Berger, but they impressed the people who mattered to me—Parks, Haines, and my colleagues, to be sure, but also some of the more cooperative officers in the Midtown North and Midtown South precincts, which shared jurisdiction in greater Times Square.

Despite the *Freep*'s less than sterling reputation among academics, and despite Parks's warning to avoid taking an academic approach to my beat, my articles enabled me to strike up acquaintances with younger sociologists and urban affairs scholars, who did not pretend to be experts about the Times Square fleshpots and scams, but who were willing to discuss their research with me.

I went out of my way to get to know many of the hardworking waitresses, clerks, and countermen in fast-food restaurants and delicatessens in the area.

I spoke to wary cashiers at Forty-second Street movie theaters, in hopes that one day they might tell me about their patrons.

As I grew more sure of myself, and as my initial jitters subsided just as they had when I was a young wire service reporter in Vietnam, I even nodded to some of the street-corner drug peddlers who were dealing crack, heroin, syringes, and needles. Their studied lack of response was clearly intended to remind me I was on their turf uninvited. In fact, the *un*welcome mat was perpetually out for all but a mark or a john, except in three instances: during the morning and evening rush hours, when thousands of commuters poured out of the nearby Port Authority Bus Terminal and overran Times Square on their way to work in Manhattan's skyscrapers. On Wednesday afternoons, when flocks of suburban matrons attended Broadway matinees. And on Friday and Saturday evenings, when poor families from the Bronx, young couples from Jersey and Connecticut, and tourists from the Midwest (who harbored foolishly outdated images of the Great White Way) visited Times Square to admire the miles of neon lights, to gorge themselves on pale hot dogs and anemic-looking pizza, and to buy mock newspapers with screaming, ribald headlines.

But the casual visitors and innocents were generally gone by eleven-thirty, and by midnight a different cast of characters began converging on the Square—youthful sociopaths from the Bronx and Brooklyn, hopheads from Hoboken and Hackensack, thrill-seekers from Staten Island and Stamford looking to buy or sell a variety of illegal pleasures. This occupying army of outlaws and outcasts rapidly changed the area's character from "naughty" to menacing, transforming it into a combat zone.

I wrote several stories tracing the decline of Times Square since its glory days, and I compiled arrest records from the two Midtown precincts to show the dangers that awaited the reckless or the unwitting, but they did little if anything to stem the nightly influx.

Using the Latin term in our respectable family newspaper, I explained how many a respectable commuter from Jersey stopped off for an early-morning blow job on the way to the office. But I made it clear that most of the serious action took place after midnight, when hard-core Times Square—the Times Square unknown to most academic theorists—sprang to life. Parking lots became shooting galleries for drugs. Convoys of cars bearing out-of-state license plates circled the blocks looking for hookers. A wide range of sex acts were hurriedly performed in the shadows of stores, apartment buildings, schools, even churches—shadows that also provided cover for muggers, robbers, and rapists.

I was mindful of those shadows when I left the *Free Press* just after midnight one evening, having labored much too long on a story about the most recent legal challenge to the redevelopment plans for Times Square. Unable to find an empty cab, I decided to walk to Forty-second and Seventh to board the Broadway local for Sixty-sixth Street, the subway stop closest to my apartment on West End Avenue.

When I reached Forty-third and Seventh a voice behind me growled, "What'd you say your name was, man?" I turned and to my relief saw Black Bart, decked out in his usual cowboy duds but now sporting a pair of red boots whose glitter seemed to reflect Broadway's neon lights.

Since I had already given him my business card, I decided to reciprocate his feigned ignorance. "Madam, I'm Adam," I replied promptly, invoking the only palindrome I could remember at that moment.

"And you're from Erehwon, I suppose," he repeated, his mahogany face as stoic as always.

Erehwon! A literary type in Times Square, of all places. I shook my head, impressed by his allusion to Samuel Butler's utopian vision.

"Then I guess I don't have a message for you," he added, finally revealing the trace of a smile.

"Who *do* you have a message for?"

It was his turn to shake his head. "The owner of this." He dangled a faded blue wallet before me.

"That's mine," I said. "How'd you get it?"

"Can't be yours," he replied, sliding it into his hip pocket. "Fellow who found it told me who to give it to, but he didn't mention any Adam."

I was about to reply when a towheaded kid in his early twenties fled wildly down the sidewalk, shoving aside pedestrians and shouting for help. Seconds later a pursuer came racing after him, naked from the waist up and brandishing a savage-looking hunting knife similar to those found in any number of Times Square shop windows.

Describing the incident in a story published later that week, I wrote that the intended victim apparently got away, because there were no homicides reported in Times Square that night, and none of the nearby emergency rooms admitted anyone answering his description. I concluded with a comment from Raymond Nelson—which I learned was Black Bart's real name—that the quarry probably got away for the same reason the rabbit in the fable eluded the fox: "Because the fox was only running for a meal, while the rabbit was running for his life."

"It's mine," I repeated, referring to the wallet. "My name's Shaw—Alex Shaw. Another way you can tell it's mine," I added, "there's forty-one dollars in it."

He eyed me carefully before tossing me the wallet. "There may have been forty-one dollars when you lost it, but all that's left is your driver's license."

I let pass his use of the word "lost," since I was happy enough about not having to make a trip downtown to the motor vehicle department for another driver's license. Still, I could not resist asking, "Who did you say 'found' it?"

"He wants to meet you. On this corner, tomorrow. Three o'clock."

"I imagine he wants a reward," I said, making no effort to disguise my sarcasm. "For finding it and returning it practically intact."

Bart—that is, Nelson—shook his head. "No reward. Just your word that you won't have him arrested or won't try to restrain him."

"Arrested? Restrain him? Who is this character, Mighty Joe Young?"

"His name's Dingo."

When he offered no further explanation I asked, "First or last name?"

"His only name."

"How will I know him?"

"He knows you."

Knows me? By sight? From my writing? I was puzzled, but it was clear that I'd have to wait at least a day for the answers. "What kind of name is Dingo?" I finally asked.

"I'm surprised that somebody who writes about wolf packs doesn't know," he said, tacitly acknowledging that he read my articles and thus had known my identity all along. "A dingo's a wild dog."

"Yeah, now I remember," I said. "From Japan . . . or is it China?"

"Australia. It's a dog with a head like a wolf," he said, enjoying playing the pedagogue. "It travels in groups and hunts at night. Instead of barking, though, it howls."

"And," I added, "it inhabits Times Square after midnight?"

Every trace of his grin disappeared. "Three o'clock," he said before turning away. "And no funny stuff."

During lunch the next day, at an Indian restaurant owned by Koreans above a porno bookshop on Eighth Avenue, I told Jill about my mysterious appointment. I thought she would be mildly interested, but I was unprepared for the shock of seeing her leave her order of paratha bread untouched as she listened in rapt silence. "Do you have any idea who it could be?" she asked finally. "Is it possible you're being set up?"

"Anything's possible here in Dodge-City-by-the-Hudson. That's why I'm telling you—so that if I wind up in concrete boots at the bottom of the East River you'll have something to spice up my obit." I took a drink of my Indian beer, rather enjoying her look of concern. "Speaking of Dodge City," I added, suddenly remembering one of my favorite trivia items, "did you know that Bat Masterson, the Dodge City gunfighter, spent the last eighteen years of his life just a few blocks from here? He was a sportswriter for the *Morning Telegraph*."

She gave me a partial smile, indicating that she didn't know if I was putting her on. "Scout's honor," I said. Then, eager to impress her further, I continued, "And one of the pallbearers at his funeral was Damon Runyon, who when he died had his own ashes scattered over Times Square by Eddie Rickenbacker."

She looked puzzled. "Who is Eddie Rickenbacker?"

Now it was my turn to wonder about being put on. "Skip it," I said with a shrug. "Some other time. For now, I have no idea who I'm about to meet. My hope is it'll be the leader of that gang of kids."

"Well, be careful," she said, patting my hand.

Even though the rendezvous was scheduled for broad daylight on one of the busiest corners of New York, I could not rid myself of the thought that less than a month earlier a teenager from Cleveland had been stabbed in the heart on that very spot in mid-afternoon, and the police could not find a single eyewitness to his murder. So I was not without some apprehension when at three o'clock sharp, with Raymond Nelson nowhere in sight, I stationed myself in front of the bank and waited.

And waited.

And waited some more.

At three-fifty I said the hell with it and started toward Forty-second Street, heading for the Port Authority bus terminal to pick up an analysis I had requested some days earlier of the number of commuters who arrived at the terminal each morning, from what cities, and on how many buses. But I hadn't gone thirty feet when someone bellowed, "Shaw!"

I spun around, only to find myself in the embrace of a guy on roller skates sporting a Mohawk haircut. His face was painted with vertical red, white, and blue stripes. As we disentangled, I heard my name again, this time from a voice off to my side.

I barely avoided colliding with two teenagers, a male and female wearing identical blue T-shirts with the same raunchy slogan, but I finally spotted Nelson through the crowd. Beside him stood the elusive little thief who had fled from me the other day.

"Shaw, this is Dingo," the photographer said, studying my reaction as I gazed at his feral companion.

"We're old friends," I replied acidly, making no move to shake hands with the Wild Boy of Aveyron. When he also made no gesture of friendship I said, "You owe me forty-one dollars."

He took a deep drag on a cigarette that did not smell like anything manufactured by the American Tobacco

25

Company, and blew a few smoke rings. Then, in a youthful voice with a slight Hispanic accent, he declared defiantly, "I don't owe you a fuckin' thing."

Nelson, amused at my surprise and discomfort, moved slowly away, struggling to keep a straight face. A nearby Senegalese peddler sniffed the air several times, then looked at the four-foot ten-inch Dingo with a broad grin of recognition.

The contrast between the boy's size and his vocabulary was so striking that I could barely contain either my laughter or my indignation. But he seemed unamused. His dark eyes darted back and forth as he stood there, back pressed against the wall of the bank, alert to any untoward movement. His shock of thick black hair featured a cowlick more unruly than most. There was the suggestion of a handsome boy beneath the dirt and dishevelment.

Dingo! His name suited him so well that I almost expected to hear him howl. But he remained silent. "Bla—" I caught myself in time. "Nelson said you wanted to see me." I waited for him to comment, but when he didn't I added, "Do you want to talk here or go somewhere private?"

At my question he flattened himself against the wall, and I had visions of him bounding up the street again. I can't remember having seen eyes filled with so much suspicion, certainly not youthful eyes. "Someplace private?" he repeated scornfully. "Like where? The police station? Or do you think I'm a fuckin' chicken?"

He was obviously no chicken in the usual sense of that word, and it took me a moment to realize he was using the word in its Times Square sense, that of a boy who sells himself to pedophiles—men, often respectable family men, known as chicken hawks.

"I wasn't thinking of either one," I said, trying to sound indifferent. "Right here suits me fine."

I assumed he was thinking it over, but he was studying

two policemen passing on horseback. As they continued up Broadway, he turned back to me. "Where was you thinkin'?" he demanded.

I hadn't any place in mind, but spotting the digital time-and-temperature clock atop Nathan's Famous across the street I nodded in that direction and said, "I wouldn't mind a hot dog. I haven't eaten all day."

He looked across Broadway at the bright green-and-yellow building, and I saw he was tempted. I didn't wonder, for he was so undernourished his rib cage showed through his torn T-shirt. Then without a word he turned and dashed into the street against the light, narrowly avoiding a bicycle messenger who was weaving recklessly through traffic and setting off a chorus of shrieking brakes and blowing horns. Shouting obscenities at the bike rider and flipping the bird at the drivers, he somehow arrived safely on the other side. I waited for the green light, a precaution only slightly less hazardous than the method Dingo chose, and entered the restaurant without a word to the boy, who followed momentarily.

At the counter I ordered a hot dog and French fries. "How many you want?" I asked, turning to Dingo.

"None," he answered, his voice dripping with youthful scorn.

I shrugged and ordered one more of each. After loading the hot dogs with mustard, but passing up the relish, which looked like it had been bathed in chlorophyll, I ordered a soda and a draft beer and looked for a seat. As I descended the broad stairway, a bleached blonde, her exposed, lumpy body a gallery of exotic tattoo designs, winked at me and rolled her tongue suggestively around her parted lips as she rode up the escalator.

I cringed from embarrassment for Dingo, but when I looked back he was still standing at the top of the stairs. Not until he had apparently satisfied himself that it wasn't a setup did he begin his cautious descent, his eyes darting non-stop around the room.

He ignored the food I put in front of him, even when I shook French fries on to his paper tray. But I was in no hurry, especially since he had asked to see me. "This place never has onions," I muttered, just before taking a generous bite of hot dog. By the time I took my second bite his resistance crumbled, and he dug into the food as if it were his first meal in weeks.

We ate in silence for a while, then I took out a notebook and flipped it open.

"What's that?" he demanded. Only then did I notice the letters D-I-N-G-O tattooed on the knuckles of both hands.

"I write my appointments in here. Time and place."

"You a reporter?"

"You ought to know, you . . ." I was about to add "stole my wallet," but I wanted to avoid an argument, at least until he explained why he wanted to see me. So I said, "You saw my business card in my wallet. I'm with the *Free Press*."

"I never heard of no *Free Press*. What kinda paper's that?"

His question raised my professional hackles. "What papers have you heard of?"

"*Daily News. Post.*"

"What about the *New York Times*?"

He wrinkled his brow, accentuating the eyes and high cheekbones that could have come from the brush of George Catlin. When I realized he was not putting me on, I could almost have kissed him for his ignorance.

"We're only about six years old," I said, surprised that I would try to justify my journalistic existence to a kid.

"That's old enough to cause trouble," he declared. "You got every fuckin' cop in this fuckin' city looking for me and my friends." By now he had finished the hot dogs and was devouring the remaining French fries, each one heaped with ketchup. All the while his eyes kept scanning the room.

I was about to ask how he knew we caused trouble if he didn't read the *Freep,* when a look of fear swept across his face. He leaped up from the table, but before he could run, a sturdy dark hand grabbed his shoulder and held him fast.

"I thought I told you to keep out of here," a wiry security guard said sternly.

"I'm with him, I'm with him," the boy protested, pointing toward me with his free hand while struggling to break the grip with the other.

The guard finally looked at me, and an expression of revulsion crossed his face. I knew immediately what he was thinking, and for an instant I thought I would lose my lunch. "Get him out of here," he said to me between clenched teeth, and it was clear he wanted me out also.

"What's he done?" I demanded. "He isn't bothering anybody."

"Not now," he replied. "Not while he has a meal ticket." With that he loosened his grip, and Dingo fell back into the chair.

The boy reacted as if slapped in the face. "I'm no fuckin' fag," he hollered, grabbing the guard's arm and trying to sink his teeth into it.

When the guard grabbed him again I shouted "Leave him alone" and grabbed his arm. When he let go of Dingo I quickly took my *Free Press* I.D. from my wallet and held it under the guard's nose. That formal-looking document had no legal value whatever, but the few times I had flashed it, it seemed to have impact. I could see the guard's eyes suddenly fill with doubt, and he became further confused when several other patrons expressed sympathy for the boy.

Throwing my press card back at me, the guard muttered something about never reading "that rag," then turned to the furious boy. "Just don't try coming in here on your own, or with that gang of yours," he warned, before walking to the escalator and riding it up to the main floor.

Dingo cursed him for several minutes, uttering an unbroken stream of profanity and threats. When the boy finally wound down, a drunk lifted his head from a nearby table with great effort and clapped desultorily. "That's telling 'em, champ," he said.

His anger spent at last, Dingo began laughing—softly at first, then louder and louder until I almost wished he would start cursing again. Finally a lone tear rolled down his cheek, tracing a path through the dirt, which prompted me to reach across the table and lay a consoling hand on his shoulder. But no sooner did I touch his arm than he pulled back. "Fuck off," he said, shoving my hand aside.

I wished we were out on the sidewalk, where Dingo's oaths would have elicited little more than indifferent glances. As it was, I was embarrassed enough by them to go upstairs for another glass of beer, and I'm not sure I would have cared had he been gone when I returned. But he was still sitting there, his back to the wall, scrutinizing everything and everyone around him.

"I didn't take your wallet," he said after I sat down.

"No?" My tone was so disbelieving that I swear a flicker of embarrassment crossed his face.

"I'm telling you, man, I didn't take the fuckin' thing."

"But you know who did."

He stared at me noncommittally, then looked away.

"You didn't really want to see me to discuss my wallet, did you," I said.

"You sure you a reporter?"

"Look," I said, irked by his inquisitorial tone, "don't you read the paper?"

"I don't read nothin' by you."

"Of course not, you're too busy reading Deep Think," I said. "Too bad Walter Lippmann's dead or you'd be in your glory."

He had no inkling that I was making fun of him, of course, but my sarcasm made me feel better just the same.

"I got a friend that needs help," he said.

I furrowed my brow. "What kind of help? Who's your friend?"

"This old guy I met a few days ago. He—"

He inhaled sharply as the security guard reappeared, but both of them avoided eye contact. I still felt soiled at the realization that the guard thought I was a chicken hawk, but before I could dwell on it Dingo hissed, "Fuckin' pig." The guard didn't hear but a woman seated near us quickly gathered her food and moved to a far table.

"Your friend needs money, I suppose."

The moment he said yes, which I fully expected, I intended to tell him to give him my forty-one dollars. Instead, he shook his head. "He needs to talk to a reporter."

"And you just happened to think of me, even though you never read the *Free Press*? Is that it?"

"Cut the crap," he said. The expression made me wince, although it was as mild as any he had used so far.

"What do you want from me?"

"Come talk with him. Maybe you can help some fuckin' body once in a while, instead of gettin' the cops on their case."

Remembering Jill's warning about the possibility of being set up, I asked, "And where is this . . . old friend of yours?"

"The Hotel Miami," he replied, naming a fleabag on Forty-fifth Street that specialized in fifteen-minute liaisons, followed by any number of communicable diseases.

"I don't imagine you'd mind if I left word with a colleague where I'm going?" I said, feeling increasingly ridiculous about my suspicions.

He did not know what I meant by colleague, so I explained that I wanted to phone a co-worker to say where I was going.

His eyes narrowed, his nostrils flared, and I could see he was still suspicious that I might deliver him to the cops. "Tell you what," I said. "I'll give you the quarter and you dial the *Free Press* and ask for Jill Leigh."

He was wary of that proposal too, but after we exited Nathan's, with Dingo flipping a farewell bird to the guard, he walked to one of the telephones on the corner and dialed the number I had written on the napkin. He fidgeted the whole time the phone rang and rang and rang. "No answer," he said finally, looking at me through narrowed eyes.

Just my luck, I thought, she's probably out buying a late afternoon repast to tide her over until dinner.

The Hotel Miami not only lacked sunshine and an ocean breeze, it was all but devoid of oxygen. The claustrophobic reception area reeked of urine, as did the dank, unpainted lobby and the graffiti-covered elevator that we took to the fourth floor—after an embarrassing cross-examination by a needle-pocked room clerk who was sure that Dingo was a chicken, that I was a chicken hawk, and that the two of us were conspiring to cheat the hotel out of the twelve dollars it charged for a thirty-minute tryst.

The musty hallway was pitch dark, although it was still light outside, yet as we groped our way along the corridor a half-dozen youngsters ran by us, playing hide-and-seek. Hallways and the streets outside the hotel were the playgrounds for hundreds of poor kids who were being housed—warehoused, actually—in rundown Times Square hotels, firetraps that charged the city as much as a hundred dollars a day per room.

I had written several stories about the so-called welfare kids consigned to such hotels, stories inspired by the death of a seven-year-old girl on Forty-third Street who was killed by a stray bullet fired during an argument over drugs. But seeing these kids running through the darkened hallway of the Hotel Miami made me realize how incomplete my articles had been. And breathing that foul air made me wish I had bought some incense from the white-robed Muslims who hawked it outside the subway entrance on Forty-second Street.

At the end of the hallway the boy stopped and knocked on a door. "It's me, Dingo," he yelled. "Let me in." He knocked again and yelled again, but still there was no reply. "Sonvabitch," he exclaimed.

"Sonvabitch," echoed a young voice from someone who had been observing us from the end of the corridor.

"Shut up," Dingo admonished. "You're too little to be using them words. Besides, girls shouldn't talk that way."

A male chauvinist at his tender age, I thought, making a mental note to ask him what his age was. "Little boys shouldn't talk that way either," I said.

"You're beginning to get on my fuckin' nerves, man," Dingo replied, lighting another joint. His match flared like a torch in the gloomy hallway, and his cowlick cast a shadow on the wall that resembled a dwarf palm tree.

After a few more minutes I said, "I'm sorry, but I've got to get to work. You know my name and number; if he shows up give me a call."

I was fishing in my pocket for a couple of quarters to

hand him when he said, "I think this is Reverend Robeson now."

I still could barely see, although I had no trouble hearing the kids racing through the corridor on the third floor. But I soon saw a shape coming slowly toward us, a large shape that seemed to be bent in two. When it got nearer a voice said, "Dingo, is that you, boy?"

"Yes, Reverend," he replied, his voice almost respectful. "I got somebody with me. Somebody who might be able to help."

"I do not know what I would do without you," the shadowy figure replied, rubbing Dingo's head. Turning to me and shaking my hand he said, "I am Willis Robeson, and I am mighty pleased to know you."

We went inside, and when he turned on the light, dim as it was, I almost wished he had left the room in darkness. The paint was pealed back in long strips, cobwebs had formed in every corner, and the lone piece of furniture was a bed that looked barely sturdy enough to sustain the weight of its large occupant. A sink, leaky toilet, and rusted shower occupied a far corner of the windowless room. A stale breeze seeped in through the open transom.

When Dingo said I was a reporter, Willis Robeson showed a flicker of interest, but he seemed too tired or too preoccupied to comment. Even sunk well down into his chair he was a huge man, six five or six six, close to two hundred forty pounds. He was as dark as the corridor, but with a thick salt-and-pepper beard and thinning hair. A crack in the corner of his left eyeglass lens resembled a miniature spider web, but there was nothing miniature about his sad, gentle face.

"Tell him 'bout Noah, Reverend Robeson," Dingo urged. "Tell him, he's a newspaper reporter."

This time the old man's expression turned downright respectful, but it was respect accompanied by an abiding melancholy. Still, I realized that I was in the presence of a kindly, decent man.

"So you are Mr. Shaw," he said. "I have been reading your stories since I got to town. They are very good, very thorough." He spoke slowly, weighing each word, shunning contractions as if to do otherwise would be to debase the language.

"You might try telling that to your little friend here," I said, turning toward Dingo. But in that few seconds he had managed to disappear. I stuck my head out the open door and looked down the hallway, but I neither saw nor heard anything. When I turned back, Reverend Robeson was chuckling softly and shaking his head.

"That boy!" he said, not without admiration. "Never saw the likes of him in all my days."

I had to agree with that, although he apparently saw more to admire in Dingo than I did. "You don't happen to know where he lives, do you?" I asked.

The minister shook his head and that look of sadness crept back into his eyes. "I asked him that myself," he said. "He gave me some address way uptown, but I learned he lives on the street—in doorways, abandoned buildings, wherever he can find a place for the night."

"What about his parents?"

"He says they have been dead a couple of years, but he will not say how or where they died. He will not talk at all about his life—will not even admit that he cannot read."

So that was it? On top of everything else, he was also illiterate? "How do you know he can't?" I asked.

"Because I showed him one of your stories in the newspaper, one about the welfare children in Times Square. He kept trying to get me to read it to him. We were right here in this room, but I had just come back from a long day of looking for Noah and I was worn out. I did not feel like reading right that moment, so I asked him to read it to me. When he just kept making excuses, I finally figured out why. So now I read to him every night he comes around, the newspaper and this mostly," he said, withdrawing a small, worn Bible from his pocket and tapping it for emphasis.

"How did the two of you ever hook up? I mean, you a preacher, him a—"

"A young boy," Reverend Robeson said gently. "One of God's children." Before he answered my question, he stood with some difficulty and poured both of us a glass of ice water from his miniature refrigerator alongside the sink. While we drank in silence I became aware of the rhythmic squeak of bedsprings in the room next door, accompanied by periodic moans and curses.

If the preacher heard the sounds, or understood their meaning, he gave no indication. Instead, he explained in his soft, deliberate manner that he was a Southern Baptist minister from a small town outside Nashville, and that he had led a mostly blessed life until his wife died three years ago, her death hastened by disappointment over their son Noah. Ever since his teens Noah had been rebellious, and by the time Noah, Jr., was born he had become an alcoholic, a drunkard who beat his wife and threatened to kill her and the boy.

For years his wife endured his drunken outbursts, followed by periods of sobriety and remorse. But one afternoon when he chased her out the door, knife in hand, his wife dashed into the street and was struck by an automobile. She died three days later, but by then her husband had vanished.

He, Willis, became legal guardian of his grandson, the minister explained, slowly, deliberately, and before long the two were inseparable. But a few months ago Noah, Jr., had received a letter from his father in New York, saying he had straightened himself out and asking the boy to join him. Willis was deeply skeptical, but when his grandson asked to visit his father the minister promised they would journey to New York in mid August. Young Noah seemed delighted at the prospect, but two days later he was gone.

"He left me this," Reverend Robeson said, handing me a note written in an immature hand. While he put a pan of water on a hot plate, I read from the letter, dated three weeks previously.

Dear Grandfather:

Im going to visit father to find out if he really is a good person. If he is I will ask him to come back home with me. Dont wory about me cause I have enough money and I will phone you from New York to tell you everything. And I will tell him everything including how sad he made all of us and how much I love you.

Your grandson, Noah.

I barely had time to swallow the lump in my throat when he removed from his wallet a snapshot showing a handsome, alert teenager with a broad, uninhibited smile. "His class picture," he said mournfully. "One of the few pictures I have of him."

"How old is he?" I asked, eager to get his mind off whatever gruesome possibilities he must have been contemplating.

"Fourteen. He was fourteen on May third."

I started taking notes, but Reverend Robeson did not seem to notice. I asked about Noah's size (four feet eleven) and weight (eighty-five pounds), his hobbies (basketball and piano), and favorite subjects (math and choir). The minister explained that he himself had come to New York ten days ago, and until today he had been out from early morning until late at night scouring the city. He was concentrating his search in the Greater Times Square area.

He had posted handbills on traffic signs and parking meters, and had stood for hours on street corners passing out leaflets with young Noah's picture and description. He showed me one of the handbills, containing the boy's school photo and description, offering a three thousand dollar reward for information leading to the boy's safe return.

"Why three thousand dollars?" I asked.

"Because that is every cent I have," he said simply.

"But why do you think he's in Times Square?"

"This was his father's return address," he said, pointing to the upper lefthand corner of the envelope, on which was scrawled the address of the Hotel Miami. Before I could comment he added, "And because Dingo thinks he saw him a couple of weeks ago."

When I looked doubtful, the minister said, "He cannot remember exactly where he saw Noah. Only that he saw a boy that looked like him, once on Forty-second Street, another time on Forty-fourth. But," he said, his voice trailing off, "he has not seen him again."

At the risk of dampening his hopes I asked, "Is Dingo charging you to help find Noah?"

"Oh, my, no, not one cent," he declared. "And he has taken me up and down streets and in and out of places I would never have known existed, helping me look for Noah."

When the water on the hot plate began boiling he got out two cups, spoons, and teabags, then wadded pages of one of the tabloids to use as a potholder while he poured.

Reverend Robeson must have read my doubts that Dingo was motivated by altruism. "You know, Mr. Shaw," he said, "I think it is tragic that Dingo and his friends run free all day and all night, without the schools or the city doing anything about it. I may be only an old country preacher, but I know a lot of time he must be up to no good." He shook his head slowly, then asked, "Did he tell you how we met?"

"No. I meant to ask you about that."

"I was handing out handbills on Forty-second and Eighth when all of a sudden I found myself surrounded by a dozen or so youngsters." He smiled at the memory. "They demanded my wallet, but instead I asked them to join me in prayer."

I almost spit out my tea. "Prayer?" I exclaimed, thinking that must have gone over big.

"They could have had my life but not my wallet," the minister continued, "because it has the reward money for information about Noah. So—"

"Cash?"

Any New Yorker, probably any resident of Nashville, for that matter, knows not to carry more money than he can afford to lose to a mugger, as he also knows not to carry too little. But this rural preacher did indeed carry cash, he assured me, cash withdrawn from a bank and from several hiding places in his modest home, cash that had been squirreled away for an old age that was suddenly upon him.

Determined to protect the reward money, Reverend Robeson fought back against his youthful attackers, although he took care to avoid injuring them. A ring on an anonymous fist cracked his eyeglass lens and an equally anonymous foot caught him in the groin. As he slumped to the sidewalk someone whistled a warning and the pack scattered.

He finally picked himself up with the aid of passersby and retrieved some of the handbills. "And there across the street was this tiny kid passing out many of the others."

"Dingo?"

He nodded. "When I approached him he said I was in a dangerous place so he and some friends would walk me home. I almost laughed out loud, he was so small. And besides, from what I could see, the only danger was from him and his friends."

Reverend Robeson laughed heartily, slapping his thigh for emphasis. But when the laughter faded he said, "Yet something had brought him back to help me pass out Noah's handbills."

"You're not suggesting that he has a conscience?" I took another unenthusiastic sip of the unsweetened tea.

"We all have a conscience, Mr. Shaw," he replied. "Fortunately, not all of us have to struggle so hard to obey it."

I was surprised to learn that Dingo stopped by the preacher's room almost every morning, helped him search for Noah a couple of hours each day, and dropped by to visit several nights a week—long enough, in most cases, for Reverend Robeson to read him the comic strips and Bible stories. In return, the boy regaled and shocked the clergyman with tales culled from his daily experiences, although Reverend Robeson was much too proper to repeat them and I was too embarrassed for him to ask. But Dingo had no further news about the person he claimed had been Noah.

"What about the desk clerk?" I asked. "Does he remember your grandson or son?"

"He claims he remembers my son. Says my description sounds like the man who registered under the name of Noah Marsh. But he caused so much trouble after getting drunk each night, they finally threw him out. According to the clerk, they evicted him just before Memorial Day—two or three days before my grandson would have arrived. But none of the people I have talked to in the hotel remember seeing young Noah."

A cockroach scurried across his floor and disappeared under the sink, but Reverend Robeson seemed oblivious. In a voice not much louder than a whisper I said, "Only Dingo saw him. One homeless stray recognizing another."

"No, you are wrong, Mr. Shaw," the minister said, shaking his head emphatically. "Dingo is a homeless stray because he does not have parents or guardians, so he runs the streets all day and half the night, and sleeps where he can. But my grandson has a home and a guardian. He is missing not because he has nowhere to turn but because something . . . something awful must have happened to him. And for the life of me . . ."

This time the tears streamed unashamedly down his cheeks. When he was finally able to continue he said, "And for the life of me, I cannot help thinking that if he is involved in something wrong, he was probably put up to it by his father—my own flesh and blood."

"You're jumping to conclusions," I said, hoping to comfort him.

"Maybe, Mr. Shaw. Each morning and night I pray that I am wrong, and that Noah will turn up safely. But with the help of Almighty God, I will not rest until I find out where he is and what happened to him."

I rwin Haines shrugged at my proposal to write a story about Willis Robeson, although his indifference quickly changed to enthusiasm the instant Kenneth Parks clasped the idea to his own ample bosom. "Let's get text and photos for at least three stories," Parks told the city editor, who made only a sheepish, half-hearted effort to convince me he had independently changed his mind about the value of my suggestion.

"The trouble is, I can't spring a photographer for two

days," Haines lamented, ticking off several reasons why not.

"What about that idea of using a street photographer?" Jill Leigh asked. While reworking the lead on her story about mismanagement in the city transit system, she was also laying waste to a wedge of pineapple cheesecake.

"While you're at it, why not a free-lance writer off the streets?" I replied. "Maybe 'Chico' or 'Fly 22' or 'Big Dick' or one of those other proud graffiti artists?"

"Speaking of 'Big Dick,' how's your story on the Freak Show coming along?" Haines wanted to know.

I explained that I hadn't had time to think much about it, except when I saw posters heralding the event on the walls of abandoned buildings and in subway stations. Before he could grill me further, Haines was called away to mediate a jurisdictional dispute between two of our newer reporters. But Jill had given me an idea, so I told her in case anyone asked about me to say I'd be back in forty-five minutes. After promising to bring her a half-pound of grapes from the Korean greengrocer in the next block, I headed back to Forty-third Street.

I wrote the first draft of my story about Robeson later that afternoon, working at poignancy but trying to avoid melodrama. I tried to capture faithfully the anguish of the poor Southern minister who had been pounding the pavements of the city's most dangerous district in search of his young grandson.

I did not mention the reward money, fearful that he would be a marked man or a corpse if the gang at Forty-second Street, a gang whose membership and motives had changed dramatically since the days when George M. Cohan was giving his lyrical regards to Broadway, knew he was carrying any part of the three thousand dollars with him. I did mention Noah, Sr.'s, last known address in Times Square. And I managed to resist suggestions from Parks that I compare Robeson to Diogenes, to Pinocchio's father Gepetto, or to other real or imagined long-suffering seekers.

I was putting the final touches on the story about noon the next day, having interrupted it the previous afternoon to write a late-breaking story about a berserk slasher at the Port Authority Bus Terminal, when the security guard phoned from the lobby to say that a Mr. Nelson wanted to see me. Since I had no appointment with a Mr. Nelson and could not recall anyone by that name, I was about to tell the guard to say I was unavailable. But then I remembered Black Bart the street photographer, and asked the guard to direct him to the fifth floor.

"How'd it go?" I asked as Raymond Nelson exited the elevator, looking as if he had stepped out of a Marlboro ad in Ebony magazine.

He shrugged. "You'll have to be the judge of that," he replied, in the best laconic cowboy tradition. I escorted him the length of the newsroom back to my desk, where he removed his ten-gallon hat, then opened the worn saddlebag that had been slung across his shoulder like a serape. Still without a word he withdrew a handful of photos.

As he spread them across my cluttered desk, it was immediately apparent that it had gone very well indeed. Here were at least a dozen good shots of Willis Robeson as he made his way through Times Square: shots of him talking with shopkeepers, chatting with cops on the beat, questioning an amiable six-foot, four-inch transvestite who hung out outside the Midtown Arms Hotel, and listening intently to a tall, slender pimp.

I heard an appreciative whistle and turned around to see Haines looking over my shoulder. "Who took these?" he asked, unclasping his hands from behind his back long enough to thumb through the photos I had finished examining.

I introduced him to Nelson, adding that I had commis-

sioned him to take the photos of Robeson. "Don't panic,"
I added. "Our agreement is that we'll pay only for what
we use."

I gave Nelson a surreptitious wink as I said it, for that
was not our agreement at all. But it was yet a little early in
the day to send Haines's blood pressure skyrocketing, and
I could tell that he liked the photos.

"They're good. Not terrific . . . but quite good," he
said, trying to climb back down from what he now feared
might turn out to be an expensive limb. "We could probably use one, maybe even two, if the price was reasonable."

"The price of my pictures is like their quality—high,"
Nelson declared, in his soft Caribbean cadence. Then,
just as softly, he named a figure that left the city editor
looking as if he had been mugged.

"For all of them, I assume," he said, once he regained
his power of speech.

"For each one," Nelson replied.

"No way. You're asking as much for each picture as
Shaw earns in two days."

"A week," I said, hoping to shame him into getting me
a raise.

"It's no concern of mine if somebody sells himself
cheap," Nelson told the city editor, surreptitiously returning my wink. He was toying with Haines, sitting back
comfortably in Jill's chair with his boots resting on the
edge of her desk. I felt a certain admiration that a street
photographer with no other apparent source of income,
appeared so indifferent about making a sale and so supremely confident about the value of his product.

Haines apparently felt the same way, because he walked
away without a word. A few minutes later, however, he
returned with Parks in tow. The managing editor, his
sleeves rolled up and his necktie askew in prescribed
newspaper manner, nodded uneasily to the black cowboy,

44

then spent the next five minutes examining the pictures with a critical eye.

When he finished he gathered up four photos and offered Nelson the amount he had asked—but for all four, rather than for each one.

When the photographer refused, Parks doubled the offer and threw in the promise of a credit line.

Again the photographer refused.

"A credit line beneath each picture," Parks said wearily, running a forefinger between his neck and his open collar, as if gasping for air. "It's my final offer. Refuse and I'll send a team of *Free Press* photographers out to get the pictures we need. Accept, and I'll consider throwing other assignments your way."

I almost hoped Nelson would refuse, and by so doing demonstrate that not everything in this town is for sale. But he reluctantly agreed, and when I thought more about it I realized he would have been crazy not to. The *Free Press* was not in the same photographic league as its newspaper rivals, in part because of our small staff, but our layout was frequently imaginative, providing an attractive showcase for what several of our more ancient reporters disparagingly termed "the shutterbugs." Besides, a credit line on photos even in the *Free Press* had to be a major step up from photographing tourists and assorted weirdos on dirty, dangerous street corners.

Nelson must have thought so too, because, although he had been blasé in his dealings with Haines and Parks, he was bursting with pride two days later when all four of his photos were used to illustrate my story about Robeson. When I met him just before noon, he had already bought a half-dozen papers and had proudly dispatched Dingo to take one to Reverend Robeson. Newly affixed to the top of the hand-lettered sign advertising his wares was a line proclaiming, PHOTOGRAPHER FOR THE NEW YORK FREE PRESS.

If the claim was exaggerated, it was not actually untrue. Besides, any number of writers who sold even a single article to a newspaper or magazine listed that affiliation for the rest of their days. So why not Nelson, whose talent even our picture editor acknowledged?

I had discovered that talent a week or two earlier when on impulse I asked Nelson if he had any photos of Dingo. He replied that some weeks ago he had offered to take the boy's photo but Dingo objected so long and so loudly that he backed away. "But these pictures might interest you," he said, reaching into his saddlebag and withdrawing two of the most astonishing handfuls of black and white photographs I had ever seen.

Here were dozens of Times Square denizens in photos that rivaled Brassai's photos of Paris's nether world: prostitutes talking among themselves or negotiating with johns . . . chicken hawks propositioning their youthful prey in video arcades . . . a grinning pimp in his customized Eldorado at daybreak . . . a deranged shopping-bag woman sitting in a doorway at dusk . . . the street-corner preachers who inhabited a slice of the sidewalk outside 1 Times Square . . . addicts shooting up in doorways . . . security guards in porno parlors perched atop towers like lifeguards, surveying their anonymous clientele . . . the rows of Senegalese peddlers along Broadway, who at the first sign of rain put away their displays of watches and rings and begin selling umbrellas.

It was all there, the whole Times Square gallery—the Black Muslims and Hare Krishnas . . . suburban matrons dressed to the nines in town for Broadway's Wednesday matinees . . . homosexual couples fondling one another in public . . . teenage spray painters, vying for a moment of recognition . . . the body of a prostitute slashed to death by a psychotic john, and the agony of a john whose penis had been bitten almost in half by a vengeful whore . . . welfare children romping in the spray from an opened hydrant . . . and the Arabs, Indians, Hell's Angels, Watusis and other characters who paraded through the sordid Crossroads of the World.

Nelson's photos were not particularly sympathetic portrayals; their genius lay in their brutal visual honesty and technical superiority. When I asked how he had captured so many candid moments—meaning, of course, how a huge black cowboy sporting an earring had managed to be at the scene of so many intimate events—he said it was by making himself so well known in the neighborhood that no one gave him a second thought, and by shooting dozens of humdrum photos for every one that was distinctive.

When I asked why he was compiling his photographic record, he replied, "Because nobody else has ever captured the inhabitants of this lost world."

A lost world, he called it, and so it was—and one not all that far removed from that other lost world conjured up by the imagination of Conan Doyle. Yet almost every night, after earning his daily bread taking portraits of tourists, and after a brief nap in his apartment on Ninth Avenue atop one of the area's few remaining fortuneteller studios that wasn't a front for a whorehouse, Nelson made the rounds of that lost world into the wee small hours, his compact 35 millimeter camera always at the ready. Occasionally, on impulse, he would close up his sidewalk studio early and look for daytime subjects to complete his photographic record.

Nelson's photos had captured on film much of what I hoped to capture in print, but because he had no outlet for his creativity I had suggested that he photograph Reverend Robeson to illustrate my story.

Judging from the reaction, it had been an inspired idea. The tip-off came when I arrived at the *Free Press* the day the article ran and the receptionist was unusually complimentary about my story. Several colleagues were also. And when Jill added her praise, on what for her was practically an empty stomach, I used the opportunity to ask her out the next night. "After dinner," I pointedly added.

I was about to head for the appropriate city agencies in search of a reliable estimate of the number of welfare kids, runaways, and abandoned children in Times Square, but before leaving the building I thumbed through my mail. I discarded unopened the stack of letters from PR agencies that I knew from experience would contain nothing of value. I tossed into my active file a reminder about the Freak Show. Then I tacked up on the newsroom bulletin board, that repository for anonymous caustic wit and solecisms culled from rival papers, a pamphlet that had been thrust into my hand the day before warning that Christ would soon show up in Times Square as a prelude to destroying it. Before posting it, I showed it to Dick Suft, the *Free Press*'s top rewrite man and resident misanthrope.

He was suitably unimpressed. "Christ wouldn't dare show up in Times Square," he assured me. "He'd know that before He could even turn the other cheek He'd be propositioned, assaulted, mugged, or maimed."

My story about Willis Robeson touched a responsive chord among readers, prompting several dozen of them to send him money in care of the *Free Press*. Parks wasted no time setting up a Reverend Robeson Fund and ordering me to write about it. But when I informed the clergyman, looking forward to his reaction so I could quote it in my story, he said he would not accept a dime. "I welcome help in finding my grandson," the minister said in his deliberate manner, "but not money."

When I pressed him as to why, he said only, "'Having food and raiment, let us be therefore content.'"

His refusal to elaborate irked Parks greatly, and his ire was coupled with incredulity when I said something about Robeson probably having faith in the Lord's willingness to provide. Nevertheless, without telling the clergyman I opened a bank account in his name with the money already contributed.

A flurry of excitement erupted the next day when crews from two local television stations got into a shoving match as they followed the minister around. Reverend Robeson was uncomfortable with the klieg lights and unwieldy television crews, but his discomfort was short-lived. Because after a brief story appeared on each station, television lost all interest, probably because the minister's wanderings did not lend themselves to the same sort of visual drama as fires, mayhem, and the other staples of television news.

I did not see Reverend Robeson for several days after my story appeared; I was busy writing about two particularly brutal murders. One involved a small-time drug dealer whose trussed-up body, with its heart cut out, had been stuffed into a trash basket on Ninth Avenue. The other was about a nineteen-year-old prostitute, found in a darkened corner of the Port Authority bus terminal, whose breasts had been hacked off before she was strangled.

Both stories were prominently displayed on the front page, and after the second story the police commissioner and the mayor held a press conference to deny what I had reported—namely, that neither murder was likely to be solved, primarily because police in both the Midtown North and Midtown South precincts were already overworked, but also because some cops on the beat felt that their limited time and resources were better spent on victims who were more deserving.

Since neither I nor any other *Free Press* reporter was invited to the press conference, I learned of it from the *Daily News* and *Post*, both of which reported the mayor's charge that "the *Free Press* reporter did not cite a single source to support his shocking charge."

That was literally true, although deliberately misleading, since the mayor well knew no cop would dare say as much for attribution. And he and the police commissioner also knew that, despite their assurances that all available manpower would be enlisted to find the killers, no manpower was available.

How could it be otherwise, I asked in a news analysis a day later, when there were not enough cops anywhere in the city? Not enough to stop the open buying and selling of crack and other drugs on street corners. Not enough to catch more than a small percentage of the "fare beaters" who went over or under the subway turnstiles to avoid paying. Not enough to cope with the aggressive panhandlers or legions of deranged men and women who wandered the city.

The mayor repeated his assurance that every murder would be investigated to the fullest, but he did not call another press conference and neither murder was ever solved. Meanwhile, I was already busy interviewing city officials about the children in Times Square—their numbers, their malnutrition, their crime and mortality rates, their inadequate schooling and medical care. I also learned that there were thousands of such kids in New York, homeless children who had run away or been tossed out and welfare kids born to mothers often as young as thirteen.

Jill gave me the names of social workers and psychologists who could help explain the many behavioral and psychological problems of these children. But what I needed to breathe journalistic life into their inanimate theories and statistics was input from the kids themselves, from Dingo or his friends. But so far, I had failed to reestablish contact with him, although I left messages with Raymond Nelson and Reverend Robeson, both of whom said he showed up almost every day. But he neither replied nor acknowledged them.

The photographer said he sometimes saw Dingo doing the usual odd jobs in the neighborhood: passing out coupons for fast-food restaurants, acting as a lookout for dealers of three-card monte, and squirting soapy water on the windshields of autos stopped at traffic lights, in return for a "tip" for wiping it off with a greasy rag.

"Any luck?" Jill asked when I returned to the office that afternoon. She knew I wanted badly to find Dingo.

I shook my head. "Nothing," I said discouragedly. "Wait, I take that back. I got propositioned."

"Big deal," she laughed, unwrapping a salami hero liberally coated with mustard. "Name one person who doesn't get propositioned in this neighborhood."

She raised the sandwich to her mouth, but instead of biting into it she said, "You think it's because of your charm, when anybody can see it's because of the size of your . . ." She paused just long enough for an impish smile to play across her face ". . . paycheck. Besides, that 'girl' who propositioned you was probably Big Dick in drag."

I started humming "Jealousy," which roused two of the older copy-editors at the front of the room from their never-ending game of chess. But when I realized Jill was too young to know that song, or for that matter any song that had a recognizable melody or understandable lyrics, I said, "This proposition was different. It wasn't made on the street or at the entrance to the coffee shop, but right inside, while I waited for my order. A woman who could have been any age from twenty to forty, so strung out she could barely stand, said she'd give me a good time."

"So even the hookers are feeling the economic pinch?" said Dick Suft. He had overheard part of my conversation after coming over to see what the humming had been about. "You can level with us, how much did you pay her?"

"A lot less than it'll cost him if he gets AIDS or some other exotic disease," Jill said.

I rolled my eyes helplessly, and after Suft departed I

told Jill that I had in fact given the woman ten dollars. When she cocked an eyebrow I explained that I had been so touched by the sight of her that if I had fifty dollars in my pocket I might have given her that.

"Oh God, not another bleeding heart beating beneath the breast of the hard-bitten journalist." She said it in mock despair, and only later did I learn that she was touched by my compassion.

I too was touched by it, or at least puzzled, because my usual reaction to streetwalkers was to ignore them—them and the many rheumy-eyed men and women in the neighborhood with outstretched hands. I managed to ignore the nun who many mornings camped outside the entrance to the *Free Press*, collecting money for the poor. So it was hard even for me to understand my concern for that pitiful creature, except that there was something haunting about her.

I had wanted for some time to write about the decent restaurants in Times Square, to speculate about their fate once the redevelopment wrecking ball dropped on the neighborhood in earnest. But my suggestion sent Irwin Haines into gales of derisive laughter, and Parks fell into one of those sullen moods that enveloped him the instant he suspected someone might be putting him on.

But I persisted, citing several such restaurants, including Sardi's, whose walls were festooned with caricatures of actors and actresses, as well as the dozen or more establishments that lined Restaurant Row, that incongruous oasis on Forty-sixth between Eighth and Ninth.

I mentioned those restaurants knowing that Parks frequented them when he wasn't lunching in the Oak Room of the Hotel Algonquin, a stone's throw from Times Square. But I also mentioned a half-dozen good ethnic restaurants that had somehow avoided being swallowed up by porno shops, hot-sheet hotels, massage parlors, peep shows, sleazy bars, and fronts for drug dealing.

Because I ate in such restaurants anyway, lunch being my big meal of the day ever since Diane moved out, taking her limited culinary talents with her, I proposed writing about one restaurant each week—an article that would be part review and part interview, allowing the owner or manager to describe the special problems of operating in Times Square. Although still skeptical, Parks eventually approved the story idea, but later he told Haines to inform me I would be reimbursed for only fifty percent of the meals.

"Nothing doing," I told the apologetic city editor when he relayed the message. "Unless you expect me to write only about Nathan's, Nedick's, and the fried chicken shops, I want my bill and that of a guest paid in full."

Haines whistled, a mannerism that somehow always accentuated his jug ears. "Listen to the poor man's Michelin," he said, adding that Parks was about as likely to agree to that demand as he was to a fifty percent pay raise. "In other words," he said, finishing the sentence by flashing a thumbs down gesture.

"Tell Parks we'll be laughingstocks if it gets into the *Post* or *Daily News* that the *Freep* is too cheap to pick up a legitimate expense tab." Hoping to make Parks squirm, I added, "I can see the *Post* headline now: 'Cheap Freep.'"

Gilbert Shipley happened to be in Parks's office when Haines recounted our conversation, and he told me the managing editor turned three shades of purple. But when his blood pressure subsided, a day later, he told Haines I could bill the paper for the cost of my own meal. "But not one cent for any goddamned groupie he takes with him," he had added.

The history buff in me admired his Pinckney-esque language, although I had never associated groupies with ink-stained wretches of the Fourth Estate, and certainly not ink-stained wretches of the *Free Press*. Besides, the "groupie" I had in mind as a luncheon companion was Jill Leigh, a trencherman of no small reputation whose weakness I shamelessly exploited by reciting portions of the menu from several restaurants on my list of candidates.

"I knew you'd be a pushover," I said after she agreed to join me.

"How'd you know?"

"I'm a student of female psychology, as well as anatomy."

"Braggart!"

"Some girls have a G Spot, you have an F Spot." When she looked at me, expecting the worst, I added, "F—for food."

Her embarrassment gave way to relief, then to feigned disgust. "I just know I'm going to hate myself in the morning," she said with a sigh.

We had by then become good friends, in part because of her interest in Dingo. Although she had never seen him, she felt as if she knew him from hearing me talk so much about him and from accompanying me several times to the Hotel Miami to visit Reverend Robeson.

As much as Reverend Robeson enjoyed our visits, he was discouraged by his failure to find even a trace of Noah. To add to his troubles, he was also deeply worried about Dingo.

"I swear I do not know what is going to become of that boy," he said forlornly one night while dining with Jill and me at a Brazilian restaurant just off Broadway. He had barely touched his black beans and rice, which he said he usually regarded as a treat. "He already smokes and uses profanity, and who knows what else?"

What else indeed, I thought. "He still doesn't tell you where he sleeps?"

He shook his massive head. "He says he lives with friends somewhere over by Eleventh Avenue, but . . ." His eyes clouded with tears, and Jill reached over and took his hand.

"No child can survive by himself in this environment," he said, sweeping his other hand and arm in a wide semi-circle. "It is a wonder he has survived as well as he has. He is a babe among wolves."

But for how long could he continue to survive, I wondered. I remembered having read that Australian men, called "doggers," went gunning for dingo scalps, for which they received a bounty. But the hunters in Times Square were far worse, often stabbing or shooting their prey just for the thrill of it.

On another night, Jill and I visited Raymond Nelson's fourth-floor walkup apartment to view his huge collection of photographs. And several nights she and I went to a quiet bar near her East Side apartment, where we drank wine and talked until well beyond the witching hour.

One sultry day we found ourselves eating lunch high above Broadway at 1 Times Square Plaza, in a pleasant Italian restaurant that was trying to make a go of it in a location where a succession of bars and restaurants had failed. While awaiting Jill's dessert we stood at the large picture window at the far end of the room and looked up Broadway—past the statue in Duffy Square of George M. Cohan, who gave his regards to a far different Broadway . . . past the statue of Father Francis P. Duffy himself, the chaplain for New York's famed Fighting Sixty-Ninth Regiment and also the longtime pastor of the red brick Church of the Holy Cross on West Forty-second Street . . . past the tourists already lined up, despite the heat, to buy half-price tickets to tonight's plays.

"'The rumble of a subway train, the rattle of a taxi,'" I

sang, inspired by the urban melody that drifted up from below.

"'The daffodils who entertain, at Angelo's or Maxi's,'" Jill rejoined, returning my look of surprise with a smile so dazzling that for a moment I feared being overcome by vertigo. As she sang her light brown hair, which fell just below her shoulders, bounced in accompaniment.

"Where in the world did you learn *that*?" I asked.

"My father used to sing it. Or was it my grandfather?" The gleam in her eye took some of the sting out of the reminder that I was forty-six and she only in her late twenties. Where in hell had my misspent youth gone, I wondered, for only the fifty-third time that week.

"The first time I ever saw Times Square," I told her, looking down on the passing crowd, "it was dusk and many of the lights had just come on. It was spectacular. The billboard over there," I said, pointing toward Forty-fourth and Seventh and thinking of Dingo's smoke rings, "used to be the Camel cigarette sign, where some pasteboard guy blew one enormous smoke ring after another, all of them perfectly round. And somewhere beyond there, an airline company put up a Super Constellation that looked big enough to fly in.

"Pepsi-Cola's billboard over there," I continued, gesturing beyond the nonexistent Camel sign, "covered an entire block and had a waterfall so big you thought you were going to get drenched just looking at it.

"I thought of it once while reading Proust . . ."

"You've actually read Proust?" she asked in that teasing voice. "I *am* impressed."

"Nobody has read all of Proust," I replied. "But there's this scene where Marcel is first invited to the home of a princess for a party, and he sees a fountain in the garden. From a distance its spray looked like a single stream of water. But from a closer view, you could see it was a constantly changing stream of water, with a thousand separate bursts.

"That was the Pepsi-Cola waterfall, a thousand separate bursts that gave the impression of a single thrust."

"That's lovely," she said, only now she was not teasing. She had been so wrapped up in my soliloquy that she did not even notice the waiter bring her dessert.

I started to reply when I spotted Raymond Nelson in the crowd below, at his usual corner photographing tourists who were blissfully unaware of the real Times Square. We watched as he took several pictures, but when we started to turn away I thought I recognized someone else.

"Dingo!" I exclaimed, pointing him out to Jill as he sauntered across Broadway to the corner opposite Nathan's. I'm not sure she was able to pick him out of the crowd, but even at that distance I knew it was he. Within seconds someone spoke to the boy, then placed a cover, probably the usual cardboard lid, atop the trash container. Then the stranger began dealing what was sure to be three-card monte, the street hustler's favorite scam. I could not see the lookout down at the far end of the street, but there was no mistaking that the lookout closest to me was Dingo.

We watched with alarm as two policemen strolled across Seventh Avenue, then I saw Dingo bring his hand to his mouth. He looked like he was whistling a warning, although we could not hear it from that distance amid the cacophony of horns, motors, and the siren atop the white and orange ambulance of the Emergency Medical Service. But the hustler had no trouble hearing, for he immediately swept up his cards and disappeared into the crowd.

Seconds after the patrolmen turned south on Broadway, Dingo and the hustler reappeared and the game continued with new players—"new meat," in the hustlers' parlance. I had few illusions about how many people read the *Free Press* or acted on its recommendations when they did read it. But at that moment I wished more of the innocents down on the street had read my recent front page article describing three-card monte as a rip-off—a dangerous rip-off for anyone lucky enough to beat the odds and foolish enough to think he would be allowed to walk away safely with his winnings.

I asked Jill to make the supreme sacrifice by forgoing dessert so I could hurry down and talk with the elusive Dingo. But she convinced me to wait, rather than risk praying whatever tenuous ties existed between the boy and me if I interrupted him while he was "working."

I agreed, since not even a young hustler would want a journalist to witness his participation in a flimflam. Besides, now that I saw him again, I felt sure he would stay around Times Square, and so I felt sure I would meet up with him in a more opportune setting.

T he *Free Press* depended on street sales for most of its circulation, and circulation surged a few days later when we ran the following double-decker headline on our front page: ORGANIZED CRIME DEEPLY INVOLVED IN TIMES SQUARE REAL ESTATE. The story ran at some length on page one, then jumped to pages six and seven, detailing the long list of buildings and sex-related businesses owned through dummy corporations by members of New York's leading crime families.

I helped with the story, and therefore shared in the byline. But Jill wrote it, and she did most of the reporting, along with Howard Eisenhart, an intelligent young reporter who less than a year ago had traded a promising legal career with a prestigious Wall Street law firm for a job on the *Freep* graveyard shift.

Dick Suft and Irwin Haines edited the story before sending it to Lawton Hickman, our timid house counsel, for the pulling and tugging between the editorial and legal departments that inevitably accompanied sensitive stories in the *Free Press*. All that saved it from total emasculation, or what Eisenhart termed "statutory rape," was Eisenhart's strenuous objections, together with his ability to cite legal chapter and verse.

The story developed when I received an anonymous letter about mob influence from someone who said that he or she liked my reporting on Times Square. Mob ownership in the area had always been a lightly guarded secret, but the usual charges lacked the specifics that made this letter worth heeding.

When I told Jill I intended to pursue the allegations as soon as I could step off my daily treadmill, she offered to make some preliminary inquiries for me—and quickly found herself up to her slender young neck in corporations with such innocuous-sounding names as "J.M.R. Inc.," "Encore Industries," and "Regional Realty."

At that point Haines assigned Eisenhart to help out, and the two spent several weeks tracing titles and deeds. They spent almost as much time huddled with Parks, Hickman, and the libel lawyers that a nervous Hickman brought in from outside.

Some allegations had to be dropped from the article for lack of documentation, while others were toned down. Nonetheless, the article showed conclusively that the principal Times Square drug and sex outlets, although ostensibly the province of individual hustlers and minor league smut peddlers, were inextricably tied to the mob families of Brooklyn, Queens, Westchester County, Long Island, and New Jersey.

I wrote a news analysis the next day explaining that even the streetwalkers along the Minnesota Strip, that stretch of Eighth Avenue heavily populated by middle-class white teenagers from the Midwest who wound up selling their bodies for black pimps from Harlem and the Bronx, were dependent on the mob in ways they probably did not understand. The mob owned many of the hotels where the hookers entertained johns who wanted more for their money than oral sex hastily performed in a darkened doorway. It owned many of the sex parlors and peep shows that lured customers to the nation's biggest sexual bazaar. And it furnished pimps with a steady supply of crack, heroin, cocaine, and other drugs that (depending on what one believed) so hooked the Midwestern teenagers that they turned tricks in return for an assured daily fix, or provided the solace necessary to cope with the realization they were not only whores but whores reduced to hustling in the worst part of town.

The story was picked up by the wire services and received brief attention from two local TV stations, both of which illustrated it by depicting buildings cited in the *Free Press* article and asking tenants what they thought of the charges. To my embarrassment, rendered all the more acute because I had been watching the late news in Jill's apartment, few of the tenants admitted to having read or heard of the article.

Even worse, as authoritative as it was, the article resulted in few reforms, in part for reasons cited by a decoy cop I had seen around the squad room of the Midtown South Precinct.

"That was a good job of reporting, as far as it went, but it's not the whole story," he said, as we talked in the precinct locker room. I had drifted in to say hello while awaiting details about the murder of an eleven-year-old girl, a welfare kid who had been raped and bludgeoned the night before.

"It's not just the mob that likes things the way they are," the cop continued, pulling on a pair of coveralls. "For years lots of landlords and developers hoped the physical and moral character of Times Square would hit rock bottom—"

"Whatever for?"

"So that after the tourists were scared off, they could pick up the abandoned real estate for next to nothing. In fact, some of them didn't even wait. A couple of years ago, you might remember, somebody ordered a wrecking ball to go to work in the middle of the night on Forty-fourth or Forty-fifth Street. The operator knocked down half a building before somebody stopped him."

"I remember," I said. "They not only didn't get a permit, they didn't even bother turning off the gas in the building, which could have blown up the whole damn block."

The cop nodded. "That's the guy. People a hundred yards in every direction would have been barbecued like Cagney in *White Heat*.

"But it's not just the developers. Some criminologists wanted to prevent dispersal of the criminals and weirdos throughout the city. Certain sociologists and for all I know some anthropologists wanted to preserve Times Square as a laboratory for their studies. So all of them argued for keeping it as it is.

"And the ordinary citizens," he said, pulling on a Steelers football jersey, "the good family men who buy coke and crack, or pay whores or uneducated Hispanic kids for quickie blow jobs, they don't want Times Square upgraded.

"Sure, they want protection from the muggers and lunatics and criminals, but not if it means *really* cleaning up Times Square. In fact, there's talk that the mob itself might start ridding the area of undesirables, to protect the value of their property. At least their property that survives redevelopment."

"What's your name?" I asked, surprised to hear that

kind of analysis outside a magazine or the op-ed pages of a newspaper.

"Rafael Sanchez. But I don't want to be quoted," he added quickly. "I still have fourteen more years before I'm eligible for retirement."

"How do you know so much about this?" I asked. Just then his partner strolled into the room carrying a lunch box. Tonight, obviously, they would pose as blue-collar workers.

Sanchez smiled. "If you were kicked and punched and shot at and pissed on night after night," he replied, "wouldn't you want to know why?"

"Tell 'em the rest of it," his partner urged. When Sanchez hesitated the partner said, "He grew up in Hell's Kitchen," referring to what is now called Clinton, a neighborhood adjoining Times Square to the west. "These streets now in the hands of animals are the streets he played in as a kid."

"I'm still playing in them," Sanchez said, reaching for his lunch pail. "Only now I'm playing for keeps."

Jill and I had not gone to sleep until four that morning, and it was almost ten o'clock when she hailed a taxi to return to her apartment. After several lingering kisses at the door I said I would see her at work, then I hurriedly showered and shaved.

I usually commuted by subway, because it was faster than the bus and because I considered the journey partial penance for my sins. I suppose other commuters did also, for why else suffer dirt, stench, aesthetic assault, blaring tape decks, swaggering youths who seemed to dare passengers to complain about their loud, profane conversation, and religious cultists who solicited money from captive audiences for what they claimed were such worthy causes as illiteracy, drug rehabilitation, or preventing kids from dropping out.

If the lights in my subway car were not burned out or missing, or if I did not pass the journey reading the scatological comments that anonymous graffiti artists had put into the mouths of the models in the subway ads, I sometimes read the latest trashy best sellers that a colleague in the book review department (she was, in fact, the entire book review department) passed along to me.

I chose some of them for entertainment, but mostly I read them to analyze the formulae for turning a literary composte heap into a harvest of gold. My distant dream was to knock off one or two such successes, then trade my press card for the literary life in the Hamptons, the Cape, or the Vineyard. That most durable of journalistic clichés notwithstanding, you would find no partially completed Great American Novel stuffed in my desk drawer, but you would discover reams of notes about how to plot and write the Great Commercial Best Seller. While the newly minted graduates who majored in English or creative writing were still paying homage to Austen and Faulkner, the border around my desk was papered with the publicity photos of the kings and queens of commercial fiction.

Viewing my literary pantheon, Jill once remarked with a shudder, "It's almost enough to make me lose my appetite." I noticed she was careful to emphasize the word "almost."

When the subway pulled into the Times Square station that morning after another ride in semidarkness, I was famished but still not hungry enough to patronize the grim subterranean bakery and fast-food counters. Instead,

I hurried up the subway stairs littered with fast-food wrappers and empty wine bottles, and emerged in the middle of the traffic island on Forty-third Street—and there outside Nathan's was Dingo, dirty, disheveled, and thrusting handbills on pedestrians.

He seemed wary at my approach, yet he pressed a handbill into my fist. "Dingo, didn't you get my message from Reverend Robeson?" I asked. "I have to talk to you."

"Not now, I'm working," he said, snapping off each handbill with a crisp crack.

"How much longer?"

"Till I give out these. And those." He indicated the stack in his hand and a stack twice as high alongside a nearby trash basket, anchored by an empty bottle of Night Train wine.

The familiar wail of a siren rent the air as an Emergency Medical Service ambulance turned onto Broadway, where it jerked to a halt while waiting for the intersection to clear. I imagined it was on its way to Bellevue or Metropolitan Hospital, and I made a mental note to see about riding in an ambulance, to profile the paramedics.

"Come see me when you finish," I said after the ambulance finally passed. "You know where I am: Forty-fourth between Eighth and Ninth."

He nodded, but I wasn't sure he did know. "Here," I said, handing him a couple of quarters. I also gave him my business card, remembering that with its usual generosity the *Free Press* had billed me for half the cost of the cards. "Phone me when you finish work and I'll take you to lunch."

"'Kay," he said, pocketing card and money without skipping a beat.

Only later, as I sat at my desk sorting the day's mail and messages, did I remember the handbill he gave me. It was an advertisement for the Freak Show, now only a few weeks away. The ad virtually duplicated the announcement on various billboards around town, but added that presentation of the handbill at the time of purchase entitled the bearer to one dollar off the admission price. And unlike the billboard ad, the handbill declared, "Thrill to the sight of Randy the Magnificent, seven feet one inch, making love to Tiny Tina, three feet, eight inches. Live, on stage. Definitely not for the squeamish."

I intended to ask Dingo who had hired him, but he neither telephoned nor stopped by. When I went looking for him about one-thirty, he was nowhere to be found. "Last time I saw him, he was watching the TV over at the Palace," Raymond Nelson said, referring to the movie theater across the street that showed film highlights on an outdoor monitor. But I could see that he wasn't there now.

Nelson glowed when I told him several publishers had telephoned to ask whether I thought his photos would make a good book.

"What'd you tell them?" he asked, mopping the perspiration from his brow and neck. It was a warm, cloudless day, one that bathed the entire city in bright sunlight. Although Nelson feigned indifference, he was pleased by the attention.

Before I could answer, however, a young woman came clacking down the sidewalk in high heels, wearing a bright red miniskirt and carrying a huge whip. Not until she passed did I realize from her feet and predominant Adam's Apple that "she" was really a "he." Then came an obese Caucasian dressed like a Sumo wrestler, complete with topknot, and with an attractive Oriental girl on one arm and a stunning black girl on the other.

Nelson and I looked at each other and shook our heads.

"Where were we?" I asked.

"You were gonna tell me what you told the publishers."

"I said you probably had several good books in all those photos. Any of them contacted you yet?"

"Nope. But when they do I mean to be prepared. Do you know a good agent?"

I told him the names of the only two agents I had ever heard of, before going on my way. But I had not gone far when I saw a familiar face: one of the kids who had attacked me the day of my run-in with Dingo and his playmates. Now he had a huge "blaster box" perched uncertainly on his shoulder, its stereo roaring full volume, as he sat on the hood of a parked car with two other teenagers.

I stopped a few feet in front of him and just stared, hoping, I suppose, to surprise him into an admission of guilt. But all three kids were so stoned that they paid not the slightest attention to me.

"Where's Dingo?" I finally shouted through cupped hands, trying to be heard above the din.

The kid I had met up with before opened his vacant eyes slowly. "Dingo? Where is that little mothafucka, man? 'Cause when I get ahold of him, I gonna slice his balls right offa him." He slurred his words, and although I could barely hear above the racket, his look left no doubt as to his meaning.

"Why?" I shouted. "What'd he do?"

He sneered, a sneer filled with hatred, but he did not reply. He closed his eyes again and began moving his head in time to the music. I noticed the three of them were wearing heavy boots, rather than the usual felony sneakers.

"What'd he do?" I repeated, just as the song ended.

"He fucked Maria, Che's sister, that's what he done," replied his companion.

None of the trio seemed older than about sixteen, but their expressions were malevolent enough for grownups.

Still, it was hard to think of Dingo, fourteen at most, making it with anybody's sister. Then it struck me that maybe Che's sister was some prepubescent. "How old's your sister?" I asked, fearing the worst.

But all Che did was rock slowly back and forth on his heels to a soft drink commercial, the blaster box still perched on his shoulder. An angry scar jutted from just under his left eye to his chin, giving him a look of exceptional villainy.

"Both balls, man," he declared, his eyes flickering dimly in anticipation. "One at a time. Zip, zip." He made an imaginary slashing movement with his left hand, in which he was grasping a brown paper bag, then he groped unsteadily for his boot and from a hidden sheath produced a bayonet-sized knife that he waved for dramatic effect.

"Maria's fifteen," his companion said. "Almost sixteen."

"Then she must be older than Dingo," I said, hoping to defuse some of Che's growing anger.

"That don't mean shit, man," he snarled. "Age ain't got a fuckin' thing to do with it."

"What does have 'a fuckin' thing to do with it'?" Even as I said it, I knew that while I might sound as tough as they sounded, life on the streets had long ago toughened them in ways I could not begin to comprehend.

"She eight months pregnant, man, eight fuckin' months," he said, "and that animal go and fuck her right in the same room wif her kids." He stuck his face into the paper bag and took several deep whiffs.

"Her kids?" I might have thought it was a put-on if Che and his zonked friends had been in any condition to joke.

"Her son and daughter," said another kid, most of whose face was hidden within the hood of his sweatshirt. Even in summer, it was a common work uniform for muggers and small-time drug dealers. I glanced up the street toward Nathan's, where the digital thermometer above the entrance registered eighty-two degrees.

"They did it right in Che's old lady's bedroom," the mahogany-skinned youngster added.

"In that hotel right there," the hooded friend chimed in, pointing to the Midtown Arms, as proud as if he were pointing out a neighborhood landmark.

As I walked away Che was still vowing to emasculate Dingo. I hoped his threats were caused by whatever he had been sniffing, but still I told Jill about them when I returned to the newsroom. She expressed immediate concern, saying we would have to find Dingo that night to warn him.

"And afterwards?" I asked suggestively, keeping my voice low enough to avoid being overheard, yet not so low she would think I was imitating Charles Boyer. Assuming she even knew who Charles Boyer was.

She smiled coquettishly. Then, in a gesture that only the two of us knew was more than a simple stretching exercise, she drew herself up at full length and thrust out her surprisingly ample chest.

"At your age," she said when she relaxed, having by then attracted the undivided attention of Irwin Haines and several other male reporters, "you should avoid cigarettes, fatty foods, and strenuous pastimes that might prove dangerous to your health."

We had no sooner approached my favorite coffee shop than I stopped short. "There she is," I said, nudging Jill, "there's the hooker I told you about."

"What hooker? Where?" Her voice betrayed her alarm at walking in this neighborhood at night.

Before I could reply, we had overtaken the pathetic creature I had once handed money to. She was wearing the regulation summer uniform of Eighth Avenue hookers, tight short-shorts and spiked heels, plus a cheap cotton V-necked blouse that revealed much too much of her sagging breasts.

This time I kept my wallet securely in my hip pocket and she did not speak, although for a few uncomfortable seconds I was afraid she might. But her bleary-eyed stare betrayed no trace of recognition, only a look so woebegone that if Jill hadn't been with me I probably would have given her money again.

"That poor woman," Jill said when we were out of earshot. "I was tempted to give her money myself."

"There'll be plenty of time for that," I assured her. "I'm reliably informed that some Times Square hookers last almost a whole year."

"Then what?" Like any good reporter she felt the urge to get on the record that which she already knew.

"Anything. Everything. Dead of an overdose. Murdered by some psychopathic john. Slashed by their pimp for not bringing in enough money."

At that moment we passed a heavily painted hooker whose limbs looked like a breeding ground for jungle rot. "Or they waste away from venereal disease," I added. "Or become so strung out on drugs and alcohol that even the cruisers who shop for sex along the Minnesota Strip want nothing to do with them."

Four unattended young girls were jumping rope on the sidewalk, chanting:

I hate your brother but he's in my class
He got popcorn balls and a rubber ass.
Jumped out the window with his dick in his han',
Yelling look out mothafucka, here come Superman.

We stopped to watch and a moment later a pregnant young woman stormed unsteadily out of a nearby bar and ordered them to get the hell home to bed, threatening "to smack you-all upside the head if you don't git," and promising she would be along home soon.

"That . . . that woman," Jill finally said, referring to the bleary-eyed whore, "she looked like she's dying, didn't she?"

I nodded, vainly trying once more to remember what there was about her.

After Raymond Nelson said he still had not seen anything of Dingo, we decided to visit Reverend Robeson at his hotel. But first I wanted to show Jill something, so we walked east on Forty-fourth. Midway between Sixth and Fifth, I stopped outside the Harvard Club. "I didn't know you were a Harvard grad," she beamed. "Now you can invite me for the club's great luncheon buffet."

"Sorry to disappoint you. I just wanted to show you these." I pointed to the three slender little-leaf linden trees in front of the building, near the curb.

She look puzzled. "Okay, I'll bite," she said finally. "You've been appointed gardening reporter?"

"Don't I wish. Look carefully," I said. "What do you see besides trees?"

"Trees with heart-shaped leaves."

She must have felt self-conscious, staring at the trees as well-dressed couples entered and left the club, but she gamely went along with my request. Finally, though, she threw up her hands. "Okay, I give up. What do I see?"

"Bars," I said simply, pointing to the five-foot-high protective metal bars surrounding the trees on all sides, anchored in metal plates embedded in the sidewalk. "The same thing over there." I pointed across the street to similar enclosures surrounding the trees outside the handsome limestone-and-marble building housing the Bar Association of the City of New York.

"Of course!" she said, smacking her forehead with her hand, as if struck by a sudden insight.

70

Then, after a decent interval, she asked, "But what does it mean?"

I took her by the arm and guided her toward the Hotel Miami. "It means nothing . . . and everything," I said as we strolled by the Algonquin. "Don't you see, it's a perfect metaphor. Here we are, in this relatively safe street, where saplings are well protected to give them a chance to grow to maturity. But less than five minutes away, hundreds of young kids, like those little girls who were jumping rope, have no protection . . . have almost no chance of flourishing."

I could see her considering my words, her expression becoming ever more pensive under the glow of the streetlights. "It might be a little subtle for most of our readers," she said finally. "But you should write an article along those lines, maybe pegged to an interview with the gardener, or whoever tends those trees."

"It might also be too subtle for our managing editor," I replied, "but it won't hurt to give it a try."

We walked the rest of the way in satisfied silence, until we reached the hotel. When the needle-pocked clerk said Reverend Robeson had not returned all day, I scribbled a note on the back of my business card and asked the clerk to drop it in the minister's message box.

"Where to?" Jill asked when we stepped outside the fetid hotel lobby, almost into the path of a lurching, shuffling junky. Fifteen feet away a bent old woman clad in rags was rummaging in a trash can, talking gibberish. I knew Jill would have preferred almost anywhere to Times Square at night, but I had to find Dingo before Che and his friends did.

I reminded her of the cliché about meeting everyone you ever knew at the Forty-second Street intersection of Broadway and Seventh, but I prudently neglected to add that today you were far more likely to see every psychopath and criminal within a hundred-mile radius of Times Square. "Maybe if we stand there a while tonight we'll see

Dingo. Anyhow, it's better than roaming the side streets, having to worry about being stalked."

If Jill had decided to leave I would not have blamed her, although she would have had to go on without me. But she stayed, relaxing our vigil just long enough to fortify herself with several pieces of fried chicken and a biscuit.

The two-man police teams posted at the intersections emboldened her to stand in the crowd viewing the scenes of kung fu action on the monitor outside the Palace Theater. When she soon had her fill of that we strolled to the corner, and, like anthropologists newly arrived in a distant land, we studied the cast of characters streaming by as we searched for Dingo.

These included a bearded three-hundred-pounder wearing a muscle shirt who sported two horseshoes suspended around his neck on a golden chain.

A tall, thin man with dirty blonde tresses, who, while balancing himself on one leg like a Dinka tribesman, stared at the window of a shop that sold exotic female lingerie.

A half-dozen high school kids, each of them bare chested and each wearing the kepi of the French Foreign Legion, bargaining with veteran drug dealers, who could scarcely conceal their amusement at the kids' swaggering gullibility.

Rastafarians in tight black dreadlocks, whose blaster boxes filled the night with reggae music.

An elderly woman with bright red hair who stood on the sidewalk facing oncoming traffic, alternately yodeling and breaking into fits of high-pitched laughter.

Shortly after eleven I convinced Jill there was no reason for her to remain longer, so I looked for a cab to take her home. Obviously relieved, she nevertheless raised a feeble protest that I had no trouble overcoming, but it proved impossible to find an empty taxi among the unbroken yellow caravan racing down Broadway.

"Let's walk to Forty-fifth," I finally said. "There are usually empty cabs at the Laney International."

Tonight I was willing to suspend my private boycott of the Laney, a sterile, modern fortress that rose on the site of three handsome, historic theaters that were laid low by the developers' wrecking balls.

We turned down Forty-fourth a short distance and cut through Shubert Alley, a block-long pedestrian walkway bordered by a new Italian restaurant on the east and a gift shop on the west. Jill hesitated at the edge of the deserted thoroughfare, but I assured her that potential muggers would be deterred by the well-lighted approaches at either end. What finally won her over, though, were not my assurances but a promise to bring her to the restaurant for lunch.

As we walked through at a brisk clip, she kept talking to keep up her courage. Then suddenly she gasped.

"What is it?" I asked. When she pointed to something or someone sprawled in the shadow near the gift shop, I was tempted to remind her that this was Times Square, not Sutton Place—although in truth the city's wretched human refuse was increasingly washing up even on New York's more affluent asphalt beaches. When I realized the prostrate figure was probably a child, for a fleeting moment I had a premonition that we had just found Noah.

Instead, stretched out cold amid several empty wine bottles, and reeking of alcohol, was a familiar grimy figure. "Dingo!" I said, kneeling beside him and placing my arm under his head.

"Dingo?" Jill asked. "This . . . this child . . . is Dingo?"

I don't think I will ever forget the astonished look on her face at that moment, as she tried to reconcile the reality of that pathetic, unconscious child with the wild boy of my descriptions.

Thank God, there was no indication that Che had carried out this threat—no sign of mutilation, no sign that his torn and ragged clothing had been slashed by a knife. There was, in fact, no sign that he was anything but dead drunk.

"What shall we do with him?" Jill asked. "Take him to the hospital in a cab? Phone an ambulance?"

My first thought was to ask Raymond Nelson if we could use his apartment, but by now he would be out shooting his photographs until morning. I considered carrying Dingo over to the Hotel Miami, certain that Reverend Robeson would welcome the boy, but that seemed a heavy burden to dump on a sorrowing elderly man. Finally I said, "Let's take him to my place."

I was grateful that Jill did not try talking me out of it, or suggest that it was a foolish idea, or raise any of a number of other reasonable objections. Instead, after wiping his soiled mouth with her handkerchief, she flagged down a taxi while I picked up the youngster and clasped him to me. Throughout the ride, during which the Pakistani taxi driver periodically glanced at me suspiciously through the rearview mirror, Jill kept her hand against Dingo's brow to comfort him.

We drew curious glances in the elevator from an elderly couple who lived on the floor above my apartment, but other passengers only scrunched up their noses at the overpowering odor of cheap alcohol, all the while staring straight ahead.

We washed Dingo as best we could as he lay sprawled on the couch. Jill removed his worn tennis shoes and faded T-shirt, a shirt depicting a spotted jungle cat and bearing the legend, "I Love Pussy." His chest and shoulders bore a half-dozen scars from knife cuts, one of them a good six inches long.

I began removing his torn trousers but when it became apparent that he was not wearing underwear I zipped his pants back up and improvised a bed for him on the floor, meantime leaving him on the couch.

Jill and I occupied the bedroom for the next hour, pausing repeatedly during our lovemaking to listen to his labored breathing. At one point, as we lay exhausted on our backs, she asked, "Do you have children, Alex?"

The question took me by such surprise that even in the near darkness she could sense my confusion. I was confused not because I had anything to hide but because my past—except for once telling her I was divorced—had not before come up during our relationship.

"Only Dingo," I said finally, hoping to strike an amusing note.

Her silence suggested she was not as amused as I had hoped. I realized she probably wanted to know why but could not bring herself to ask.

"I wanted kids," I said, breaking the silence, "a house full of them. But a reporter's salary is not exactly the answer to tuition bills and braces—not even the salaries of two reporters."

"Your wife was a reporter, too?"

"A television reporter."

"Alex!" She sat upright in mock astonishment. "You of all people, married to a *television* reporter."

"Worse than that," I admitted, gently pushing her back down onto the bed. "She became an anchorwoman. She still is, or was, the last time I heard from her."

"Next you're going to tell me you were married to Connie Chung, or Diane Sawyer, or one of those other brainy beauties."

The way she said it I had the impression she somehow felt inadequate, even though she could hold her own in looks and intelligence with any television newswoman.

"No such luck. Her name's Ann, and she never made it to the networks—only to Kansas City and Albuquerque. She was never even as famous as Kris Carten," I kidded, naming a New York TV reporter who was notorious among print journalists for her banal questions, her overbearing personality, and her ability to outdo most of her colleagues in "wrapping up" stories by using anonymous quotes that just happened to convey her own point of view.

Having told Jill that much about Ann, I proceeded to tell

her a little more about our marriage and eventual break-up. I said that with both of us dedicated to our careers, and neither of us willing to compromise, about children or much else, it was only a matter of time before we drifted apart.

"Neither of us had somebody else," I said. "There were no ugly scenes, and no dramatic parting. Emily Dickinson had it about right, in our case at least, when she wrote, ''Tis not love's going that blights my days/but that it went in little ways.'"

She was silent an unusually long time. Finally she said, "That's not much of a blueprint for the future, Alex."

Only then did I realize that that explanation hurt her more than if I really had been married to Connie Chung or Diane Sawyer. But I did my best to convince her that the failure of my marriage was a page from the past, not necessarily a blueprint for the future.

She snuggled closer to me, and I felt a tear drop graze my chest. Just when I thought she had drifted off to sleep she looked up and said, "Compared with the problems of that little boy in the next room, almost everything else sounds trivial, doesn't it?"

Instead of answering I patted her on the head to indicate agreement, agreement with which I'm sure Ann also would have concurred.

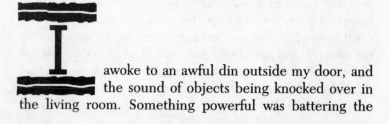

I awoke to an awful din outside my door, and the sound of objects being knocked over in the living room. Something powerful was battering the wall, trying mightily to break it down. I leaped from bed and threw on the switch in the living room—in time to see Dingo racing around in panic, hurtling from one corner of the room to another like a wild animal who had just been enclosed in a cage.

"Dingo, it's Alex," I said, "It's Alex." I stuck out my arm to restrain him as he barreled past again, but his compact body knocked it aside.

"He doesn't see you," said Jill, who huddled in the doorway. "He looks like he's in a trance."

I let him run, hoping that with the lights on he would avoid running into my few furnishings and hurting himself, and hoping also that he would soon unwind. But when he finally came to a stop some minutes later he crouched in the far corner and began howling—I don't know how else to describe it—and making other animal noises.

I approached him cautiously and tried draping my arm around him, but he shrugged it off in a single motion and stared at me with eyes filled with fright. When he began howling again, provoking angry thumps on the ceiling from the neighbor above, Jill approached him and said something that soon had a calming effect. When she put her arm around him he whimpered, then rocked back and forth, but he made no attempt to remove it. As his fright began to subside he held his head and groaned while Jill and I stroked him and tried to soothe him.

"Take me home," he begged before long. "Take me back home." It was heartbreaking to listen to his childish, plaintive voice.

"Soon, Dingo," I promised. "I'll take you home soon."

"Now!" he demanded, his voice filled with urgency and fright.

"Let's have breakfast first," Jill said. I thought she was only trying to get him to relax, but later she said she was also struck by how malnourished he looked.

He grimaced, and at that moment I again caught a strong whiff of alcohol. "I'm too sick to eat, lemme go home," he protested.

"Where's home?" I asked, with little expectation that he would tell me.

"I wanna go to Reverend Robeson's," Dingo said, pulling on his panther T-shirt. "I wanna tell him I saw that kid last night who might be his grandson."

"Where? Where did you see him?" Jill asked excitedly.

Instead of answering he dropped his head into his hands again and groaned. "Take me out of here," he pleaded. "Lemme go home."

I saw nothing to be gained by keeping him against his will, not in his state and not with at least one irate neighbor, so I decided to try to bargain: "Take a shower. Go in there and wash the dirt off you, then I'll take you right home." When he just looked at me with a puzzled expression I added, "It'll help make your headache go away."

When Dingo finally spoke he said, "Alone?"

"What do you mean, alone?"

"Where will you be when I'm inna shower?"

Jill and I exchanged puzzled glances. "We'll be sitting at the kitchen table drinking coffee. Unless you need me in there to hold your hand."

The boy was not amused. "If I take a stinkin' shower," he said, glowering, "I want you to keep the fuck outta the room."

His profanity and tough-guy manner were hard to take, but I did not want to scare him away. I still had a hundred questions I wanted answered, and on top of that I felt a degree of responsibility toward the boy. "With Jill as my witness, I promise not to leave the kitchen table," I vowed.

I gave him a clean towel, and, after he cast a slightly suspicious glance at Jill, Dingo fairly slinked into the bathroom. He ran the water in the tub for at least five minutes before the door flew open and he stuck his head out, signaling me to come there.

"Where's the fuckin' hot water? And how do you work the fuckin' shower?" he demanded.

"I'll show you . . . if I'm allowed in."

He stepped aside slowly, grudgingly allowing me entry into his sanctum sanctorum. He was wrapped in a bath towel almost as wide as he was long, which he cinched tightly under his thin arms. After showing him how to operate the mixing spigot, and how to divert the water flow to the shower, I left him to soak to his heart's content.

When he emerged twenty minutes later he was wearing the same soiled clothing. I had nothing his size to give him, but while he had been in the shower I told Jill that I planned to buy him clothes that very day, and she offered to help me shop for them.

I was embarrassed to be seen walking to the corner in a respectable neighborhood with him wearing that raunchy T-shirt, but Dingo seemed oblivious. When he asked me to buy him a pack of cigarettes I offered to give him the money, but I said he would have to buy them himself.

"I ain't old enough," he protested.

"Then you're not old enough to smoke," I declared in my best Dutch uncle voice. But he had been through quite enough for one night, so I relented. At a nearby deli I bought him the cigarettes and picked out an assortment of pastry for Jill. When I handed Dingo the pack he tore it open without a word, after removing the cellophane wrapper with his teeth. Three, four, five times he drew deeply on the cigarette, inhaled with his eyes closed, then exhaled. I have no doubt that tobacco causes cancer and a dozen other ailments, but that cigarette helped restore Dingo to his old self, a self about which I had certain obvious reservations.

Jill took a cab to her apartment and we flagged down a taxi for Times Square. We hadn't gone fifty yards when the driver directed our attention to the NO SMOKING sign pasted on the glass divider. Dingo ignored it, and when he scoffed at the driver's order to extinguish the cigarette the cab pulled to the curb and the cabbie cut the motor.

Picking up a heavy-duty flashlight and slapping it menacingly against his palm, the driver said, "I got emphysema and can't breathe if somebody smokes in my cab, so either the cigarette goes out or the two of you, out."

"Tough shit, buddy," Dingo said, taking a provocatively deep drag. "'Cause I ain't gonna put out this cigarette and we ain't getting the fuck out of here."

Pocketing his keys, the angry driver got out of the cab before I could apologize for Dingo's behavior. Threatening to call the cops, he walked to a pay phone at the corner. Dingo sputtered and threatened defiance, but I finally managed to convince him of the wisdom of beating a strategic retreat.

As we made our way across town in another taxi a few minutes later, Dingo cursed nonstop, interrupting his denunciation of the first cabby just long enough to berate me for not punching him out. I tried to explain that the driver was under no obligation to take passengers who did not obey the posted regulations, but Dingo was in no mood to listen. Instead, he lighted another cigarette and alternated between blowing smoke at the new driver's neck and out the side of his mouth at me.

When we arrived at the Hotel Miami, where a derelict lay sprawled on his back in a corner of the lobby, Reverend Robeson had already departed on his daily rounds. Only as we groped our way down the darkened hallway did Dingo tell me that the kid he thought might be Noah had denied it. "Said his name was Richard. But fags always lie," he added.

"How do you know he's a 'fag'?"

He gave me a look of such scarcely veiled contempt that I was sorry I asked.

"He was outside where all the games are, where lots of fuckin' chickens hang out," he said, a cigarette dangling from his lip. "After I talked with him he went off with some crazy fuckin' guy from Jersey that most chickens won't go with no more."

I could scarcely believe I was hearing all this from a child, but as we turned the corner into Broadway we came face to face with a string of X-rated movies and X-rated shops whose windows overflowed with mammoth phallic vibrators, stilettos, and serrated jungle knives— merchandise a world apart from that displayed in the toy stores of suburbia, or even in the toy stores on the East Side.

But Dingo was energized by being safely back on home turf. His anxiety and headache vanished, and he appeared as happy as I had ever seen him. "Look," he exclaimed, coming to an abrupt halt and staring up as a huge flock of pigeons flew in a lazy circle toward the reflecting glass near the top of the Laney International, before continuing up Broadway and regrouping.

"Jeez-us," he exclaimed.

"Impressive, isn't it?" I said, delighted with his appreciation of nature.

"Yeah, man. I just wish I had a gun," he replied, cocking both thumbs and firing his index fingers at the flock.

I bought an I LOVE NEW YORK T-shirt at the corner stand, the only T-shirt they had in his size, and invited Dingo to breakfast. When he chose McDonald's on Seventh Avenue, I agreed, provided he change into the clean T-shirt. And for once he obeyed without an argument. When he peeled off his old shirt and left it on the sidewalk, I asked, "Don't you want to save that? You can have it washed."

"It stinks," he said. "Besides, I got lots more where that come from."

"Where did it come from?" I asked, gingerly picking up the shirt and depositing it in a nearby trash can. But when Dingo answered with a laugh, I knew better than to persist with the questioning.

Dingo had wanted a Big Mac but this time of morning McDonald's served only breakfast. After reciting a few choice swear words, he settled for two Egg McMuffins and coffee.

I hesitated to return to the subject, but I needed to know more about chickens and chicken hawks so I could write about them with some authority. After we were seated, I asked Dingo to tell me what he knew about the boy who said he was Richard rather than Noah. Then I asked why boys became chickens. "Money, man," he replied, "what else? Who gonna take all that hassle if he ain't making lots of money?"

I'm still not sure if I asked the next question for professional reasons or out of curiosity, but, keeping my voice down so none of the half-dozen other customers could hear, I finally said, "Are you a chicken, Dingo?"

He looked at me with disgust. "Do I look like a fuckin' fag?" he demanded.

I assured him he did not, but in the next breath I asked, "Not all chickens are gay, are they? You said yourself they make a lot of money."

Several businessmen who had stopped in for breakfast on their way across town seemed amused by Dingo's language, if not his execrable table manners. Even though I could understand why they found him amusing, their muttered comments annoyed me. But Dingo appeared not to notice. After draining every drop of orange juice from his cup, then wiping his mouth on his brown arm, he said, "No fuckin' man is ever gonna fuck me."

A startled blue-collar worker two tables away glared at

me with undisguised loathing. I was tempted to get up and leave, and the temptation grew as Dingo continued to speak as loudly as if he were back in my apartment.

"A couple months ago," he said, "some fat sonuvabitch from Brooklyn or somewheres like that, he tried to get me to go down on him in his car. Said he'd give me fifty dollars for two minutes work."

I studied Dingo carefully to see if he was trying to shock me or the other customers, but he seemed unaware that he had said anything shocking. He interrupted his tale long enough to fish a mangled piece of Danish from his pocket. "Want some?" he asked.

I shook my head. Even if I hadn't just eaten, the sight of it would have ruined my appetite. "Where'd you get that?"

He smiled. "That store where you bought the cigarettes," he replied proudly. "Got this, too," he said, pulling cheap salt and pepper shakers from his other pocket.

Before I could sermonize about theft, or worry about what he might have stolen from my apartment, he resumed his story. "I fixed his fat ass," he said, chewing as he talked. "Told him to take out his dick so I could see it first, and when he pulled it out, outside of some hotel on Forty-sixth Street, I kicked 'im right in the balls. He fell like a ton of shit, man. I ran away, but I heard him yellin' in pain for a whole block. Served that fat fuck right."

Even the guy two tables away seemed amused, but I had visions of that fat guy retaliating, possibly by hiring a couple of goons. Then I remembered Che's threats.

"He's been braggin' for a long time he gonna cut my nuts off," the boy said when I told him.

"You're not worried?"

He shook his head. "He tried it before. Sliced up my hand pretty good," he said, extending his left palm for examination while holding the cup of coffee with his other hand. "But that time he surprised me, him and that nigger friend of his, Ozzie. This time I'll be ready."

"Dingo, don't use that kind of language. Names like 'nigger' and 'fag' are insulting."

He looked puzzled. "What do you call niggers?"

"'Blacks,'" I said impatiently, hoping the worker across the way, himself a dark Hispanic, could not hear our conversation.

Dingo shrugged. He had never heard "blacks" used for niggers before, he said, but if it made me feel good he'd try to remember to use it.

I assured him it would make me feel good, then I asked, "How will you be ready for him this time? Che, I mean? He carries a knife almost a foot long in his boot."

"Don't worry, I got me a pig sticker, one of them big push-button knives, and if he come after me again I'm gonna carve him into a thousan' fuckin' pieces, the way he carved up that ol' drunk."

"What old drunk?"

"I don't know his fuckin' name, just some drunk that Che stabbed a few months ago."

I wasn't sure I wanted to pursue the matter, but since I had gone this far . . . "How do you know he stabbed him?"

He looked at me as if I were a simpleton. "I fuckin' saw the body, that's how. Che showed it to me in a empty lot. He said he done it."

I shuddered. "He killed him?"

Dingo took another bite of food, then nodded. "Must of bled to death, he had so many holes in him."

"Maybe Che was just bragging," I said, not wanting to believe something so terrible about a youngster who was still walking around free.

He shook his head. "The night before, he tole me he was gonna smoke that guy."

"Smoke?"

He sighed. "Waste. He's killed a couple-a drunks. Him and Larry killed an old man that they mugged right near your newspaper. Knocked his brains out with a tire iron."

"You mean that retired NYU professor?" I asked, remembering that brutal unsolved murder of a few months ago.

"I don't fuckin' know what he was," Dingo said wearily. "They just tole me they smashed an old guy's head in with a tire iron, and the next day everybody on the street was talkin' about the murder."

For a few minutes I didn't say another word. I was appalled at how casually Dingo spoke of the most heinous crimes—and, if what he said was true, of how casually some Times Square kids carried out those murders. Finally, no longer able to pursue that subject, I asked Dingo, "What happened to your mother?"

He looked off in the distance for some time, apparently summoning up courage to talk about her. "She died a couple years ago, when she was havin' another kid," he said finally. "I come home from school and there was all these people in the apartment. One of them tole me, he said she kept sayin' my name. The baby died too. He was a boy."

I wanted to ask more—about his mother, about Che, about Che's sister, about that whole youthful Times Square subculture. But he was fighting back tears, and I saw he was impatient to leave. "Before you go, Dingo," I said. "Where do you live? Where do you sleep?"

"With friends," he replied without hesitation. "I got this friend who's got this big apartment uptown, I stay there lotsa nights. Lotsa other nights I stay at some other guy's apartment."

He was a practiced but unconvincing liar, although I thought it best not to press him too hard—nudge him, perhaps, but not press him. "What about the nights you don't stay with your friends?"

He eyed me suspiciously. "You ain't writing a story bout me, are you Alex?"

I shook my head. "Not about you, Dingo. But I want to offer you a job."

I was relieved when our disgusted Hispanic neighbor finally left, yet his departure did nothing to allay Dingo's apparent suspicions. "What kinda job?" he asked.

"To tell me about life on the street. I want to meet for breakfast or lunch each day where I can ask questions about—"

"So that's it, you want me to be a fuckin' squealer."

"No, I *don't* want you to squeal," I said, afraid he might bolt for the door. "I'm not after any names. But I want to know how kids survive on the street—straight kids, hustlers, chickens."

"What you wanna know for?" Sitting at that table, that improbable fifty-eight-inch sovereign had the upper hand and he knew it.

"Because I want to understand street life, I want to write about it."

"Why?"

I could have told him because that was my assignment, but what would a kid his age understand about newspaper beats?

I also could have told him I hoped that by writing knowledgably about the grim lives of runaway and abandoned kids in the midst of one of the richest cities on earth, maybe the mayor or the governor or even the president might do something to help them.

Or I could have told him I cared about Dingo, a sentiment I'm sure would have evoked a torrent of scorn and curses from the boy. It was true, though. He was a dirty-mouthed urchin, without any doubt, but he had not always been dirty-mouthed, or an urchin, and there had been no decree that he had to remain one.

In the end, though, I told him none of those things.

Instead, I said, "Because I want to understand the kind of life Noah might have gotten himself involved in." I thought up that explanation at the last second, but it was not untruthful and it seemed to appeal to Dingo.

"I could tell you some things if I wanted," he said, sounding thirty years older than his actual age. "But not at no breakfast."

"Lunch, then," I said, feeling like a fisherman after his first nibble of the morning. But when Dingo remained noncommittal I added, "I'll also pay you a salary."

That perked him up. "How much?"

"What's fair?" I had a figure in mind, but I wanted to hear what he expected.

"Ten bucks an hour."

"Five," I quickly countered, for I had no illusions that Kenneth Parks or Martha Liston would reimburse me one red cent.

"Five, your ass. I can make more'n that handin' out leaflets."

"Five, plus lunch."

"And a pack of butts each day."

What the hell, I reasoned, it was his funeral—although I doubted that smoking was much more hazardous to his health than the accumulated assaults of living in Times Square.

We had no sooner agreed to terms than I wondered if even five dollars might not be too much for a kid Dingo's age, but before I could think it through he was leading me out the door of the restaurant and bidding me good-bye the instant we reached Forty-second Street.

Happy to be back home, he took off down that perilous thoroughfare exuding complete confidence. I watched him disappear into the crowd, and at that moment he reminded me not of a dingo but a shark, a creature that must keep moving or die.

For two days I saw nothing of Dingo, although the next afternoon I ran into Che and his cohorts outside the video arcade on Seventh Avenue, their blaster box still blaring as they passed a joint from one to another. All of them looked stoned, but the sight of me perked up Che sufficiently to repeat his threat against Dingo.

"Fuck off," I told him, using language I knew he would understand. I was not anxious to antagonize him, after what Dingo had told me about him murdering the derelict, but after some indistinguishable muttering Che picked up a bottle wrapped in a brown bag and proceeded to drink from it.

I wondered why they were making themselves so conspicuous when just the night before a group answering to their description had robbed two tourists on Broadway, beaten and robbed an unsuspecting couple who had remained talking outside a theater, and terrorized passengers on the IRT subway line between Times Square and Penn Station. Yet clearly they were making no effort to keep out of sight.

Outside the Hotel Miami a couple of five-year-olds stopped playing tag over the prostrate body of a drunk long enough to fix me in the sites of their "guns"—in actuality, their index fingers—and tell me I was dead. Inside, Reverend Robeson was awaiting my visit.

"I'm glad you got my message," I said, surrendering my hand to his usual powerful grip. To my surprise, however,

I realized that much of the strength had ebbed from his handshake, as had much of the energy that had radiated from the rest of him when we first met.

Kenneth Parks and the *Free Press* accountants be damned. I invited the minister to breakfast at the Rose Room in the Hotel Algonquin. Only a brief walk from the Hotel Miami, it was a world away in every other respect. I had long wanted to take him there, but had hesitated out of concern that he might feel out of place—not for racial reasons, although there was only one other black customer that morning, but because breakfast at the Rose Room, with its linens and fine china, cost almost twice as much as his nightly hotel room. Even though I intended to charge it off to the newspaper, I did not want to make him ill at ease.

But if Reverend Robeson felt out of place, it did not show. He ate a generous breakfast of eggs, ham, hash browns, and toast, pausing every few minutes to admire the crystal chandeliers and the full-length wall mirrors that reflected the bright red chairs and benches. For the prices they charged, which in fact were on a par with those of other first-class New York restaurants, I almost expected to see Robert Benchley, Dorothy Parker, or other literary wits of the Algonquin Roundtable. But Reverend Robeson enjoyed it so much I was sorry I hadn't invited him earlier.

"I never saw anything as fine looking as this," he said each of the four times the waiter refilled his coffee cup from a sterling silver pitcher. He especially admired the pink carnations at each table, and when the maître d' offered him one to wear in his frayed lapel he was overjoyed.

Raymond Nelson soon joined us, causing some raised eyebrows. I couldn't tell whether the reaction was related to his race or to his earring, but soon we were so engrossed in our own conversation that I forgot about it. A few more eyebrows shot up when Reverend Robeson said grace, but afterwards an elderly black waiter at another table, a white-haired man with a gentle manner, came by and said a heartfelt, "God bless you."

When the main course arrived I said, "Reverend Robeson, Raymond has something to tell you."

"Dear God, you have located Noah!" he said in a faltering voice. "You know where my grandson is."

Hope turned to heartbreak when we told him we had not been able to find a trace of the boy, and he lapsed into silence until Nelson told him he wanted the clergyman to move into his apartment. "If you can put up with my upside-down work habits, and don't mind stepping over some photo equipment, you're welcome to stay as long as you want," the photographer said.

Knowing the minister was running out of money, I had invited him several weeks earlier to share my apartment. But no doubt because he understood my situation with Jill, he declined the offer. He also wanted to remain in Times Square, he said, because, "I am too old to commute here every day."

Jill and I then thought about helping to pay the clergyman's rent, until I remembered Raymond Nelson's nearby apartment. When I asked if he would accept the clergyman if Jill and I paid his room and board, Nelson said he would be pleased to have him as a roommate, on condition that he live there rent-free.

"But since it might look like discrimination if I refused to let two ofays help a brother," he added, barely keeping a straight face, "you can split the cost of his food with me if you want."

It was then that I suggested the breakfast meeting so Nelson could break the news.

Reverend Robeson listened to Nelson's offer without comment, but tears gathered in the corners of his eyes. When he spoke he raised any number of objections: he would be a bother. He snored. He stayed in the shower too long. Nelson would not have as much privacy.

When the photographer brushed aside each objection, the old man asked, "What about your wife or girl friend? What will they say about you having a boarder?"

Nelson laughed aloud, a warm, hearty laugh with a Caribbean lilt. "I had two wives and both are long gone," he said. "I'm not planning to have another for a long, long time. Right now I'm married to my camera."

"But you have to have a woman," he protested. "It is not right, a fine young man like you not having a woman."

"I didn't say I didn't have a woman," Nelson quickly replied. "I have . . . oh, let me see, three or four. Five, if you count the waitress at that fish restaurant on Eighth Avenue who's engaged to the boss." He laughed, drinking in the memory.

"Well there you are."

"It's no problem, I tell them I'm married so they don't ask to come to my apartment. I go to theirs."

Far removed by age, occupation, and outlook from that kind of thinking, Reverend Robeson was puzzled. "You mean you say you are married and it does not bother them? And why do you want to tell them that?"

"So they won't want to move in with me. So I can develop my pictures without having them beg me to come to bed. So I can come and go when I want."

Nelson started to bite into his English muffin, but seeing the older man's puzzlement he stopped. "It might have bothered women in your day, Reverend," he explained, "but women today like it when they think you're married. It's more exciting."

The preacher did not understand, nor did he approve, yet he had to smile at the explanation of his new landlord.

Later that morning I helped move him the half-mile from the squalor of the Hotel Miami to his clean new home. "Raymond told me I can look at his photographs whenever I want," he said, in what I assumed was intended as an explanation for his decision to move in with Nelson instead of me.

I returned to the *Free Press* soon afterwards, anxious to finish a story about the dangers of working the night shift in a Times Square subway booth. The article was pegged to the recent fiery death of a clerk at the Seventh Avenue IRT booth after two teenagers squirted lighter fluid through the booth's token and change slot, then set it on fire.

But just as I switched on my word processor, Irwin Haines ambled up, hands clasped behind his back, to say that Parks wanted a story for tomorrow on the Freak Show.

"Why the rush?" I asked. "It doesn't open for a few more weeks. The dates are on the flyer." I had given him a copy of Dingo's handbill, which repeated the original promises but added several additional sexual feats, including the one involving Randy and Tina.

"He's afraid one of the other papers will write something about it," Haines said, shrugging his shoulders warily. "So your first story should announce that the show will be here, when, hints of what it's likely to include—"

"I know, I know," I said impatiently. "Who, what, when, where. I don't think our readers need to know 'how.' At least not the ones who are thinking of attending."

"Parks also wants a denunciation from the mayor," he said, pretending not to have heard me.

"Wait a minute," I protested, "I'm a reporter, not a scriptwriter. How do we know the mayor gives a good goddamn about another sex show in Times Square, much less that he'll denounce it?"

"Alex, how long have you been a journalist?" His manner suggested that I should know better than to ask such a naive question. "It's all arranged, Parks has taken care of it."

"So I write the score for his melody?"

The city editor closed his eyes and I could almost hear him counting to ten. "You know Parks wouldn't care if CBS showed freaks fucking live and in color during prime time every night of the week," he said patiently. "But if he thought he could steal a beat on the *Times* he'd call out the infantry, the artillery, and the air force. So pamper him. Indulge him in his fixation and maybe he'll let us keep our jobs."

I had to laugh at Haines, even though I was boiling at having to write a rehearsed story about the mayor's ostensible moral outrage.

"I'll only do it on one condition," I said at last.

Again Haines closed his eyes, only now he stood with his hands clasped before him in prayer. "Give it to me gently," he said. "I can hardly bear the suspense."

"If you're praying for a raise, it won't do you any good," Dick Suft quipped as he hurried past.

"He's praying that he hits the lottery," said one of the copy-editors, who himself never bought fewer than fifteen lottery tickets a week.

After the irreverence had subsided I said, "I want your promise that Parks will nominate the piece for a Pulitzer."

"Sure, son," Haines replied, laying a reassuring hand on my shoulder, "the Pulitzer and maybe even the Nobel. Meantime, see if you can hold it to five cents," he added, using *Free Press* argot meaning five hundred words.

I did as ordered, of course, producing another of those *Freep* hybrids mixing news and commentary on which we seemed to own the copyright. And of course the mayor just happened to have an extemporaneous response to my telephone inquiry, denouncing anyone who would try to make money by exploiting the physical defects of others.

The lead editorial in the *Free Press* a day later likewise denounced the Freak Show, concluding with a ringing demand that it be banned. I didn't have to write about that in the news columns, but my story that day, about a new wave of assaults by youth gangs that roamed the side streets of Times Square brandishing clubs and chains, did contain an insert (a "reefer" in journalese) directing readers' attention to the editorial.

The following day, Dingo had still not been heard from. Jill and I were walking east on Forty-fifth Street toward an Argentinian restaurant when someone called to us from a doorway. Not until Jill said "It's your friend" did I recognize the strung-out streetwalker. What, I wondered, was she doing so far from her usual haunts?

"He's upstairs, up there," she said in her raspy voice, poking her thumb behind her.

I was about to humor her so we could move along when she repeated her statement.

"Who's up there?" I finally asked.

"Your friend. That preacher man."

I was so surprised that she knew who Reverend Robeson and I were, or knew who *anyone* was, for that matter, that I did not for a moment doubt that the clergyman was upstairs. And the instant I saw the sign in the second floor window, offering cash to blood donors, I realized why.

Jill and I climbed the stairs in silence. When we reached the entrance to the blood bank, I no sooner pulled the handle on the fragile wooden door than it opened and out came Reverend Robeson. When he saw us he was rendered speechless.

I was afraid Jill was going to break down and cry right there, and thinking about it even days later still brought tears to her eyes. I too was overwhelmed by sorrow. I knew the minister was running out of money, but it never occurred to me that he had been selling his blood—especially since, at his age and after a lifetime of toil, he looked as if he could have benefitted from a transfusion.

It was a painful, embarrassing moment for everyone, yet none of us acknowledged our embarrassment. With his cracked left eyeglass lense, Reverend Robeson looked especially pathetic. Yet he offered neither explanation nor apology, nor did Jill or I hint that anything was amiss. Instead, all of us acted as if we had met there by prearrangement. And even during lunch, at which we persuaded him to join us, we talked about his new apartment, about the differences between New York and Nashville, and ultimately about Noah—about everything except the sorry state of his finances.

"I have a feeling that I am going to find that boy very soon," he said of Noah as he buttered a roll. When we looked surprised he explained, "I have always had faith, but what I feel now is special. I am convinced . . ." He lowered his voice so that I could barely hear him. "I am convinced it is the presence of God."

His eyes shone with a bright, new intensity. "The last time I felt it this strong," he continued, "Noah's father was thirteen or fourteen years old. A friend of his came running up to the church hollering that a gang of white boys had grabbed him off the street and said they were going to lynch him.

"I rushed outside and then started racing downtown, almost crazy with fear, when all of a sudden a voice as clear as a bell told me my boy was not in danger. But I still ran every step of the way, and when I got a block or two from downtown he was walking toward home. He was scared and shaken, but unharmed. The boys said they had just been playing a practical joke."

"Some joke," Jill said, shuddering as though from a sudden chill.

"With Noah, Jr., this has been going on too long to be a joke," the minister said. "But I have the same feeling that he will also turn up unharmed." At that, although lunch was almost over, he bowed his head and prayed briefly.

We told him we were sure his optimism would be rewarded, for it was impossible in his presence not to share some degree of his faith. But later that night we concluded that we were much less optimistic than he. We also resolved that night to find a face-saving way to give him enough money to live on so that he did not have to sell his blood.

When the security guard telephoned and said there was a kid in the lobby wearing an obscene shirt who claimed he knew me but wouldn't give his name, I hesitated before telling him to let Dingo come up. Only as I headed for the hallway to await the elevator did I wish I had said I would meet him downstairs.

As I waited I felt oddly ambivalent, glad that Dingo had finally contacted me but uneasy about inviting him on up. Like all newsrooms, ours was a magnet for many of the city's weirdos and malcontents, but I could not remember having seen any street kids wandering through it.

Even before the elevator doors opened I heard his voice, angry and profane. When the doors parted he stepped out without the slightest acknowledgment of my presence, took a deep drag on his cigarette, then turned back. The doors just started closing when Dingo blew a jet stream of smoke into the elevator and simultaneously thrust out the middle finger of his left hand at the occupants, pumping it vigorously up and down.

I did not recognize either of the male passengers, but there was no mistaking the female who stared at me in shock just before the elevator doors slammed shut: Martha Liston, publisher of the *Free Press*!

"That'll show that bitch," he snarled, taking a final drag before flipping the lighted butt onto the floor.

Fearing the worst, I nevertheless managed to ask, "Show her what?"

"Bitch said I'm too young to smoke and it's against the law to smoke in elevators. Where the fuck's she get off, bossin' me?"

I started to reply but, noticing his T-shirt, was rendered speechless. It read: SHOW YOUR TITS.

"It *is* against the law," I said when I recovered my breath. "Elevators, stores, banks, certain sections of restaurants—you can't smoke in any of them."

"Law!" he spat. "What ain't against the fuckin' law?"

At that moment I got a whiff of his cigarette. "That goes for pot as well as tobacco," I said.

Apparently pleased that I recognized the pungent odor, Dingo unwound a little. "Get off my ass," he said, but most of his anger was now spent. "Joints don't give you cancer."

Part of me wanted to smile, but I was heartbroken that this child was already so worldly-wise. Without another word I led him back to my desk and pulled up Jill's chair. He plopped down like he owned it, settling so far back that he almost disappeared. But his eyes continued to check out the largely deserted newsroom, much the same way they had scanned Nathan's, taking in each detail.

"Well?" I asked finally.

Instead of answering he lighted another joint, expelling a thin stream of smoke through his nose. Howard Eisenhart threw puzzled glances at us from across the newsroom as he sniffed the air, and I realized how ridiculous it must have looked, a mere babe seeming to hold court.

"Where've you been these last two days?" I asked.

"Around." He took another drag and again I noticed his raunchy T-shirt.

"I thought we agreed to meet for lunch every day."

"I don't wanna," he replied. "Not for five lousy bucks a day."

"Five lousy bucks plus a pack of cigarettes—although God knows why I agreed to that."

"Look at this place," he said, referring to the *Freep*'s modest surroundings. "Your paper's loaded, man. I want twenty bucks."

"My paper's not paying you, *I'm* paying you, out of my own pocket." Out of a pocket that might become empty very quickly, I was tempted to add, if Martha Liston ever suspected we were friends.

That gave him pause, but not for long. "You're rich too," he said. "I seen your apartment, remember?"

I was surprised by his impression of my modest one-bedroom apartment, furnished in thrift-shop chic, but compared with his everyday world of hunger and homelessness I was indeed rich.

I glanced at the newsroom clock before remembering that, like both newsroom copying machines, it had not worked in weeks. "How about continuing this conversation over a hamburger?" I said, pushing a button and consigning the story I had been working on back to the electronic memory of the word processor.

But Dingo was not yet prepared to back down on the matter of high finance that had brought him to my office. "Since *you're* payin' me, make it fifteen a day," he said, in what for him sounded like a conciliatory tone.

"We'll talk about it at lunch," I replied, standing. "I never discuss money on an empty stomach."

As I started toward the elevator, with Dingo trailing far enough behind to enable him to give the once-over to each desk we passed, Bessie Gath practically dashed across the newsroom toward me. "Mr. Parks wants to see you," she said, her mouth twisted into what was intended as a warning.

It didn't take long to discover the reason for the summons. "Why have you invited that . . . that juvenile delinquent into the newsroom?" Parks demanded even before I could close his office door.

"I didn't invite him, at least not today," I said. "That's the kid from the gang that attacked me. I'm trying to talk him into explaining the customs and scams and folkways of the kids in Times Square."

"Folkways! Customs! You're talking like an anthropologist." He was pacing the floor, livid and looking very much like someone who had just been called on the carpet himself. "If you were doing a story on death row, would you invite convicted murderers into the newsroom?"

"What should I have done, told the guard he couldn't come up? After searching for him for two days, should I send him packing?"

I could see Dingo watching us through the clear glass window that surrounded Parks's office, and I hoped he would not learn the conversation was about him. When Parks also saw him, a small, forlorn-looking sight, some of the editor's anger dissolved.

"I wouldn't mind so much," he said, reaching for a cigarette from the pack on his desk, "but do you know what he said and did to Martha Liston on the elevator?" He dangled the cigarette from his lips, but, as usual, made no effort to light it.

"I saw, but didn't hear. I can imagine what it was like, though. That's the way these street kids are, crude and unmannerly. They're a social tinderbox, and there are going to be lots more of them unless this city does something."

"But giving Martha Liston the finger and saying what he said to her," Parks continued, shaking his head in disbelief. "I never even heard a *man* use that word around a woman until a few years ago. She's so furious she wants him out of here, this minute."

"We were on our way out when you sent for me," I said. I was curious about what Dingo had called the publisher, yet I knew I would sleep better at night if I didn't ask.

"She wants me to order the guards to keep him out. She said—"

Bessie Gath sounded a warning, but too late. The office door burst open and there stood Dingo, the message on his T-shirt glaring like a neon sign. When I recovered my composure enough to introduce him to Parks, neither moved to shake hands.

"Well?" Parks asked finally. "What do you want?"

"Got a joint?" the youngster asked.

Parks furrowed his brow. "A what?" He turned to me as if to an interpreter.

"A cigarette will be fine," I said. I indicated the pack on his desk.

"Son . . . of . . . a . . . bitch," Parks said, drawing out each word. "You barge in here in that smutty T-shirt asking for a joint, a little piss-ant barely out of diapers. Well here," he said, sliding the pack of cigarettes toward the boy. "Sorry I don't have your usual brand, but maybe this'll do. Save yourself another trip, why don't you, take three or four."

Dingo gave the room his usual once-over, then warily took five cigarettes. He turned back to the portrait of Martha Liston hanging behind Parks's desk and studied it a few moments, but did not comment.

"I suppose you want a light? Well, I don't have one." But Parks's sarcasm was lost on the boy, who carried his own matches. After lighting it and taking a few drags, Dingo instinctively cupped the cigarette in his left hand, protecting it the way he did out on the street.

"Let's get outta here," he said to me, indicating the open door.

Parks started to speak to me but instead just shrugged

his shoulders, signifying the sooner the better. I excused myself and followed Dingo out to the elevator, where, after pushing both the up and down buttons, he asked, "That your boss?"

"That's him. And his boss is the woman you insulted on the elevator."

"What woman?" he demanded, raising his voice. "I didn't insult no fuckin' woman."

"I saw you give her the finger."

"Oh. Her," he said dismissively as the bell rang and the light atop the elevator door flashed red. "That bitch insulted me."

We stepped on—and there at the back of the elevator stood Martha Liston! I managed to stammer "Hello," to which she responded with a perfunctory nod, then occupied herself with avoiding further eye contact. I doubt if Dingo recognized her, although once again he filled the elevator with smoke.

Not since the days of Elisha Graves Otis had so short an elevator descent taken so long, and as I hurried past the publisher's limousine outside the entrance—hoping that by distancing myself from Dingo I would avoid giving the impression that we were together—I wondered what other disaster could possibly befall me. I didn't slow my pace until I reached the corner and turned south on Eighth Avenue, a one-way street northbound, meaning Martha Liston's limousine could not follow.

When Dingo caught up, we walked a block or so in silence before somebody called his name. The boy spotted her immediately, a plump and obviously pregnant young Hispanic girl. "Where you been, Dingo?" she asked pleasantly. "I been lookin' for you ever'where."

"What for?" he scowled, glancing toward me in discomfort. I decided to stay right there, to watch him squirm.

The girl laughed, a hearty sound that caused her distended belly to shake. "You know what for." She nudged him playfully with her elbow, the way adolescents do the world over.

Dingo moved away, but I hoped to prolong his unease. "Aren't you going to introduce us?" I asked. He glared at me, but said nothing.

"I'm Maria," the girl said, favoring me with a smile.

"And I'm Alex Shaw."

"Alex Shaw." She laughed as she repeated the name. "Let me warn you, Alex, you wasting time with Dingo. He *straight*." She batted her penciled eyebrows but that seemed only to infuriate him, as her implication that I was a chicken hawk infuriated me.

"Shut the fuck up!" he hissed.

But Dingo's anger did not bother her, nor did I, whom she sized up as a pedophile, seem to be beyond the pale. "At least he straight 'til my brother catch him," she said. "Che, he say he gonna cut Dingo's balls right off of him."

She laughed again and executed a two-step right there on the sidewalk, to the amusement of an overweight hooker who was lingering outside the nearby bar. "I axed Che, how you gonna find his balls, they so small?"

"You didn't think so the other night," Dingo spat, quick to defend his flowering manhood.

Maria threw back her head in laughter. But when she brought it forward she screamed. "Run, Dingo, run. It's Che, it's *Che!*"

It took Dingo only a split second to size-up the situation, and a split second later he was across Eighth Avenue and dashing up Forty-fourth with Che and two others in pursuit. I took off after them, without thinking what I would do if I caught up and they pulled the knives they were surely carrying. I didn't need to be convinced any longer that they had stabbed the life out of Times Square derelicts, but all I could think of at that moment was that Dingo's life was in danger.

I rounded the corner in time to see one of Che's henchmen disappear down the subway entrance, but by the time I arrived none of them was anywhere in sight. I hurdled the turnstile, imitating the fare-beaters I had written about so often, and ran along the platform. "That way, officer," a fine-featured young black woman said, pointing to the tunnel that led to a maze of passageways that eventually wound up at the Port Authority Bus Terminal.

I hurdled another turnstile and raced through the tunnel as fast as my out-of-shape legs would carry me. I hadn't gone fifty yards when I overtook Che's accomplices, spread-eagled against the tunnel wall, cursing two seedy-looking characters who had pistols trained on them.

"There's one more," I panted at Rafael Sanchez, one of the decoy cops. "And watch out, they carry knives."

"You're telling us!" Sanchez said, indicating two knives on the floor whose serrated blades looked like they were designed to scale the Loch Ness monster.

"The other one got away," said Sanchez's partner, who also recognized me. They had seen the chase on the street and followed the trio underground, he told me; now they would hand the prisoners over to the transit police.

"What about Dingo? Did you see the kid they were chasing? He's maybe thirteen or fourteen, wearing a blue T-shirt?"

"He ran past us like a shot," said Sanchez, who then ordered the captives to stop whispering.

"I have to find him," I said. "I'll come by the precinct later, to charge them with attempted assault or whatever."

As I started toward the bus terminal the partner came over and introduced himself as Frank Baylor. He added that there was no need to worry about the prisoners, because they couldn't book either one. Seeing my puzzled look he said simply, "Under age."

"They're not too young to run around with carving knives, threatening to cut the nuts off another kid. What about possession of a deadly weapon?"

"The only law that applies to knives," he said, with a patience borne of resignation, "is a state statute against carrying a switchblade, a cane sword, or a gravity knife. These guys didn't have any of those. Besides, the offense for criminal possession is a misdemeanor."

"What about threatening bodily harm? Isn't that a crime in the Big Apple?"

At that both of us turned toward Che's defiant accomplices.

"For minors? You gotta be kidding. We book 'em, they go before a judge in juvenile court whose calendar is overflowing with rape cases, assault with intent to kill, even murder, some of it committed by kids as young as ten. So what's the big deal about a threat?"

Sanchez tried for a second time to contact headquarters on his portable radio, but the return message was indecipherable.

"Even if he sentenced them," Baylor continued, "there's no room in the detention centers. When you detain somebody these days, to make room you just about have to release another criminal, and sometimes that criminal's worse than the new guy."

"So you're going to let them go, just like that?"

"Off the record?" He looked first at his partner, then at the prisoners.

"On the record."

"No way."

When I shrugged, implying grudging acceptance of his terms, he said, "Transit cops go through the motions of arresting them, even fingerprinting them. But they'll be back on the street within hours. Once word gets around that we arrested them, the drug dealers they work for get their lawyers to spring them. They'll say your friend tried to rob them at gunpoint, so they chased him down the street."

The passageway was little used at this hour, and the sight of a scruffy-looking adult standing armed guard over two spread-eagled youths sent most pedestrians scurrying back in the direction they came from.

"These kids work for drug dealers?"

I hadn't the courage to ask about Dingo, but I kept scanning the passageway for signs of him.

Baylor seemed surprised I didn't know. "A lot of the kids who hang out in Times Square work for drug dealers, at least part time," he replied. "They don't sell the stuff, just act as lookouts or couriers, hauling it around Times Square as needed, transporting it by subway from Harlem or the Bronx, or running it crosstown. Even if they get caught, what can you do to a minor?"

All the rest of the day I remembered that conversation, and it inspired me to arrange interviews with several juvenile court judges. But my overriding concern was Dingo, whom Raymond Nelson said he saw shortly after my encounter with Sanchez and Bradley.

"Was anybody after him? Was he okay?"

The photographer laughed. "Just suffering from a nicotine fit, at least until he bummed fifty cents from me for a few cigarettes." As Nelson adjusted the nearby signboard advertising his wares, I remembered that Times Square vendors often sold cigarettes one or two at a time to their down-and-out clientele.

"Come to think of it," Nelson recalled, "he did hang around here longer than usual. You know Dingo—'hello,' then zap, he's gone. This time, though, he came back even after buying the cigarettes and he hung around talkin' and smokin', before sayin' he was going huntin' some more for Noah."

"Noah?" I suddenly remembered that since Dingo's disappearance I had not given much thought to Reverend Robeson's son and grandson.

"That's what he said. But that's Dingo—one minute he's as obsessed with that kid as Reverend Robeson is, passin' out handbills about him, next minute he's passin' out leaflets about some damn Freak Show. Other times he helps the old man search for any scrap of information about Noah, next day he's a lookout for a three-card monte dealer."

A middle-aged tourist in a loud blue jacket asked Nelson to take his photo with a heavily made-up Hispanic hooker. Gathering up his camera the photographer said, "It's hard to believe Dingo's just in his teens. That boy's as complicated and troublesome as any three eighteen-year-olds."

J ill and I slept late on Saturday, and after awakening and hearing the rain beat against the windows we made love and once again snuggled against each other. But not even the blissful exhaustion that follows lovemaking could lull me back to sleep this morning, nor could Jill's naked body against mine inspire a repeat performance. When she finally asked what was the matter, I replied, "Old age."

The answer amused her, but she knew the real cause of my anxiety. Squirming around to face me she said, "You care a lot about that boy, don't you?"

Some women I knew would have been offended by the truth at a time like that, but not her. "I think he's on my mind so much now because it's raining," I said. "I can't stand knowing that he may have had to spend the night in the rain. Or if he's lucky, sleeping in an all-night movie theater or on the subway. I wish I knew where the hell he *does* spend the night."

Later, when we were in the shower, I said, "What bothers me is that I care about Dingo, with all his faults, but I care almost as much about the kind of person he could have been. Does that make sense?"

"Perfect sense," she replied, soaping my chest with a soft, circular motion. "Why couldn't he be one of the millions of kids who live with one or both parents, and who sleep in beds each night?"

"Kids who acquire their values and vocabulary at home and in school," I added, "rather than on the streets. And who do not have to spend each day surrounded by violence and depravity."

Our taxicab to the *Free Press* splashed through streets that were practically deserted. Many windows were still covered with metal gates and shutters, and even the umbrella vendors seemed to be sleeping late this Saturday.

Before I met Dingo, I had always welcomed rain. I felt refreshed after even the briefest shower, and I cherished the speed and thoroughness with which it washed away the stench. Were it in my power, I would have ordered a shower first thing each morning, but only after Dingo was safely up and about.

As soon as the cab crossed the Avenue of the Americas—unlike most New Yorkers, I preferred its official name to the more familiar Sixth Avenue—this dreary morning seemed even drearier. Several strung-out hookers and addicts were already camped in doorways along Forty-fifth Street, including the doorway of the Hotel Miami.

Stan Lassiter, who covered city hall for the *Freep*, and who I suspected had the hots for Jill, viewed us with more than passing interest when we arrived at the office together on a Saturday, after a soggy dash from my coffee

107

shop. "I thought you'd be soaking up the pleasures of Times Square before they uncage the animals," he said to me in a tone of voice that bordered on hostility.

"And what do the denizens of city hall do when it rains?" I asked with studied indifference as I leafed through my telephone messages.

"Neither rain nor snow nor dark of night keeps them from squandering taxpayers' money," he said. "Oh, by the way, the mayor liked your account of his reaction to the Freak Show."

Jill, about to bite into a cinnamon roll, made a wry face at the same time I did. "Did I say something wrong?" Lassiter asked.

"Not a blessed thing," I assured him. "But it was not exactly my finest journalistic hour, having to act as a conduit between him and the editorial page."

"The man talks like a virgin," he said, turning to Jill. Then, turning back to me, he said, "His aides say hizzhonor asked his legal staff to find some law that will let him bar the show."

"If he does, our editorial writers will recommend that his term be extended for life. And," I added, remounting one of my favorite hobbyhorses, "those hyenas who deliver the editorial comment on television will go absolutely bonkers."

"But you can't blame the mayor for not wanting a bunch of freaks fucking on the Broadway stage, can you?" Lassiter said.

"In contrast to simulating it Off-Broadway?"

"Such as?"

"Such as *Down and Dirty* or *Dreams of Havana*," I replied, naming two long-running scatological reviews.

"Jesus, Shaw, you're not really comparing nudity and dirty language to freaks fucking and going down on stage, are you?"

I was tempted to say that I damn well was, but I damn

well really was not. I shook my head. "Maybe the Freak Show should be banned," I conceded, "since I can't think of any redeeming value it could possibly have. But that show is scheduled for only two hours a night for a week, before moving on, whereas the welfare families and homeless kids are a permanent fixture in Times Square. But who's concerned about their welfare? What politician or talking head is demanding laws to protect them from exploitation and degradation?"

"'The poor will always be with us,'" he said.

I looked for a hint of irony, a suggestion that he might only have been trying to goad me, and when I discerned neither, the anger I had manfully repressed only minutes ago boiled to the surface.

"They'll always be with us if enough people have your attitude," I said, my vehemence catching him by surprise. "They'll be with us for decades because those kids out there right now, the three- and five- and eight-year-olds, they're the next generation of street kids—boys who will steal and rob and mug, girls who will turn to prostitution. And both will turn on to drugs, using them and selling them."

"I only meant—"

"It isn't just you, Lassiter, it's all of us. We close our eyes to that army of ragged, dirty kids drifting through our streets, looking for spiritual nourishment as well as food, sometimes looking for just a kind word . . ."

As I spoke I tried to arrange my phone messages in approximate order of importance, but I was too wrought up to concentrate.

"Hell, I spoke a kind word to one of those little black bastards over by the bus terminal," Lassiter said, "and when I turned my back he tried to slice my wallet out of my pocket."

He seemed hurt that neither Jill nor I was amused.

"It's too late by the time they're on the street a month,"

I said. "By then they have had to survive any way they can. Survive nights of cold and days of hunger, survive in the rain with mattresses made of paper and a piece of plastic for a sheet."

I felt Jill's eyes on me and I knew she was also thinking of Dingo. "Just take a walk through Times Square after it stops raining," I continued. "Look at the kids on every street corner, in the arcades, huddled beneath movie marquees. Then ask yourself how long it will be before New York—before America—ends up with millions of abandoned children, like India or South America."

Lassiter was silent a moment; with any luck he was reflecting upon what I had just said. Finally, though, he just shrugged. "Beats the shit out of me," he said, before stalking off toward his desk across the room. Minutes later, clutching a street-corner umbrella for which he paid three dollars, he left the newsroom, headed for the elevator.

When I asked if I had overreacted, Jill assured me my message was faultless.

"For that deft insight, I'm awarding you one of my doughnuts," I said, even though she had just polished off two of her own. "As Reverend Robeson might say, 'Greater love hath no man than he give up a raspberry-filled doughnut for a friend.'"

"You're too good to me," she replied, oozing insincerity, "but I don't dare. It'll ruin my appetite, and I have a lunch in forty-five minutes."

"Tell me who it is and I'll break both his legs," I joked. "Or if he's bigger than me, I'll have both his legs broken."

She fluttered her eyelashes. "Who said it's a he?"

It was none of my business, of course, yet now I seemed caught up in a question-and-answer session from which there was no immediate withdrawal. "Is it?" I asked. When she nodded, I asked the predictable question: "Anybody I know?"

110

Jill shook her head. "Only by name."

If that cryptic reply was designed to whet my interest, it succeeded. "Who is it, the mayor?" I asked.

"Worse than that." She hesitated, then flushed. "Donald Driggs."

Donald Driggs? "Donald H. Driggs the Third?" I asked, supplying the byline that for many years I had heard him—in a transparent imitation of Edward R. Murrow—declaim on the CBS radio and television network. A talking head, no less.

"It's just a lunch, Alex," she said, in a voice that I wanted to believe was tinged with guilt.

I shifted my weight in the chair. "What else?" I replied airily. To show my indifference I began opening the mail piled on my desk, a pile that was less a tribute to my ability to inspire readers to take pen in hand than to the laggardness of the clerks to distribute mail that had accumulated for days.

Most of my mail consisted of the usual pitches from public relations agencies, indecipherable press releases, and letters from cranks. But one letter managed to take my mind off my hurt feelings, and I set it aside to reread.

"Anything interesting?" Jill asked in an amused tone as I stashed the opened pile into the trash can beneath my desk.

"A few crackpots and the usual fan mail," I replied.

She turned up her nose playfully, and all at once it struck me that she had quite an attractive nose. It also struck me that I hadn't paid a bit of attention to her nose until she mentioned Donald H. Driggs III, with his trademark white brush mustache and his overlay of pomposity.

Was it possible that while I was worried sick about what had become of Dingo and Noah, had worried over Willis Robeson, and couldn't understand why nobody was doing anything about the kids who roamed Times Square—was it possible that during all that time Jill had wanted me to

111

praise the shape of her nose? And because I had not done so was having lunch with Donald H. Driggs III? Would that pompous bastard take time from solving the city's and the world's and the universe's problems to praise her nose? More to the point, would he praise her nose if he succeeded in getting what he obviously had in mind when he invited her to lunch?

Before my Rabelaisian imagination took full possession, a cheerful voice rescued me from gloom and self-pity. "Your friend's got a good touch, Alex. Bring him around so I can offer him some assignments."

It was the photo editor, Edmundo Burke, who had grudgingly looked through Raymond Nelson's portfolio at my request.

"You really like him?"

He nodded. "He's good and he's soon going to be a lot better. Another Eisenstadt, maybe, or Gordon Parks."

"Another Edmundo Burke?" Jill enjoyed bantering with him, because although he was supremely self-confident, he still enjoyed laughing at himself.

"I said he was going to be *good*, not *great*," Burke said, a smile lighting up his handsome Hispanic features. Even if he had not discerned greatness in Nelson's self-taught work, he had clearly seen talent. Because I imagined the rain would keep Nelson from his usual street-corner studio, I told Burke I'd try to bring him by the newspaper.

The letter I had set aside was from the advertising agency representing Miura, an up-and-coming Japanese manufacturer of jeans and sports clothes. Its client was so touched by my stories of Willis Robeson, the agency's account executive wrote to me, that it wanted to run a photograph of Noah on its billboard in Times Square for one week.

Miura's was not the biggest sign on Broadway, but, soaring three-quarters of the way up the northern face of 1 Times Square Plaza, it was one of the most conspicuous and expensive. I could hardly wait to see Reverend Robeson's reaction when I told him the good news.

I debated whether to show the letter to Jill, but my happiness for the minister outweighed my bruised feelings. When she returned it to me she was beaming. "It's a generous offer," she said, "and a tribute to your persuasive writing."

"It's also a good way for an unknown Jap company to get lots of free publicity—us ink-stained wretches writing about their big corporate heart, and television slobbering all over itself to run their story," said Dick Suft. He long ago perfected the knack of passing colleagues' desks whenever something delicate, unsavory, or gossipy was being discussed. I started to tell him there was probably some truth in what he said, but by then he had moved on to eavesdrop on another conversation.

I told Jill I would see her after lunch, and when she asked if I'd wait a few minutes so we could walk out together I had to decline. "Gotta go now," I said, gathering up my umbrella. "By the way, where's Donald H. Driggs the Third taking you? The CBS cafeteria?"

"Four Seasons."

"I'm impressed," I said, emitting a spiteful whistle. "I'm also late," I added, looking at my watch.

I hurried toward the elevator but on an impulse I stopped and turned back. "Okay, I admit it," I said, as if continuing a prior conversation, "you do have a nice nose."

She looked at me as if I had flipped out, but before she could say anything her telephone rang. When she said, "Oh, hello Donald," I felt the need for fresh air, even fresh air mixed with auto exhaust and uric acid.

On my way down in the elevator, I prayed that Jill would unleash on Donald H. Driggs III the full fury of her ravenous appetite.

It was still drizzling when I walked out of the *Free Press* that afternoon, the foul weather complementing my mood perfectly. Someone called to me from across the street. I thought I recognized Dingo's voice but could not see him until he opened the door of a luncheonette a crack and beckoned to me.

I was shocked when I saw him for he had a nasty cut over his right eye, a swollen lip, and scratches on the back of his hands. He appeared to have gotten much the worst of a fight, but did not appear to have been badly injured. I restrained myself from offering him sympathy.

He was wearing the same clothes he had had on the last time I saw him, only now they were dripping wet. One hand gripped a blue and white container of coffee adorned with a Greek temple; the other was cupped around a lighted cigarette. Despite the steam rising from the coffee, Dingo was shivering so hard he was trembling.

I nodded to the store owner, a heavyset man whose facial scars left him with a perpetual scowl. I wanted to embrace the frail, shivering child, but I had come to understand that like many other street children, Dingo, except in his dealings with Reverend Robeson, mistook kindness for weakness and then moved rapidly and unerringly to exploit it. So I resisted the urge to greet him warmly and ask what happened. Instead, I waited for him to speak.

"Okay, Alex, we'll make it fifteen bucks," he said finally when I continued to stare at him in silence. "Fifteen

114

bucks and the cigarettes, but that's as low as I'm gonna fuckin' go."

At the sight of that tough-talking, battered tatterdemalion trying to bargain with me, his small, undernourished body trembling with cold, my resolve came dangerously close to breaking down. I was overjoyed to see him safe if not sound, and I was aching to ask how he had escaped from Che, where he had gone, how he had been. I was also aching to accept his offer on the spot, then take him to a restaurant to get some decent food into him.

Instead, I said, "Thanks, Dingo, but I don't need your help now. Maybe some other time."

My reply shook him right down to the worn soles of his sneakers, and for a moment I thought he would break out in tears. Instead, he flew into a rage. "What you mean you don't need my help?" he demanded. "You still gonna pay me, ain't you?"

"Pay you for what? I just said I don't need you now. I decided I'm not going to write anything about the Times Square kids at the moment."

In a flash of anger he drew back his container of coffee. "You're lying," he threatened. "You're just sayin' that 'cause you got somebody else for less money. Who is it? Tell me who it is and I'll kill the cocksucker. Is it Che? It's Che, ain't it? I knew I couldn't trust you, you motherfucker." His voice rose to fever pitch.

The store owner walked quietly toward the cash register and ran his hand under the counter, as if searching for a weapon.

Dingo's hand was still shaking, but I wasn't sure whether it was from cold or red hot rage. Either way, prudence suggested that I try to calm him down.

"It's not Che," I said, affecting a placidity I did not feel. "It's not anybody. It's just that for now I have other stories

115

to write. Here's one of them," I said, fishing in my shirt pocket for the letter from the ad agency.

I started to hand it to him when I remembered that he was illiterate, or at best barely literate. So after satisfying myself that he was unlikely at that moment to dash the container of steaming coffee in my face, I read the letter aloud. When I finished I said, "Great news, isn't it? It means they'll display Noah's picture there for at least a week."

When I asked if he wanted to come along to tell Reverend Robeson the news, his fires banked before my very eyes, and a few face-saving seconds later he lowered the container to the counter. "Do your stories on the kids now, Alex," he pleaded. "Fifteen bucks, it's a real bargain. I won't bullshit you like lots of these jive-asses do. An' I'll show you lots of whores and chickens."

"How about lots of normal kids?"

The irony so completely eluded him that he could not think of an answer.

After several more minutes of feigned indifference I agreed to pay twelve dollars, and on that note we left the deli and headed for Nelson's apartment. It was still sprinkling, although now the rain felt more like a typical summer shower than a wind-whipped, cold downpour.

The nearby check-cashing store was deserted except for the pasty-faced teller behind the bulletproof glass, who also sold food stamps and lottery tickets. A boy clad in tight-fitting jeans and a middle-aged man walked together into a two-story sex shop, no doubt to avail themselves of its private booths. And under the canopy of a Korean grocery store a fifteen-year-old whore of Dingo's acquaintance was negotiating with a john who, Dingo said, "likes to have his ass stomped."

For some reason as we walked I thought of Diane, mostly at how quickly I had gotten over her, and therefore how shallow my feelings for her must have been.

What I could not decide was whether such detachment, at my age, was something to be proud of or to worry about. I prided myself on detachment from political or ideological dogma, but detachment—which my ex-wife Ann called lack of commitment—topped the lengthy bill of particulars she handed me the day our divorce became final.

It could have been worse, I suppose; she could have run it as an ad in the paper I worked for at the time. But its implications were disturbing, for if true it suggested I would soon tire of Jill also, even though I thought it more likely that she would tire of me. And if I tired of Jill, would I then also tire of Dingo and Reverend Robeson?

At that moment I felt my usual exasperation with Dingo, but certainly not boredom. I also felt oddly protective of his sensibilities, so I tried to divert his attention from the bedraggled man on the corner snorting cocaine—a scene he must have witnessed hundreds of times before.

I asked Dingo why he wanted money so badly and I was surprised when he said he wanted to buy a bicycle. I was even more surprised when he explained that he wanted the bicycle so he could get a job as a messenger.

"It'd be great, ridin' all over town," he said, his brown eyes fairly glowing. "I'd be the fastest motherfucker on two wheels, zoomin' in and out of traffic, makin' money."

"Then do it," I challenged him. "With the money you earn working for me and handing out leaflets"—I was tempted to add "and running drugs"—"you ought to be able to buy a bike in a few weeks." Only much later did I even think about where he would keep the bicycle after he bought it.

"Really? Only a few weeks?"

I had rarely seen a child more excited, unless maybe on Christmas Eve, until sadness suddenly enveloped his bruised face. When I asked what was the matter he replied, "I don't know how to ride a bike."

As it turned out, he had been on one only once in his life. "When me and Che stole two of them outside a pizza joint," he said, cherishing the memory. "But I couldn't ride so I crashed it into a car and wrecked it."

As we approached Ninth Avenue, in the shadow of Manhattan Plaza with its two modern towers rising high above the surrounding brownstones, the rain had almost stopped, but there were as yet few signs of life on the streets. "Teach me to ride, Alex," Dingo said, reverting to his habit of demanding things.

Had it been my own child, or almost anybody else's, I would have agreed readily. But Dingo, a product of one of the meanest neighborhoods in America, was still testing me, still probing for weaknesses, so for his sake and mine I did not dare to appear conciliatory. "Get Che to teach you," I said, stifling a strong urge to ask if Che was responsible for his injuries.

"Che!" he spat. "If I ever find him without his fuckin' bodyguards, I'll waste him." He patted his pants pocket, apparently indicating where he carried a knife. When I just laughed at his bravado he said again, "I wanna learn to ride a bike, Alex. Teach me."

"There are other ways to make money."

He looked extremely doubtful. "How?"

At that moment we stopped outside the fortuneteller's studio, on top of which was Nelson's apartment. "As a lookout for three-card monte dealers," I answered, making no move to enter the vestibule.

"That don't pay shit."

"Delivering drugs for the big boys."

"Too dangerous, man," he said. "Junkies always rippin' you off. Lots of kids get beat up and robbed."

"Then you could always be a pimp."

I still don't know why I said it, except that we were in pimp territory, and because I had recently written an article quoting a city councilman's denunciation of Times

Square as "the domain of the pimp, prostitute, and ped-erast." But no sooner were the words out of my mouth than Dingo began calling me every vile name he could think of. I stared in stupefaction as he paced in a wary semicircle, much as he and his friends had done the first time our paths crossed. One thing was certain: this was no act, or a rage born of frustration, like his temper tantrum in the delicatessen. This anger erupted from his very soul, and I was thankful no one I knew was around to hear it.

"Don't ever say that to me again, you motherfucker," he yelled. "Don't say it or I'll waste you." Before I knew it he had his knife out and was waving the blade from side to side. I should have been scared, I suppose, but I was so fascinated by this second Jekyll-Hyde routine literally within minutes that I felt more like a spectator than part of the main event. That feeling intensified when he soon turned his rage on pimps.

"I'll kill 'em," he screamed, standing in a puddle of es-pecially muddy water. "I hate every fuckin' pimp who ever lived and their whore mothers. I'll kill 'em, I'll kill 'em."

One would have had to see Dingo to understand the depth of his anguish and hatred. Circling and groaning as if in agony, now whimpering, now hollering, his body had been transformed into a veritable Saint Elmo's fire of rage. Asian faces pressed against the window of the gro-cery store across the street, watching Dingo's remarkable performance. A cab driver rolled down his window as he cruised by, but seeing Dingo brandishing a knife, he kept right on going. If Che and his sidekicks had come along at that moment, even a dozen strong, I have no doubt Dingo would have attacked them without hesitation.

But the only person who came along was Willis Robeson, protected by a rain hat and leaning lightly on his walking stick. He stopped before he descended the stairs,

119

probably because he heard the yelling, but when he recognized Dingo's voice he resumed his journey.

Only a moment earlier I would not have believed it possible, but the sight of the old preacher hobbling toward us had an instant calming effect on Dingo. He folded his knife and slipped it back into his pocket; seconds later all that remained of his outburst were red-rimmed eyes and a jaw that he clenched to control his anger.

Reverend Robeson could not have failed to hear Dingo's tantrum, or to notice his battered condition, yet he greeted us as warmly as if we had just entered his church. "What brings my friends here today?" he asked with his usual courtesy.

When I explained that we were on our way to see him and Nelson, he said that Raymond had been out since dawn taking pictures of homeless people in the rain. I showed him the contents of the letter from the ad agency, and tears of gratitude began flowing down his face. When he could speak he said, "I was just on my way to church, and now I have even more reason to give thanks."

I said I would join him, and to my further surprise Dingo also decided to come along. As we headed toward Forty-second Street I said, "I didn't know there was a Southern Baptist Church around here."

He chuckled. "Thank the Lord you are not the religion reporter," he said. "While I am staying at Raymond's apartment I attend the Catholic church across from the bus station."

Besides admiring his broadmindedness, I could not for the life of me remember a church across from the bus station. Moments later, however, we stood before the oldest one in Times Square, the Church of the Holy Cross. Hemmed in by parking lots between Eighth and Ninth Avenues, and less than two minutes from the city's principal open-air sex and drug bazaar, the church somehow was still intact. Equally amazing, I learned later, almost directly behind it, on Forty-third Street, the church operated a red brick school for children who live in Times Square and nearby Hell's Kitchen—or Clinton, as the developers and newly arrived Yuppies insisted on calling it.

We climbed the church steps, on which two derelicts were sleeping it off, and I noticed on the signboard that three of the eight Sunday masses were in Spanish. I paused long enough to jot down the name of the pastor, thinking I would interview him about the difficulties of running a parish in such an environment.

When we did talk several days later, he told me that prostitutes regularly propositioned his parishioners, that derelicts and winos often slept in the church pews, and that transvestites and prostitutes even brought customers into the confessionals during cold or rainy weather.

"But what stretches my Christian charity to the limit," the soft-spoken, white-haired priest said, "are the presumably upstanding citizens who proposition our school children, boys and girls in blue and white uniforms who could not possibly be mistaken for anything but students."

The article based on that interview was received with unusual warmth by my colleagues, for even those who had lived in New York all their lives had forgotten that this was the parish of Father Francis Duffy, the chaplain of the Fighting Sixty-ninth Regiment. And only a few of them knew that Father Duffy's statue still stood where it was erected years ago: in front of a granite cross in Duffy Square, a tiny traffic island at Forty-seventh Street between Broadway and Seventh Avenue, where long lines of tourists bought half-price Broadway tickets for same-day performances.

The instant I set foot inside Holy Cross and saw taped to the glass partition at the rear of the church posters of Noah and two other missing children, I knew this was no ordinary church and no ordinary parish.

The church itself, as I wrote in a subsequent article,

was a treasure of vaulted ceilings adorned by frescoes, stained-glass windows, and mosaics. On one side was the shrine of Our Lady of the Miraculous Medal; on the Epistle side was the shrine of the Infant Jesus of Prague, carved in oak. Above the altar hung a painting of the Crucifixion, flanked by one picture of the Emperor Constantine seeing a vision of the cross and another depicting Saint Helena finding the cross.

"I get goosebumps in this church," Reverend Robeson whispered, his hands locked in devotion. Looking sidelong at him, I could not help wondering how much prejudice and discrimination that pious, decent man must have suffered for much of his life, merely because of his pigmentation. And I marveled that still he had managed to pursue a life of Christian faith and love, devoid of any bitterness.

Even Dingo seemed impressed by the place, although he did not say a word. He had not spoken the entire time, in fact, and I could not tell if his head was bowed in prayer or lingering anger. Afterwards, however, as we walked in a fine mist back toward Ninth Avenue, he said to the minister, "What was you prayin' about? Noah?"

Willis Robeson draped a massive arm around Dingo's shoulders as we sauntered along. "I was indeed praying for Noah," he said. "Praying that Merciful God will return him safe and sound. But I was also thanking God for my blessings."

"What blessings?" I blurted out without thinking.

He halted a moment, leaned against his walking stick, and looked at me with a winning expression. "For many things," he replied softly. "For good friends like Raymond, who have given me a roof over my head. Like Dingo, who has taken me places I would never have known existed. Like you, who wrote about me and worried about me."

He resumed walking, continuing to talk at a measured

pace. "Then there is Jill," he said, "who stopped by so many times to check up on me, even though she is scared to enter my hotel. And to kind strangers I run into on the street each day—black and white, rich and poor, men and women."

Two winos on the corner of Eighth Avenue were weaving uncertainly as we approached, and as we drew near the larger one stuck his hand in front of us like a traffic cop, signaling us to stop. "God bless you, my son," Reverend Robeson said, tipping his rain hat.

Perhaps thinking the minister was mocking him, the drunk let loose a torrent of slurred profanity, before reaching out and seizing Dingo, who was bringing up the rear.

I turned when I heard the boy holler and lunged for the wino's hand, intending to bend his fingers back until he loosened his hold. But before I could get a grip he crumpled to the sidewalk, clutching his groin and screaming in agony.

"Keep your fuckin' hands offa me!" Dingo warned, cocking his foot to kick his prostrate attacker again.

I bumped Dingo hard enough to knock him off balance, and from the anger that flared in his eyes I thought he would turn on me. But when he saw Reverend Robeson taking it all in, the boy calmed down. A policeman rushed over from across the street to see what had happened. He recognized us, and when Reverend Robeson explained, the cop radioed for a squad car.

The wino made an unsuccessful attempt to rise but sank back flat on the sidewalk, still groaning but now clutching his groin with both hands.

We gave the officer our addresses and he waved us on our way, wishing the minister good luck in his search. None of us spoke as we splashed along Forty-second Street, except when the minister returned greetings from some of the drug dealers and three-card monte dealers. When Dingo could no longer bear our withholding approval of his action he said, "He shouldn't a-grabbed me."

I did not reply, but Reverend Robeson said, "No, he surely should not have done that."

"I had the right to defen' myself," the boy insisted, again clenching and unclenching his jaws, which made his swollen lip look even bigger. I knew he was dying for a cigarette and I wondered how long he would abstain out of respect for the clergyman.

"You surely did have that," the minister agreed.

We passed several prostitutes in short-shorts, shivering beneath transparent umbrellas.

"I coulda killed him for that," Dingo continued.

This time the minister stopped and fixed Dingo with a look of great concern. "Killed him? Killed an unarmed drunk? Kill a creature of God?" He said it almost in a whisper, but the words landed—on my ears, at least—with explosive force.

"How you know he was unarmed?" Dingo asked, ignoring the more important point.

Reverend Robeson rubbed his chin thoughtfully. "Seems to me when somebody is talking about killing, it is up to that person to prove the enemy is armed, armed and ready to use his weapon. 'Whoever sheds the blood of man, by man shall his blood be shed; for God made man in His own image.'"

Dingo shifted his weight from foot to foot, a mannerism he sometimes resorted to when he was forced to explain himself. Finally, in a tone just this side of defiance, he said, "Nobody has the right to grab you."

"No indeed," the minister agreed. "You did what you thought had to be done. But murder? Taking the life of another human? Wanting to do what only God has the right to do? 'Take heed what ye do: for ye judge not for man, but for the Lord.'"

Dingo kept shifting his weight, and I swear I saw his

cowlick begin to rise. "But people kill other people here every week—sometimes every day," he protested, sweeping his hand in a wide semicircle. "I seen a guy stabbed to death last night, a drug dealer stabbed him right in the guts. Last week I seen a bag lady stretched out dead a couple blocks from here. Her throat was slit wide open."

For a change he was not being argumentative; rather, his recitation of violence seemed an effort to understand why Reverend Robeson and God valued life so highly when everywhere else in his experience it was dirt cheap.

"You *saw* that man stab another man to death?" the minister asked.

"Sure. Me and my friends seen it. I seen lots of dudes killed. It's no big deal."

"Did you report it last night?"

"Whadda ya mean, report it?"

"To the police. Did you tell them what you saw."

Dingo looked to me for support, but I remained noncommittal. "'Course I didn't tell no cops. Wasn't my business, so why would I tell 'em?"

The minister apparently saw the hopelessness of trying to explain the legal facts of life to a kid who lived largely outside the law. And just minutes later we passed three pushers, none much older than Dingo, each of whom chanted a variation of that familiar street-corner mantra, "Crack, coke, acid, joints!"

Two boys about fifteen who were lurking in the shadows of a video store studied us with amused interest as we passed. "Dingo," one of them called in a teasing, effeminate voice.

Dingo's jaw clenched again, yet he did not reply. But the instant Reverend Robeson was not looking he turned and flipped them the bird, then grabbed his crotch with his other hand and shook it vigorously up and down.

The boys laughed heartily at his response. Their reaction was hardly surprising, but I was quite unprepared for

125

the expression on the face of that ubiquitous prostitute, the one who had tipped off Jill and me that Reverend Robeson was in the blood donor center. She had been watching from beneath the marquee of the nearby porno movie theater, whose current XXX-rated attractions were *Horny Sluts* and *Wet Dreemz*.

I would have guessed that she too would have found Dingo's response amusing, but her blotched face registered disgust and disappointment. Thinking about it later, I could not understand why a veteran streetwalker would be put off by something so commonplace in Times Square as an obscene gesture by a youthful ragamuffin.

The next several mornings Dingo proved as good as his word, conducting me on a tour of a Times Square that even I scarcely knew existed.

He showed me burned-out and abandoned buildings where runaways and other homeless kids, presumably himself included, took refuge on winter nights.

He took me on a spelunker's expedition through the maze of subway tunnels in Times Square, where he demonstrated how to suck tokens out of turnstiles, a talent that netted as much as twenty-five dollars a day when he sold the tokens to riders who did not want to stand in line at rush hour.

He told me of the scams that took place at the row of shoe-shine stands along Eighth Avenue, across from the bus station, where some bootblacks sold whisky without being hassled by the law, in exchange for informing the police about runaways.

Dingo pointed out several shops that sold fake I.D. cards to minors, and several more that were actually shooting galleries for drugs. He showed me a half-dozen respectable-looking New Jersey commuters who regularly paid homeless kids for quickie sex behind doors or in hallways.

I had a hard time realizing that Dingo was not exaggerating for my benefit, but much of what he told me squared with what I had learned from the police. Besides, he wanted money to buy the bicycle, and he must have realized I wouldn't pay for a tissue of lies and exaggerations. Yet he often stretched the truth in matters concerning himself. He said, for instance, that he hated drugs and drug dealers because many of his friends were addicts and a few had died from overdoses. But when I asked whether he ever acted as a courier for pushers, he swore on his mother's grave that he never did.

One afternoon I was typing up notes based on the most recent tour with my half-pint cicerone when Reverend Robeson showed up at the *Free Press*. "I apologize for disturbing you at work, Alex," he said as he stepped off the elevator at the fifth floor and pumped my hand. "But I need your advice and I did not want to discuss it by telephone."

There was no need to apologize, I assured him, adding that I was honored by his visit. When he walked into the newsroom many heads turned to look at the distinguished elderly man of such bearing and commanding presence. With his walking stick, he looked like an African chieftain—one no longer spry enough to kill a lion with only a spear, perhaps, but one who in his day had clearly been a match for man or beast.

"How have you been, my girl?" he asked as Jill, interrupting her kibitzing with Dick Suft and Howard Eisenhart, rushed joyfully across the room to greet him.

"Wonderful," she replied, hugging him like an admiring granddaughter. "How have *you* been?"

"Like a man twenty years younger," he said with a grin. "Did Alex tell you that Noah's picture will soon be shown on Broadway?"

She nodded, saying how happy she had been to hear it. Then we laughed and chatted until I finally asked to what we owed the pleasure of his company. "This," he said with a grave expression, extracting an envelope from his vest pocket and handing it to me.

The envelope bore a *Post* return address, as did the enclosed letter, which I read with mixed feelings before passing to Jill. "You have to do it, you have no real choice," I said to the clergyman. "It's a great opportunity. I just wish the *Free Press* would match it."

"I did not expect they could," he said softly. "Three hundred dollars for one column a week is a lot of money—too much money, in my opinion. But my loyalty is to the *Free Press*, to you, Alex, for writing about me when no one else paid any attention."

"You don't owe us anything, Reverend Robeson. You owe it to yourself and Noah to do the best you can." I remembered how forlorn he had looked coming out of that blood bank.

He shook his head. "To Noah," he repeated. "And to Dingo."

"Dingo?" I glanced at Jill, who seemed equally baffled. "Why Dingo?"

"Because the boy wants a bicycle, and—"

"He's working for that. He'll soon have enough saved."

"He will also need money for books and lunches at school. And clothes."

If I had not known Reverend Robeson, I would have thought he was being ironic. "I doubt if a squadron of truant officers could keep that boy in school for more than a day," I declared. "He said he'll never return."

A twinkle lighted Reverend Robeson's eyes. "Not now, maybe," he said. "But school does not start for more than a month, and I am convinced he will change his mind."

He was deluding himself, in my opinion, yet who was I to tell him so? Especially after his grief and worry about Noah, and especially when he still faced pressing financial problems. A week earlier Jill and I had tried to contribute a modest amount toward Reverend Robeson's rent, in addition to our share of his food bill, but Raymond Nelson had refused our offer. So we added it to the fund we had earlier established for him, hoping one day we could talk him into accepting it.

Now, though, the minister sat holding a letter from the editor of the *Post*, offering him a weekly column in which to write about the search for his grandson. Furthermore, the column would be ghostwritten by a member of the *Post* staff.

Under the circumstances, who could object to the clergyman's accepting that veritable king's ransom? But Kenneth Parks took great offense. "Those motherless bastards are trying to steal our columnist right out from under us," he charged, managing to sound personally affronted and betrayed. The more he felt that way the better I liked it, for that was the reaction I had hoped for when, leaving Jill and the clergyman deep in conversation, I fairly swaggered into Parks's office to show him the *Post* letter.

"They're not satisfied to imitate us by beefing up their own coverage of Times Square," he shouted, pounding his desk. "Now they're trying to run off with one of our most important discoveries."

I pretended for a few minutes to sympathize with him, then I said, "I know Reverend Robeson would much rather write for us."

That seemed to come as a surprise to Parks, whose eyebrows did a quick little dance in response to the news. A second later, though, he said, "But he's too rich for our blood."

We were a frugal paper, as the wire service I had worked for was frugal, but we were certainly better heeled than Willis Robeson. Why should he in effect subsidize the *Free Press* by working for less than the going rate, even if that rate was established by our competition? "If we made him a competitive offer," I said, "I know he'd choose us."

I would have loved knowing precisely what went through Parks's mind those next few minutes, when he had to balance his natural stinginess against competitive considerations. Meanwhile, his eyebrows bounced up and down like slinkies, and I almost expected to see them begin descending the stairs.

"Offer him a hundred a week," he said finally, "and tell him you'll write the column for him."

I'm sure Reverend Robeson would have taken it for a hundred, maybe even for nothing, had I so much as hinted that he had a moral obligation to the *Free Press*. Instead, I said to Parks, "Two-fifty is his minimum."

"Two-fifty? Screw that. For two-fifty I can take my pick of a hundred columnists. At least those the *Post* and *Daily News* don't already have under contract."

"*Syndicated* columnists," I emphasized. "But this would be a local column, a Times Square column. Besides," I said, ruffling the *Post* letter, "our competition seems to think he's worth two-fifty, and then some."

It drove Parks berserk when anyone described the *Post* or the *Daily News* or the *Times* as competitors. Our role, he said ad infinitum, was not to "compete" with them, but "to fill the gaps in their coverage."

His rationale made a certain sense, I suppose, but most *Freep* reporters certainly regarded those other papers as competitors, and some of us were busting our butts so our rivals would regard us as competitors.

"Someday," Parks said angrily, "some goddamn day, I'm going to run a paper that doesn't have to pinch every penny and squeeze every nickel. But it hasn't happened yet." He breathed so deeply I was afraid he would begin to hyperventilate. "All *right*," he said melodramatically, "offer him two hundred. But that's it, take it or leave it."

When I told Reverend Robeson the news I expected that, given the precarious state of his finances, he would react like someone who had just won the New York State lottery. Instead, he thanked me quietly and said he would have to think it over. I didn't have to think it over to realize that his response disappointed and annoyed me.

Granted, the offer was not as generous as that of the *Post*, but I had personally braved Parks's not inconsiderable wrath to get even that much for him. So when the minister thanked me again I asked, "What is there to think over?"

Oblivious of my irritation he replied simply, "I have to ask God for guidance."

His reply filled me with instant shame, but I kept at it. "What objection could a merciful God have to your writing a newspaper column about searching for your grandson?"

"Not writing about it, writing about it for money," he said. "'Set your affection on things above, not on things on the earth.'"

"But without money you won't be able to continue the search," I protested. "Surely your God knows you're not searching for Noah for the money."

"Alex, why do you say *your* God? Is He not your God also?"

His question took me aback. It had been years since I had agonized over questions about God, yet it would have taken a far more determined cynic than I, and probably even Dick Suft, to remain in the presence of that devout man and not credit the source of everything he held dear, the source of everything that had sustained him through so much grief and adversity. So I nodded and said, "You're right, *our* God. *Our* Father, Who art in Heaven."

At those words he bowed his head. Looking around I saw Jill's eyes lowered also, out of respect for the minister. Everyone in the newsroom was looking at him, and such was his presence that even those who did not know who he was were respectful. Never before had I seen such reverence in a newsroom, where the typical invocations to God are loud and obscene, and become louder and more obscene the closer it gets to deadline.

The photograph of Noah Robeson created an instant sensation when it made its Broadway debut. From atop 1 Times Square Plaza, the handsome teenager gazed down on the Great White Way with eyes as piercing and as haunted as those in that familiar photograph of Kafka.

The photo was all the more conspicuous surrounded by the large illuminated Coke sign at Forty-seventh and Broadway, by several enormous billboards angled against the sky depicting young men and women frolicking in only their jeans, and by flashing ads for film and electronics products. And it was all the more arresting because the photograph included a digital printout saying that Noah was missing, giving his vital statistics, and asking anyone with information about him to contact the police at the number listed.

Dingo and I saw the sign each morning when we met for breakfast, and I saw it again each evening on my way home. Day and night, Noah kept a silent vigil over the expanse where thousands of people gathered in the days before television to watch the moving billboard atop the building spell out election victories, flash the results of championship boxing bouts, and herald the latest Allied victories.

The minister turned up often at Nelson's "office" to sit in the folding chair that the photographer kept available for more formal poses, and there he would stare for hours at the electronic likeness of his grandson. His appearance unfailingly attracted well-wishers, many of them legitimate shopkeepers and workers in the neighborhood, but occasionally even prostitutes and drug dealers.

One afternoon, after he had dozed off in the sun, the minister awoke to discover a twenty-dollar bill and a ten-dollar bill tucked in his partially clenched hand. Less than ten feet away a band of teenage idlers were sizing up the money—but also sizing up the baseball bat that Raymond Nelson was nonchalantly holding in his hand.

Nelson professed ignorance of how the money got there, for fear Reverend Robeson would try to return it, but he told Jill and me the twenty dollars was a gift from the six-foot-six-inch transvestite who often hung out near the Midtown Arms. And the ten-dollar donation came from a passing sidewalk preacher who had witnessed the unusual initial transaction.

"I know what I am going to do with this," Reverend Robeson said, before disappearing into the nearby bank. Soon afterwards, just as I was telling Raymond Nelson that another page of his photographs was scheduled to run in the *Free Press* the next day, the minister emerged wearing a satisfied smile. When I asked what trouble he had been up to, he handed me two crimson passbooks. The first page of one read, "In Account with Willis Robeson as custodian for Dingo (full name to be supplied), a minor under the N.Y. Uniform Gifts to Minors Act." The second was for Noah. And each listed balances of fifteen dollars.

"Once my column begins," the minister said proudly, "I will donate one-quarter of the money for each boy."

I clasped his hand vigorously, wanting to convey my own pride and pleasure. "Speaking of your column," I said, reaching into my pocket for the essay I had written to appear under his byline.

But before I could produce it, Reverend Robeson said, "That reminds me, Alex, I wrote my first column last night."

I don't think he noticed my surprise when he handed it to me. And I don't know whether it was arrogance, or something much worse, that led me to assume I would write the column to which he would simply affix his name. Whatever the reason, I dreaded having to read what he had written. For in spite of God's admonition to "Be clothed with humility," an admonition I had once heard the minister invoke, I felt mildly miffed that a layman would presume to invade my professional domain.

I promised to read his column that day after I checked on the status of the Freak Show, which had lately drawn the editorial fire of both the *Daily News* and the *Post*. A cartoon in one of those papers parodied the banquet scene in Todd Browning's macabre movie, *Freaks*, except that here a virtually naked pinhead said to the partially nude limbless woman, who was sprawled on her belly like a snake, "Isn't it great that New York City decided it can't ban us? But did they have to say we're protected under the same laws that protect pornography?"

I had not gone fifty yards down the street, giving wide berth to a grungy man urinating from the doorway of a grocery store, when I prepared to detour around a body sprawled across the sidewalk. Similar obstructions had become such regular fixtures of the urban landscape that I rarely noticed them any more, but this time something impelled me to glance down. In that split second I recognized the prostitute with the haunting look, a look the Mona Lisa might have had if it had been painted by Toulouse-Lautrec.

She was cut and bleeding and appeared to have been beaten into semiconsciousness, rather than being strung out on drugs or alcohol. I bent down to examine her and she looked at me through the one eye that was not yet swollen shut. She worked her battered lips in an effort to speak, and eventually I thought I heard her say "Shaw."

"Can I do anything to help?" I asked, but she just groaned.

Someone behind me said, "Oh, look what that bitch did to her." I turned and there high above me loomed that huge transvestite, his face wrought with anger and concern.

"He beat her up again," he told me as he dropped to one knee beside the woman. A handful of welfare kids stopped playing tag in order to stare at the three of us, but a half-dozen adults walked by without a second glance.

"Who beat her up?" I asked.

The question annoyed him but once he realized I really did not know he said, "Motion. Her pimp."

"Motion?"

"That's his name, Motion," he said, cradling the battered head in his lap. "He's got a violent temper. They say he killed a couple of his girls, and a couple others who wouldn't be his girls." The transvestite smiled at the whore. "But Iris here, she's tougher than he is, ain't you, Iris?"

Iris tried to smile through puffed lips, but she was in great pain. When the transvestite, who said his name was Celeste, said he could carry Iris back to her room, I offered to help. Don't ask why, because I had no desire to get mixed up with the likes of either of them. I'd like to think I volunteered out of concern for my fellow man, or because I remembered the story of Jesus and Mary Magdalene.

But my motive might also have been curiosity, because I suddenly realized I had never been in the Southland, the most infamous of the city's many infamous welfare hotels.

The Southland failed to live up even to my lowly expectations. Iris lived in a rancid one-room apartment on the eleventh floor, bare except for a bed that sagged, a rickety table, two chairs, and a dresser that had avoided a paintbrush for decades. Kids raced through the graffiti-scrawled corridors on almost every floor, and every few minutes a woman in the distance crowed like a rooster. Compared with this place, even the Hotel Miami was a five-star dwelling.

The elevator was broken, so Celeste had to carry Iris up all eleven flights of stairs. Inside her apartment he settled her gently into bed, then turned on the faucet in the rusted sink. There was no hot water, and the cold water did no more than dribble out. Unable to find a cloth, Celeste soaked my handkerchief and applied it to Iris's mouth.

Despite an overpowering urge to escape that dark, dank, hotel, curiosity forced me to remain. "Why'd he do it?" I whispered. "Why'd Motion beat her?"

Celeste looked at me again with that quizzical expression. "You don't need to whisper," he said, looking to the moaning woman. "Iris ain't ashamed of what happened. He beat her 'cause she didn't bring him enough money. It's the rules of the hustle, man. All the pimps do it and all the ladies 'spect it when they get old or wore out. But Motion, he like to kill his ladies when he beats them— 'specially the old . . . the older ladies."

There was something so touching about his use of the word "ladies" that I wondered if it was his own expression or street parlance for a hooker.

Iris nodded in agreement. "When Motion beats, he don't never let up," she said, removing the handkerchief and speaking with great effort.

"Now don't you be talkin' when you should be restin'," Celeste said solicitously. "Soon you gonna be as good as new." The transvestite lit a joint and placed it between

136

her lips. Iris spoke but was drowned out by the sounds of kids fighting and cursing in the hallway.

After a few deep draws she said, "Motion, he ain't so bad. I seen lots worse'n him. But Leonardo, he don't believe me," she continued, the smoke belatedly escaping from her mouth and nose. "He says he gonna kill Motion if it's the last thing he does. I hear Leonardo got hisself a piece, so he can pop Motion."

Celeste laughed loudly, his voice high-pitched and affable. "She-eet, you don't have to worry none. Leonardo, he couldn't hurt Motion."

"But Motion could hurt my boy," she said. "He *would* hurt him, if Leonardo has a piece. He'd kill him, even, or get Che to."

The moment I set foot in this run-down, overcrowded hotel, whisking past the sullen room clerk who knew better than to cross Celeste, I had realized I had to write about it. About the kids who lived amid squalor, vice, and danger. About the worn-out hookers like Iris. About the broken elevators and frequent fires. About the drug dealing and shooting up in full view of children.

I knew the answer to my next question—I knew it empirically, theoretically, and intuitively, yet the journalist in me had to ask anyhow. "Why do you stay with Motion?" I said. "Why don't you leave him?"

That human rooster crowed again in the distance.

"Why *do* you, Iris?" asked Celeste, although presumably he knew the answer as well as anyone. "I told you, you can move in with me. You can still go your own way and I'll go mine, but Motion won't bother you no more." His eyes turned cold and menacing. "If he even talked to you, I'd wring his neck like this," he said, twisting his huge hands in opposite directions.

"You're a good frien', Celeste," said Iris, who seemed to perk up after a few puffs. "I know Motion's no good, but

I'd be lost without him. He takes care of me, buys me things—"

"With your own money!"

"Besides," she added, not bothering to deny the obvious, "your place is too small for me and Leonardo."

Celeste stood and placed his hands on his hips. "Tell me," he demanded like an indulgent headmistress, "when was the last time Leonardo slept in this room."

Iris shrugged. "A week. Ten days."

"How about ten months?"

"Uh-uh, Celeste. He slept over on my birthday, and—"

"How old is Leonardo?" I asked, increasingly curious about this mystery child.

"What's he, twelve, Iris? Fifteen? I can never keep up with nobody's age. Least of all my own," Celeste laughed.

Iris squinted at me through the cigarette smoke. "He's fourteen. Didn't he tell you?"

Her confusion was understandable, after what she had just been through. I shook my head. "I don't believe I know him," I said.

She studied me for a moment, then began choking on cigarette smoke. When she could finally speak she gasped, "Don't give me that, Mr. Shaw. He said you one of his best friends." Worry wreathed her distended face. "He told me you was gonna buy him that bicycle. If you ain't been giving him money . . . I wonder where did it come from?"

I was dumbstruck. How did this quasi-bag-lady know my name, I wondered. And what was this about Leonardo and a bicycle? "The only person I'm helping buy a bicycle," I said, "is . . ."

It took almost ten seconds before I could bring myself to ask, "Is your son . . . is he named . . . Dingo?"

"Dingo?" Iris laughed, shaking her head slowly. "My boy is Leonardo. Leonardo Ruiz. He said you his best friend—you, your girlfriend, some preacher, and that photographer." She pronounced it "photo-GRAF-er."

"Leonardo!" I knew he had a real name, of course, but I had long ago given up trying to find out what it was. "Leonardo Ruiz!" The boy who swore on his mother's grave.

"I was gonna name him Francisco, after my father," she said, talkative now despite her pain. "But Leonardo was the name of the conductor who delivered him."

"Conductor?"

"He was born on the subway," she said proudly. "The A train. I was on my way home from . . . from work one morning and he was born, just like that. Two weeks early."

Celeste laughed exuberantly. "On your way home from work!" he repeated. "You mean you was almost nine months gone and you was still workin'?" He slapped his knee appreciatively, and I was afraid the concussion might blow the door open.

Iris grinned, showing traces of what had probably been a winning smile. "Had my last customer 'bout an hour before Leonardo was born," she boasted. When she saw Celeste shaking his bewigged head in wonder she added, "You be surprise' how many men, they like it when you're pregnant."

"Even when you're out like a balloon?" He lit up another joint and passed it to her. Shouts and the sound of breaking glass echoed through the hall, but neither of them paid attention.

"That excites some men," she said. "'Course, I was a lot younger then. Even a little bit pretty."

"She-eet, Iris, you still pretty," Celeste lied, patting her needle-pocked arm.

The prostitute raised her swollen eyes with their fake lashes, shaking her head from side to side. As she did the tears again streamed down her cheeks.

"Where is Dingo, Mrs. Ruiz?" I asked. "I mean Leonardo. Where does he live or sleep?"

"That boy, he gonna be the death of me," she sobbed.

139

"Where does he live?"

She bit her lip. "With friends, he says. But . . . he lives on the street, mostly. He comes home to change his clothes every once in a while, to get a new T-shirt. He has lots of T-shirts, says somebody gives 'em to him. I try to get him to stay, I tell him to come just to sleep if he don't want to stay. But—"

"Tell him the truth, Iris," Celeste said. Then, turning to me, the transvestite said, "Leonardo don't like Motion."

"Hates him," Dingo's mother added. "Says he's gonna kill him. I tell him he can't kill Motion 'cause Motion is his father."

"His father?" I gasped.

Iris shrugged. "He could be. In this job . . . who knows? But I say it so he won't kill Motion. Or so Motion won't kill him. And so Motion won't let Che kill Dingo. Che, he'll do anything Motion says. He wants to be like Motion when he gets older."

"What does Dingo say when you tell him Motion's his father?" I asked.

"I don't say it no more. Last time I did he liked to go crazy. Screamed and hollered at me, shouted it's a lie. The room clerk came up and said shut up, and Leonardo ran at him with a kitchen knife, but the clerk ran downstairs. Leonardo stayed away a long time after that. When he came back, he told me 'bout his friends—you and that girl, what's her name?"

"Jill."

"That's it, Jill. Says you are both important reporters." She struggled to open both eyes for a better look at me. "You with the *Daily News,* right?"

"The *Free Press.*" Even in that squalid environment I was not safe from insult.

"Oh, that one I never see. But Leonardo says he was in the building. 'Magine that, inside a real newspaper. Said he even met the owner, and another big wheel there offered him a cigarette."

"People like Dingo. I mean, Leonardo."

"Motion don't. Says I spend too much time worrying about him. An' 'cause Motion don't like him, Che hates him too."

Celeste soaked my handkerchief again and Iris applied it to her closed eye.

"I do worry," she resumed. "I worry 'bout him mornin' and night. Worry 'bout when he's gonna go to school. Worry that he'll get mixed up with bad people. Worry 'bout this neighborhood."

"She worries too much," Celeste said. "If it's in the cards for him to grow up good, this neighborhood won't hurt him. And if it's in the cards for him to grow up wrong—"

"Like me," Iris said.

"Me too," said Celeste. "You think my daddy, God rest his soul, would be proud of me? No way! Why if he ever saw me in a dress, he'd have killed me faster than Leonardo says he'll kill Motion." He smoothed the front of his dress as he spoke. "One day my sister, she was eight or nine then, she tells my daddy that Ben, my oldest brother, touched her private parts. Daddy took and broke two fingers on Ben's right hand. Just bent 'em back till they snapped like Popsicle sticks."

The thought of it made me nauseous, the way violence invariably did. It was partly to overcome that fear that I had requested assignment to Vietnam, but all I had managed to do there, maybe all that most journalists had managed to do, was to sublimate my own fear by writing about the fear and courage of others.

I was thinking of what to say next to Iris Ruiz when the door flew open. "What the fuck is this?" Dingo demanded, glaring at me with a look of betrayal. Before any of us could reply he noticed his mother's battered face.

"Motion! I'll kill that fuckin' bastard," he hollered, turning and running out the door.

"He didn't do it, Leonardo," Iris screamed, jumping up and staggering to the door. "It wasn't Motion, it was a john," she hollered after him.

I thought later of what an extraordinary scene that would have been in a civilized setting, a prostitute trying to protect her pimp from her son by blaming her beat-up condition on one of her customers. But civilization ended a few blocks from Times Square, at some ill-defined border within sight of the illuminated billboard flashing the photo of Noah Robeson.

D ingo didn't kill Motion—he didn't even meet up with him as far as I know, because after searching for the boy a good part of that afternoon and evening I checked the police reports at both Midtown precincts and found no one answering to their descriptions. But I was relieved, nevertheless, when the next day Raymond Nelson said he had seen Dingo that morning, headed toward Sixth Avenue with an armful of leaflets advertising the Freak Show.

I told Nelson how much I liked his photos in the *Free Press* that morning, a full-page spread showing some of the homeless and welfare kids who struggled for existence in the shadow of Broadway and the gleaming Laney International Hotel. In fact, my brief text accompanying the photographs pointed out that incongruity—with the result that Gilbert Shipley told me when I arrived at work that several theater owners had threatened to withdraw their advertising. If winter comes, I mused, could Lester Kable be far behind?

Dick Suft advised me to tell them to fuck off if they phoned me to complain, and Jill promptly seconded the motion. Yet Parks, to my astonishment, never mentioned the protests. And the rest of my colleagues, including Edmundo Burke, who stopped by my desk to remind me that "one picture editor is worth a thousand words," were highly complimentary about Nelson's photographic talents.

I was tempted to ask Jill what Donald H. Driggs III thought of it, but at some point we had tacitly declared him off limits as a topic of conversation, so that like the man in the nursery rhyme he simply wasn't there. If avoidance put something of a strain on our relationship, that very strain, or perhaps the uncertainty it created, had an aphrodisiac effect on me. All of a sudden I was more passionate, persistent, and potent than I had been in several years.

"Casanova," Jill called me, after I tapped her on the shoulder the third time in a single night. Had I not been too impassioned at that moment I might have pointed out, as a good copy-editor would have even in those circumstances, that the Casanova of legend was famous for variety rather than for endurance.

The telephone awoke me from a sound sleep, its incessant ring sending me crawling in the darkness across the still-sleeping Jill. After finally grunting "hello" into the receiver, I recognized a familiar voice. "I am sorry to be calling you at this hour, Alex," Reverend Robeson said, "but Raymond is still out and I did not know what else to do."

"Do about what?"

"Dingo. He is here in the apartment. He has been cut.

143

He said four kids attacked him with knives, and he is bleeding."

"Call the Emergency Medical Service immediately, tell them to take him to Bellevue. I'll come right over there."

"He will not let me call an ambulance or the police . . ." His voice trailed off and I could hear muffled conversation in the background. At the same time, I knew from the changed rhythm of Jill's breathing that she was awake, listening to my anxious instructions.

Before long the minister returned to the line. "Alex, he said he wants you to come over."

"Shouldn't you get him to the hospital right away?"

"Alex, the boy has been slashed, he is bleeding, but he wants you."

It was the sharpest tone of voice I had ever heard from Reverend Robeson, and it ended any further thought of argument. "I'll be right there," I promised.

I had no sooner finished the sentence than the lamp clicked on, flooding the bedroom with light. Jill was sitting up, the sheet clasped modestly to her breast.

"Dingo?" she asked.

"Who else?"

Seeing that it was not yet five A.M., I suggested she sleep a couple more hours, but she would not hear of it. After a few hurried ablutions—the word that Ben Rocha, our irreverent religion editor, often used to describe even the washing of hands—we managed to hail a taxi almost immediately for Ninth Avenue. A sleepy Jill snuggled against me in the early morning silence, broken only by the drone of an all-news station on the car radio.

My mind wavered between erotic memories of the last few hours and concern about Dingo, so I did not hear a word the announcer said until he mentioned "freak show." Listening carefully, I thought I heard something about a protest rally, but I could not be sure.

Raymond Nelson met us at the door with the good news

that the wounds appeared to be superficial. Inside, Reverend Robeson greeted us warmly, but Dingo sat silently on the edge of the bed, looking frightened and vulnerable—looking, in short, like a fourteen-year-old.

For someone who had asked to see me, Dingo gave no hint that he was glad I came. He nodded to Jill but never even acknowledged me. When I asked to see his wounds he extended his left forearm and I saw four slashes, each several inches in length. "Hurt?" I asked, touching the blood, which had begun to congeal.

He clenched his lips and shook his head, but tears welled in his eyes. Almost any other time I would have enjoyed seeing him cry, would have enjoyed seeing an end to his tough-guy exterior. But not now. I did not want him to sob in front of the four of us, lest he never forgive himself or us. "They'll be healed before you know it," I said, turning away as if I had just examined something as inconsequential as a blister.

Seeing Dingo's face drop at my cavalier dismissal, Jill asked, "Was it Che?"

He nodded. "Che an' three others. Motion tole 'em to do it, I bet. That moth—" Cleaning up his usual language just in time, in deference to Jill and Reverend Robeson, Dingo continued, "Che don't have the guts to come after me hisself, so he attacked with his gang."

"It is this blighted neighborhood," the minister lamented. "No child should be exposed to this lawlessness and vice."

"I ain't no child," Dingo protested. To underscore his boast he tapped a cigarette from its package and boldly, almost defiantly, lighted up.

"What you say is not far from the truth," Reverend Robeson conceded, laying his hand on the boy's back. "Noah is a child, at least he *was* a child, compared to you. But you already know things that most adults in Nashville cannot even imagine."

Dingo remained adamant that he would not go to a hospital emergency room or to a doctor. All he needed, he said, was a cup of coffee to go with his cigarette and an hour's rest. I worried that his wounds would become infected, but I also worried that if I insisted he seek treatment he would disappear again.

We adults were too emotionally drained to sleep, so while Dingo finally slept on the couch we sat around the kitchen table talking and drinking coffee. Raymond said a number of people had stopped to congratulate him on his layout in the paper, and someone from the Mechanics Institute Library had suggested to him the possibility of a display in the library's six street-level windows, west of Fifth Avenue on Forty-fourth. But he seemed especially proud when Jill told him, as she had earlier told me, that it was the most dramatic photo display she had ever seen in the *Free Press*.

Reverend Robeson was likewise proud when I told him his first column was wonderful. When I promised to bring him the copy-edited version later that day for his approval, he modestly said, "I just wager you had to edit plenty."

"Not at all," I replied, and it was the truth. "I only made a few cuts for space reasons, and the copy-editors made a couple of changes to conform to our style. But it's your column, your words, exactly as you wrote them."

While I had helped shape the piece, eliminated several duplications, and rescued some participles left dangling in midair, he proved, despite my initial misgivings, to be a natural writer. From the opening paragraph, which explained his decision to come north in search of his grandson, his writing style was an extension of his speaking style—logical, direct, and fully comprehensible. I realized immediately that a heavy blue pencil would only drain it of much of its vitality.

Several times I went over and looked down at the

sleeping Dingo, hoping to see a dirty-faced cherub at rest. Instead, I saw a child with a worried look, his breathing fitful and uneven, periodically shuddering in his sleep, other times talking incoherently.

I felt pity for him, and deep anger that a city government, a state government, a federal government, and a private sector had not yet found ways to cope with the growing number of Dingos in our inner cities. Cops would justifiably label them delinquents, psychiatrists would diagnose many of them as sociopaths, and either way they were trouble. If they were no longer youthful innocents they were still kids, who deserved far better than the neglect to which they had been subjected since birth.

I was examining the sleeping boy's arms with the light from Raymond's flashlight when the photographer said, "You won't find any."

"Any what?" Jill asked.

"Needle marks." He smiled. "I already looked."

I lowered Dingo's limp arm with a sigh of relief, which was echoed by Reverend Robeson. "Well," I said, "that's something in his favor." I left unexpressed the opinion that it would not have been surprising if Dingo, like his mother and so many other habitués of Times Square, had shot up regularly.

As I returned to the kitchen table I said aloud, "Now if I can just get him to give up crack and booze."

"Good luck," Raymond said, reminding me that bad habits were easy for kids to acquire in this neighborhood but next to impossible to break. "By the way," he added, "I saw Iris today. She's back on the street, even though she's still black and blue."

"What about Motion?" I looked anxiously toward the sleeping Dingo. "Is he around?"

"When he ain't off somewhere teaching Che the tricks of his trade. He and Iris are partners again, least 'til she stops bringing in any money. He was acting just like her business agent until he saw Celeste walking toward them, then he hauled his superfly ass down the street."

I laughed at the image of Celeste in high heels pursuing the pimp in his platform shoes. I didn't yet understand the motivation or modus operandi of pimps—that was a subject I hoped eventually to pursue—but I knew enough to know they were a parasitic and often brutal bunch.

I also did not know enough about the prostitutes themselves, but neither did the clergymen, academicians, or reporters who purported to be experts. Some of the women probably wound up on the hustle because they were physically coerced, but drug addiction, poverty, and lack of education accounted for many more. Some others were probably attracted to prostitution "for kicks," or because they viewed it as an escape from boredom. But rather than write articles filled with the usual platitudes, I refrained altogether from writing much about the role of hookers in the Times Square mosaic.

Meanwhile, I hoped some day to understand the twisted values that allowed Iris to forgive the pimp for whom her son had a consuming hatred.

I had just hung up the telephone, having been told by the security guard that two policemen were on their way up, when Bessie Gath buzzed to say that Parks wanted to see me. My priorities were obvious, and before long the managing editor thrust the editorial pages from the *Daily News* and *Post* under my nose.

"What about this?" he demanded.

Their headlines left no doubt that both papers wanted the city to ban the Freak Show, but I could not understand what that had to do with me. "I'm a reporter, not an editorial writer," I reminded him. "If you have any doubts," I added, "look at my paycheck."

"Cut the bullshit," Parks said, with the subtlety for which he was noted. "We're getting beat on our own story."

"We're *not* getting beat on the story," I insisted. "We're getting beaten on the reaction to it. But that's a problem for our editorial writers, not us."

He sat down heavily and leaned far back in his chair, clasping his hands behind his head and drawing anxiously on his unlit cigarette. "Spoken like a good journalism school grad," he said sarcastically, "but—"

"Liberal arts," I interjected. "With a philosophy major." I had actually majored in English, but since I had heard Parks did also, I picked a discipline that would be more likely to impress him.

But he seemed not to have heard me. "My problem, which makes it your problem, is that Martha Liston thinks otherwise," he continued, "and she signs the paychecks. She feels that if we write an editorial now, it'll look like we're following our rivals, whereas at this point it looks like they're following our lead."

"An astute analysis for a publisher," I said, the thought of the policemen cooling their heels having made me unusually bold.

Parks gave me a long hard look. "Maybe you *should* have gone to J school," he said icily. Turning back to the *News* and *Post* he said, "I hear both papers are sending reporters and photographers to do a series on Times Square, and they're both also assigning teams to dig up what they can about the Freak Show."

Suddenly I wasn't quite so flippant. I had confidence in my ability, God knows, but God also knows that teams of eyes and legs have a decided advantage over a lone reporter. On the other hand, I told Parks, I doubted that either paper had that kind of manpower to spare. "If I had to guess," I said, "I'd bet they'll assign one full-time reporter each and maybe a part-timer to rewrite my clips for whatever they miss."

"We'll be ready for them," Parks vowed, slamming his fist on the desk. "The first sign that they're beating us, or even catching up, I'll assign Jill to work with you." His eyebrows bounded like a trampoline, before coming safely to rest.

"Why not Howard Eisenhart?" I asked.

He emitted a knowing laugh. "Over so soon? That stuffed shirt at CBS, I suppose?"

"You suppose wrong," I snapped, still thinking of the waiting cops. "Eisenhart because not only is he a good young reporter, but Times Square really is as dangerous as my stories suggest. Or haven't you read them?"

"You're sexist and a chauvinist, Shaw," he said. "Don't the cops use policewomen and female decoys in Times Square?"

They do, but I pointed out that the female law officers were armed with guns and a radio, while Jill had only a press pass for protection.

"Well, well. Speaking of guns and cops, what have we here?" Parks asked as two large policemen appeared at Bessie Gath's desk.

"They're here to see me."

"What did you do?"

"I beat a hooker out of her money after an all-nighter."

His eyebrows sprang to life again. "I know that's a lie," he said, "because you're not up to an all-nighter."

I was tempted to ask who had been telling tales out of school. Instead, I mumbled something about not judging others by oneself, then excused myself to go talk with the law.

We went into the cramped interview room adjoining the newsroom, but the officers declined my invitation to be seated. They were polite but firm, saying they understood I knew the whereabouts of the young boy called "Dingo" and they wanted his address. When I asked why, they said they had a warrant for his arrest—for shooting another boy.

"Shooting? Are you serious?" Even had I not known they were serious, it would not have been the most imaginative of questions.

"Dead serious," said the larger of the two, a granite-looking cop who was as big as Celeste. "The victim was only grazed, but he lost a lot of blood."

"And a lot of his natural bad-assedness," quipped his partner, a muscular black no more than thirty years old.

"Who was the victim?" I asked, certain that it was Motion.

"A real nogoodnik named Che," the partner replied. "He's into drugs, muggings, some pimping, chain snatching—murder, too, from what we hear. We can't prove murder, but a mound of circumstantial evidence points in that direction. He's the protégé of a scumbag named Motion, Dingo's mother's pimp."

"Now what about it? Where can we find Dingo?" asked the cop who looked like a defensive end for the Giants.

I might not have lied to protect Dingo, but neither did I want him arrested. "If I knew, I couldn't tell you," I finally said. When they looked at me quizzically I added, "It's privileged information."

"Harboring a fugitive is not privileged under New York law," said the partner. "It's like a bank robbery. You can write about it, but you can't drive the getaway car or refuse to divulge the license number."

His analogy made me uncomfortable. The fact is, I was still not sure where my duty lay in the matter of Dingo. He was a kid with many good qualities and even better potential, but he was also dangerous as long as he packed a gun. If caught with it, he could be sent to prison or reform school. Yet if I told the cops where they might find him, Dingo would never forgive me—and I'm sure I would never forgive myself.

"I don't know where he is, that's the truth," I said finally. "But if I find out, I don't promise to tell you."

A scowl enveloped the big guy's face, but his partner handed me a card. "Here, in case you change your mind."

His name was Buckholtz, and, I discovered later, the bigger cop was aptly named Savage. "Is this something new?" I asked, examining the business cards. "Or just for cops in these swank precincts."

They laughed. "It's a public relations gimmick some con man sold the commissioner on," Buckholtz said.

"I'll bet the bag ladies are impressed."

"Charmed," Savage said. "Yesterday I exchanged cards with three winos, two crazies, two muggers, and a drug dealer."

After we laughed again Buckholtz said, "You're doing a good job, all the guys in the precinct read you. But you can do that kid a favor by persuading him to turn himself in."

"A favor? What would you consider a bad turn?"

"You *would* be doing him a favor," Savage said. "Because it's just a matter of time before he uses that gun in a robbery, or to shoot somebody who pisses him off. This guy Che is okay, but he came within a quarter-inch of permanent paralysis."

I promised I would talk to Dingo when I saw him again, but I had no expectation that he would pay attention. With Che on the road to recovery and with Motion still sending Dingo's mother out to peddle her wasted flesh, the boy would almost surely feel he had greater need of the pistol than before.

When the cops left I returned to my desk and tele-

152

phoned a newspaper in Canada, where the Freak Show had played for several weeks. Jill bounded into the newsroom. "Were they here to see you?" she asked, swinging her backpack onto her desk. "Is Dingo in trouble?"

I put down the receiver and told her about their visit. "Alex, you have to do something about that boy," she said with a troubled look.

"*I* have to do something? What can I do? What can anybody do?"

"Take him places. Keep him occupied. Show him an alternative to Times Square. Why not take him to Yankee Stadium? Why don't we take him to Radio City Music Hall? The Empire State Building? The Statue of Liberty? All the tourist places that he's probably never seen?"

I had been so busy covering my own little journalistic universe that I simply hadn't thought of the obvious. "There's just one small problem," I said, now that I did think of it. "He's wanted by the police."

I caught up with him that day outside the luncheonette on Forty-third Street where he was talking with a couple of older drug couriers, including a Hispanic kid who Dingo once told me wore a ring embedded with tiny razor blades. Dingo's laughter rang through the street, above the noise of traffic and above the shouts and laughter of young children playing hopscotch, and I surmised from his gestures that he was holding forth on the subject of Che. I didn't want to approach him then, for fear of sending him scurrying, so I ducked into the shadows.

"Alex, how you been?" a familiar voice asked. "Haven't seen you in a while."

It was Celeste, dressed in a simple summer dress that looked so dainty on his muscular, ebony body that, had he been a foot smaller, I might have laughed aloud. Instead, we shook hands and after exchanging pleasantries he asked if I had heard what they were saying on the street—

153

that Motion had dropped Iris from his stable, and that she was sick with worry. "It's just like a man," Celeste added, rearranging his hose. "Wear you out then they throw you out. They're such bitches."

"Does Dingo know?"

"I don't think so."

Both of us looked as the boy continued holding forth on the sidewalk, clasping what appeared to be a bottle of beer. Lowering his voice, although Dingo was well out of earshot, Celeste confided, "The word is that Dingo's the reason Motion kicked her out—he don't want no hassle, don't want to have to waste a young kid."

"Waste?" Would even a pimp seriously consider killing a fourteen-year-old? Especially a fourteen-year-old who might also be his son?

Celeste nodded gravely. "He's been puttin' the word around that if Dingo comes after him, he's dead. And I believe him, 'cause he's one mean mother. Now that Dingo shot Che, they may not even wait for Dingo to make a move."

I looked again toward Dingo. Suddenly the air around Dingo's face exploded in a big orange-blue flame, which billowed into a great ball of heat and hot air. I remembered a flame thrower hurtling its boiling fire through the jungles of Southeast Asia, and for an instant I sought cover.

"Je-sus Kee-rist Almighty!" Celeste exclaimed, invoking the Savior's name in the only context he knew.

My knees were still shaking when more flame spewed out, followed by a lesser burst and still another. At each eruption the kids cheered and shouted, and each time the billows subsided there stood Dingo wreathed in a triumphal smile.

Celeste and I took off at the same moment, sprinting up the street, him trying to keep up with me in his high heels. The kids scattered toward Eighth Avenue until

Dingo whistled, much as someone had signaled the youthful wolf pack the first time our paths had crossed. Coming to a sudden halt down the street, the kids now observed us from afar.

"Good trick, ain't it Alex?" he said proudly as I pulled up, winded and shaken. "Now I'm gonna earn me enough money for a bicycle—two if I want 'em. And money for whatever I want."

"What are you doing, Dingo?" I demanded. "You're lucky you didn't burn your face off."

"Or blow your brown little ass sky high," said Celeste.

Dingo smiled, relishing equally our censure and the admiration of his friends, who were warily circling back toward us. "Let's see you try it, numb-nuts," he taunted the Hispanic kid, a boy about eighteen whose cheeks bore the marks of ritual scarification.

"You fuckin' crazy?" the awed and horrified kid said. "I ain't doing it. Not me." He backed up a step.

One by one Dingo's companions declined his challenge, leaving Dingo bursting with pride. When I repeated my warning he brushed it aside. "Why don't you try it, Alex?" he asked. When I told him it was dangerous and stupid, he retorted, "It's simple, man, watch."

Before I knew what he was doing he squirted fluid from a can into his mouth. Striking several matches simultaneously, he held the flame eighteen inches from his face, then propelled a thin stream of liquid straight at it.

The instant it touched the matches the liquid burst into flame, completing its fiery journey in the street, onto the hood of a passing taxicab. The startled driver slammed on the brakes, threw open the door, and started to run for his life until the flames finally sparked, sputtered, and went out. Before he could restart the motor another firebrand landed on the hood of his cab, and sparks rained against his windshield.

I don't know what prevented the flame from flaring back into Dingo's face and throat, or why he did not become violently ill from the fumes and liquid. Nor can I explain why he himself did not ignite when he lighted a cigarette moments later. I do know that Celeste couldn't get out of there fast enough, and soon after he left I began to wish I had done the same. I was about to lecture him when I looked up the street and saw officers Buckholtz and Savage ambling in our direction.

Turning to Dingo I said, "Quick, get inside there and hide, and don't ask questions."

It must have been the sense of urgency I conveyed, because the boy had never before obeyed me without an argument. This time, though, he entered the Southland Hotel immediately, and after exchanging a few words with the room clerk he walked behind the desk and disappeared into a back room. As the police approached, Dingo's playmates drifted away.

The cops greeted me pleasantly enough, and Buckholtz told me about the arrest that morning of a mugger who had trained his parrot to say on command, "Give me all your money!" I probably didn't appreciate it as much as I would have if I hadn't been scared they would discover and arrest Dingo.

"By the way," Savage said, as they prepared to continue their patrol, "you don't happen to know where that kid is, do you?"

"What kid?"

Buckholtz rolled his eyes. "I'll take a wild guess—I think he's talking about Dingo."

"I wish I did," I replied, telling the literal truth.

"Think he might be staked out, or cleaning his weapon?" Savage asked.

"For what?"

He looked at me oddly. "You do know who his mother is, don't you?" When I nodded he said, "Her pimp beat her up one night and tossed her out. She begged to be taken back, but after a few days he unloaded her again."

156

"Why'd he do that?" I asked, wondering if they would corroborate what Celeste told me.

"The word on the street is she's got AIDS," Buckholtz said. "They also say she's now turning car tricks at the Holland Tunnel."

"God Almighty!" I exclaimed, shocked by the thought of her carrying a fatal disease, and by the image of her at rush hour alongside the road to the tunnel, giving head at cut-rate prices to commuters who didn't even have to leave their cars."

"It'll *take* God Almighty to help all the johns she must have infected," Savage said.

"She's a modern-day Typhoid Mary, from what I hear," Buckholtz added. "But she's still that kid's mother, and her pimp is bound to be his enemy."

"So is the pimp's protégé, Che, when he gets back on the street," Savage said.

Both of them made a few more jokes at Iris's expense, but I was so worried Dingo might overhear that I tried, unsuccessfully, to change the subject. After what seemed an eternity they finally departed, laughing and joking as they strolled toward Eighth Avenue, their movements closely watched by every junkie on the block.

I f Dingo overheard the officers' conversation, he never hinted as much. After he emerged from his hiding place I steered him toward a fried chicken restaurant on Forty-second Street, in the opposite direction from the two cops. As we passed in front of a shop with T-shirts with raunchy messages displayed in the window, Dingo said, "Wait a minute," entering the store while I cooled my heels on the hot sidewalk. While waiting I watched from a safe distance a three-card monte game that several times threatened to erupt into violence.

Dingo finally emerged wearing a new maroon T-shirt that declared, "Sure I Want It, Only Not With You."

"So this is where your wardrobe comes from," I said. "How do you get so many shirts?" I was tempted to ask if he stole them.

"The guy gives 'em to me," he said. "I do him favors and he gives me shirts."

I was wondering what kind of favors when commotion arose from the three-card monte players, and at the same time a mounted policeman cantered toward them. Dingo shouted something I couldn't understand and in a flash the dealers and two lookouts scattered in different directions.

"What did you tell them?" I demanded as we walked toward Broadway.

"I warned 'em the cops was coming."

"Why? You weren't involved."

"'Cause Darwin pays me to look out for cops sometimes," he replied.

"Was he paying you now?"

After viewing the empty cartons, the policeman rode on. As he passed, Dingo stepped off the curb to pet the horse's shiny brown flank.

"He wasn't payin' me tonight," the boy said when he returned. "But if the cops arrest him, he won't be 'round to give me no work for a couple days." After mulling it over a moment he added, "That guy who was arguin' with Darwin should have gave me some money 'cause I saved his ass."

"How's that?" I asked above the sound of the street preachers at 1 Times Square Plaza, bellowing into their bullhorns.

"'Cause Darwin is a bad motherfucker," Dingo said. "I seen him knife two guys who said he cheated them. One he slashed 'cross the face and like to cut his nose off of him."

I cringed at how casually the boy spoke of violence. I could not help thinking of the contrast between all that Dingo had been exposed to and how upset my nephew had been when he was about six and I took him to see a Disney movie. Outside the theater a couple of fathers began arguing about cutting the line, and soon they were trading punches. When one of the combatants wound up with a bloody nose, my nephew and another kid in line began crying.

They, of course, were middle-class kids whose proper middle-class parents probably agonized over whether to expose them to something as traumatic as the animated death of Bambi's mother. Dingo and his Times Square companions, by contrast, had grown up among murderers, muggers, slashers, and crazies—the whole panoply of pathologies compressed into a living laboratory in less than one-quarter of a square mile.

As we walked and talked, Dingo readily admitted shooting Che, but said he didn't feel like talking about it. When I told him the cops were after him and his gun, he, like a half-pint Billy the Kid, shrugged and said they would have to catch him. Then he badgered me for five dollars to play the arcade games.

I felt conspicuous and soiled, waiting in the arcade where several chicken hawks were sizing up their prey. But Dingo went through the money quickly and when I wouldn't give him more we left.

He became much more expansive when I asked about the flame-thrower routine. It required only lighter fluid, matches, and controlled breathing, he explained, forgetting to add "plus total disregard for one's safety." He had learned it from a street kid from Mexico, he said, who had spent a few nights in Times Square before hitchhiking to

Los Angeles. Now Dingo was making plans to cash in on his newly acquired talent.

At dinner that night, at a small Mexican restaurant just off Ninth Avenue, it was all Jill and I could do to keep him from putting on a demonstration right there and then. He restrained himself again that evening, outside the Shubert, Broadhurst, and Majestic theaters, but only because Jill implored him to, and, I suspect, because he feared attracting the wrong kind of attention. The night before Che slashed him, he recalled for us with a laugh, two squad cars had screeched to a halt outside Holy Cross Church, where a crowd had gathered to watch him shoot flames.

"How did you get away?" Jill asked. From the way she kept sizing him up you knew she still had trouble reconciling his reckless deeds with his age and size.

Dingo smiled that disarming smile. "Everybody else ran away, so I run alongside a couple of big guys and they never seen me."

Ran alongside, Dingo, I said to myself. All the people *ran* and the cops never *saw* you. Grammar had no value in his present sordid world, it was true, but a minimal facility was necessary to escape Times Square and its counterparts in other cities. I had no expectation that Leonardo "Dingo" Ruiz could become a Hispanic Eliza Doolittle, but the pedant in me still harbored the hope that Jill and I could help him improve.

To our amazement, Dingo agreed to move in with Willis Robeson and Raymond Nelson. At first he agreed only to spend one night in the apartment, at the minister's request, but he returned the next night to sleep on the bed they fixed for him on the worn couch. Then he came back the third night, and the fourth and the fifth.

Jill and I took him and Reverend Robeson to dinner each night for about a week, and Jill invited them to Sunday dinner at her apartment. At those times, Dingo, washed clean and his hair more or less combed, could have passed for a Latino version of our son. But at the end of each evening he insisted on saying good-bye to us and disappearing for hours, after our usual visit to an ice cream shop.

Each evening Reverend Robeson urged Dingo to return to the apartment with him, but he had to be careful not to frighten the boy or give him reason to think of the apartment as a place of confinement. So after stopping off at Holy Cross for a few final prayers, he went home and read the Bible until he heard the boy's footsteps in the hall, usually not before three or four A.M. Then he closed the book and pretended to be asleep.

To the minister's distress, Dingo usually returned reeking of alcohol and what the clergyman described as a pungent, sour smell that I assumed was marijuana, if not something stronger. Dingo usually dozed off immediately, but sometimes he talked or hollered in his sleep, thrashing from side to side. One early morning soon after Raymond Nelson returned home, Dingo began swearing and yelling. When Nelson realized the fitful boy was having a nightmare, he held him in his arms until he calmed down.

Dingo usually slept until about eleven-thirty, then left for the day. Some afternoons he passed out handbills for the Freak Show, sometimes he worked as a lookout for Darwin's three-card monte scams. But each lunch hour, I eventually learned, he performed his flamethrower routine for growing crowds at Grace Plaza, at the corner of Forty-third and the Avenue of the Americas. An instant success, he was usually well rewarded when he passed around an empty shoe box.

A red-faced businessman in the crowd offered Dingo twenty dollars to go back after lunch to his real estate office in a nearby high-rise and perform on the roof garden for his colleagues. When the boy departed less than thirty minutes after his arrival, he had collected another fifteen dollars in tips.

A week later, though, when he and the businessman entered the empty elevator to return to his office the man offered Dingo thirty dollars for a blow job. The boy did not just angrily refuse, showering the man with curses, he whipped out the can of lighter fluid and brandished it. "I'll set *you* on fire if you ever come 'round me again, you fuckin' fag."

"Okay, take it easy," the man pleaded, frightened by the menace in the youth's voice. "I didn't mean anything by it, I just thought you . . . you street kids picked up extra money any way you could. My mistake."

At the twenty-seventh floor the elevator opened directly into the office of the real estate agency, where a receptionist sat in front of a low, clear-glass partition. The man hurried away with as much dignity as he could muster, hoping no one would see Dingo or associate the boy with him. But he no sooner reached the receptionist desk when Dingo, his foot preventing the elevator door from closing, shouted at the top of his voice: "That cocksucker just offered me thirty dollars to go down on him!"

"Why didn't you just let it go," I asked when he told me about the incident, "instead of humiliating him in front of his co-workers? Wouldn't his shame have been punishment enough, knowing that you know what he was after?"

He gave me a look of contempt. "If I didn't do what I done," he said, "he'd be out on the street tonight tryin' to get some other kid to go down on him. You don't know them guys, they think they can buy anybody."

I was briefly annoyed at that pipsqueak telling me I didn't know "them guys," but he was right. For all my worldliness, I really did not know any more about pedophiles than I knew about the sexual preferences of Celeste and Iris. I saw both of them frequently, as I often saw the kids who rented themselves to pedophiles, but by no stretch of the imagination could I say I knew them.

For that matter, could I truly say I knew Dingo, except as a very complex personality? Ever since he had learned to make money as a flame thrower and moved into Nelson's apartment, he had stopped eating with me. But we continued our working relationship, moving it at his insistence to early evening instead of morning. I agreed, on two conditions—that he continue living with Raymond and Reverend Robeson, and that he surrender his gun.

I expected him to spurn my offer but he agreed on the spot, although he swore he had tossed the pistol down the sewer. I wasn't sure I believed him, but like Reverend Robeson, who tolerated Dingo's staying out late in return for his eventually coming in off the streets, I decided a cross-examination might drive him back into the arms of Che or the police.

Reverend Robeson roused Dingo out of bed early that weekend, although not without considerable effort, and with Jill, we set out on a typical sightseers' tour of Gotham—or maybe an atypical tour, since none of the tourist brochures mentioned Times Square, crime, drugs, pimps, or prostitutes.

In two days we covered a lot of ground, ascending to the observation deck of the Empire State Building, eating lunch atop the World Trade Center, taking the ferry to the Statue of Liberty, attending a matinee performance at Radio City Music Hall, and visiting the Museum of Natural History.

Dingo enjoyed most of it, although he was wary of heights and was forever looking around him as if he were being followed. But he was overawed by the dinosaur bones in the museum. He never said so, but he also must have been impressed by how clean all these places were compared with Times Square, whose streets and sidewalks were a monument to fast-food wrappers, used condoms, empty beer cans, and broken wine bottles.

Reverend Robeson, who until now had spent his entire visit looking for Noah, was fascinated by each new glimpse of New York. He was more excited than Dingo when I said we would attend a baseball game at Yankee Stadium next Saturday and visit the Bronx Zoo the following day.

Dingo's behavior during our excursions was good by his standards, but it was hardly exemplary. His conversation, out of Reverend Robeson's hearing, was filled with profanity. He treated as nonsense my pleas that he not litter. And at the World Trade Center he took instant offense when a bespectacled kid about his age, looking from Dingo to Jill to me to Reverend Robeson, asked his embarrassed mother, "Is that kid black or white?"

"I'm a fuckin' half-breed, you four-eyed dick," Dingo shouted at him, clenching his fists. "You got any fuckin' objections?"

The frightened boy's frightened mother whisked him away before Dingo could say another word.

At the museum, several members of an Indian family crowded in close while Dingo was pressed against the restraining rope around the bones of a *Tyrannosaurus rex*, so that Dingo was somehow maneuvered to the rear. "What the fuck is this?" he demanded when he realized what had happened. Angrily shoving aside an older boy, he automatically assumed a street-fighter's stance.

The startled youth looked as if he could easily have whipped Dingo, but he just stood there, transfixed by those eyes that brimmed with hostility and contempt. Dingo calmed down only after Jill talked with him, finally drawing his attention back to the dinosaur, giving the older boy and his family time to move discreetly away.

Jill usually had a calming effect on Dingo, who respected her as much as he did any woman. But that was a backhanded compliment, considering that his general

164

opinion of women had been shaped on the streets, where females were invariably items of commerce—for sale to whoever could scrape up twenty bucks (fifteen, some nights) or some coke.

One night before dinner at a simple Italian restaurant in Greenwich Village, after Jill and Reverend Robeson had gone to wash up, Dingo asked, "Is she a good fuck, Alex?"

I wanted to wash his mouth out with soap, but I detected no sign of a smirk.

"Is she, Alex?"

"Dingo," I said with some annoyance, "that's not a question you ask somebody."

"But she ain't here, Alex, she can't hear."

"It still isn't something you ask. What a man—"

"Shove it, then," he said angrily, bumping the glass of water near his elbow. "It wasn't no big deal, I just asked—"

"I know what you asked, Dingo," I said, hoping to sound conciliatory. "But you don't ask that about a woman, you—"

"Who *do* you ask it about? You think lots of people didn't ask that 'bout my mom? You think even Che's close friends didn't ask me that 'bout Maria? They even ask *Che* that, 'cause he fucked Maria lots of times."

"How do you know that?" I sputtered, barely able to disguise my incredulity and disgust.

"She tole me, how you think?" he replied. Then, returning to the main subject, he said, "Big fuckin' deal, she's a woman. Don't women like her fuck?"

I thought about telling him his mother and Maria were hardly models of womanhood, but fortunately I held my tongue.

Dingo lapsed into sullen silence when Jill returned, and it persisted even after Reverend Robeson rejoined us. I made several unsuccessful attempts to draw him into the conversation, and just as I moved my attention to Jill,

Dingo turned and began looking for an exit as two disheveled workmen approached our table.

"'Evening, Mr. Shaw. And Reverend Robeson, I presume. And Dingo."

It took several seconds for me to recognize Rafael Sanchez and Frank Baylor, whom I introduced to Jill without mentioning they were decoy cops.

"Jeez, Shaw, why'd I ever think all journalists look like you?" Baylor asked, staring appreciatively at Jill.

"He's been practicing that line for weeks," Sanchez said. I could see that he also appreciated Jill's looks, including, no doubt, her graceful nose.

I could also see that Dingo was scared to death that the strangers knew him, strangers who, his intuition told him, were cops or people equally to be avoided.

They chatted easily with Reverend Robeson, asking about his progress in tracking down his grandson. Although the minister had no idea who they were, he replied in his usual courteous manner, thanking them for their concern.

"That was a powerful column you wrote yesterday," Baylor told him, "about your reaction to seeing Noah's face gazing out over Times Square."

"Well now, I surely do thank you," the minister replied, as he had replied to me when I had complimented him. "I am not a writer yet, like Alex here," he said. "But I might learn to express myself if I keep practicing."

We chatted a few minutes more until Sanchez said they had to be going. Turning to Dingo he said, "Take care of the three of them, won't you?"

"Especially the young lady," Baylor added.

Jill looked heavenward. "With your approach," she said, "you're either a defrocked priest or a cop."

The lawmen looked at each other, then at me, and laughed.

They were barely out of earshot when Dingo hissed, "Cops. Dirty, stinkin' cops, ain't they?"

"Cops, yes," I answered. "But not dirty, not stinking. Just a couple of guys doing their duty."

He scoffed. "Duty! They shake you down. They take money from whores and pimps, and they arrest anybody that don't pay up."

"Those two guys?"

"Them I don't know," Dingo replied. "But lots of others."

"How do you know that?" Jill was positively wide-eyed at what she was hearing.

"My mo . . . the hookers tell me."

"And is what they tell you reliable?"

"That part is."

"What a terrible thing for a child to have to hear," Reverend Robeson said. His words and gestures made clear that he had never come to terms with Times Square and probably never would.

Jill's smile announced the waiter's arrival with the antipasto, but it faded when Dingo then said he wanted to leave. We tried talking him out of it, appealing in turn to his appetite, to his conscience, and to his pocketbook. "If you leave before we eat," I declared, "I won't pay you for tonight."

But his fear that the decoy cops would return and arrest him was stronger than the lure of money, and he rose to leave. I soothed the waiter's wounded pride with a generous tip when we decided to accompany Dingo home. When the train screeched to a halt in Times Square he exited onto the platform and bounded up the stairs out of sight.

We settled for pizza and salad at a restaurant off Broadway, and during dinner we discussed ideas for the clergyman's next few newspaper columns. Afterwards we stepped out into the warm, languorous evening. When we reached Broadway the three of us instinctively looked up at the electronic Noah, his dark eyes radiating trust and innocence.

A minute later Jill gasped. "Oh God, what a desecration," she exclaimed. It took a moment to understand what she was talking about, then the word "freak" leaped out at me. The digital billboard under the portrait of Noah was proclaiming the merits of the forthcoming Freak Show, saying that a limited number of seats were still available for most performances.

I should have passed up my doughnuts that morning, because of the several pounds I had gained from so many big meals during the past few weeks, but I didn't want to give up my morning coffee also and I was too much a creature of habit to buy one without the other. Which explains why instead of going directly from the subway to the *Free Press*, I triumphed over my guilt feelings and stopped off at my favorite coffee shop for my usual morning fix.

Having just pocketed my change, I was walking to the door when one of the half-dozen pimps who were congregated there that morning came up to me.

"Alex Shaw?" I was still looking him up and down when he added, "My name's Motion."

He was slender but wiry, with a large, springy Afro and a cocky air that I associate with most lawyers, many low-level politicians, and certain young reporters. I could understand right then why Dingo hated Motion, quite apart from the pimp's exploitation of his mother. Since I did not care to shake his hand, but did not know him well enough to hate him, I replied, "That's your problem," and walked out the door.

I hadn't gone ten yards when he was beside me, hardly contrite but no longer smirking. "Listen, man, I don't give a fuck what you think of me, you and that wild animal you trying to tame," he said. "I want you to give Iris some money from me when you see her."

I had been prepared to ignore him, to blot him out of my consciousness the way I blotted out so much else of the squalor of Times Square by day's end, but this was too, too much. I stopped then and there, letting my arms slump to my sides in disbelief.

"Well, isn't that just too generous for words," I said. "Conscience money for Iris. Money you withheld from her earnings? Money from the asses of your other hookers? Enlighten me, maybe I'll write an article about it."

Mention of an article just popped out, but it had a sobering effect on Motion. His eyes narrowed, his nostrils flared, and his hair bobbed ever so slightly. In addition, his cockiness had given way to apprehension.

"I don't owe her a fuckin' thing, honky. She'll tell you that herself. But she need money to buy her shit ever' day, and I hear she ain't working." He was not good looking but his thin moustache and light skin made him look vaguely like a stereotypical Latin lover.

"You 'hear' that, do you?" I said. Slowly I removed the doughnut from my bag and stuffed it into my pocket, powdered sugar and all, so I could have quicker access to the lid of my coffee cup in case Motion or his pimp friends decided to run roughshod over the First Amendment . . . or the closest embodiment of it. "I thought *you* were the reason she wasn't working. Didn't you fire her after you beat her black and blue?"

"I beat her 'cause she tried to cheat me," he said indignantly, although lowering his voice when he realized we were drawing funny glances from passing strangers.

"Look," he said, his several gold crowns glinting in the mid-morning sun, "I carried her for a couple of years, paid her bills, bought her coke and junk, fed her—and got nothin' in return. I didn't expect nothin'. You seen her. What guy who wasn't stoned out of his mind would pay for her pussy?"

His voice was rising again in righteous indignation, and as he uttered that last sentence a woman I knew only as Bea, who worked in the *Free Press* payroll department and handed out our checks each Thursday, hurried by. Recognizing me as a colleague, but apparently unaware of the beat I covered, she gave me a look of outright disgust. Then she hotfooted it up Eighth Avenue, weaving her way past a wino who yelled obscenities and a derelict who stood in the middle of the sidewalk apparently trying to stroke life back into his limp penis.

When I turned back to Motion I had to admit to myself that Iris, except for that haunted look I found so mesmerizing, was indeed a pitiful sight. I wasn't about to tell that to her pimp, or former pimp, but my silence gave him the opening he wanted in order to press his argument.

"I don' expect Dingo to understand about his mom," he said. "Even she don't want to face it." He turned away long enough to signal to a figure loitering outside a bar across the street. The hooker nodded, then began strolling the avenue.

"Iris tell Dingo lots of crazy things about me," he resumed. "That's cool, I can handle that. Same way with all that shit you newspaper guys always write about pimps— 'bout how we hold those innocent Midwest white virgins in captivity. How we force 'em to become hookers." He laughed aloud, an empty staccato laugh that barely altered the scowl on his face.

A large cream-colored Cadillac pulled up at the curb and the pimp at the wheel raised his head slightly. Motion understood the message and secretly conveyed one of his own—probably assurance that everything was under control, because then the car drove slowly away. A figure sat huddled in the darkness of the back seat, and I thought I recognized the profile of Che.

I had heard a rationale similar to Motion's a couple of weeks earlier from members of the vice squad, but then they proceeded to rip it to shreds. "You might not hold them in captivity," I said, echoing the cops' argument, "but you get them hooked on drugs, then you exploit them, especially their lack of self-esteem."

"If exploiting 'em means making my services available, then I'm guilty," he replied airily, straightening the bright red handkerchief in his vest pocket. "If it means giving 'em the satisfaction their parents and friends couldn't give 'em, I'm guilty.

"If their parents and friends gave 'em satisfaction and self-esteem, and they still need to sell their ass on the street to please this tall, skinny black man with a ninth-grade education, well then I guess I don't feel no guilt."

Infatuated by his own voice and logic, Motion's scowl had been replaced by an expression of quiet satisfaction. He fit to a tee his self-portrait as a tall, skinny black man, but of course he was more than that. As his disingenuous remark about his ninth-grade education implied, he was a street-wise strategist, amateur psychologist, and fabulist par excellence.

When I didn't reply, Motion, after rapidly scanning Eighth Avenue, told me I should write a *true* story about pimps. "I'll tell you things, and I'll introduce you to some of my business associates," he said. His eyes showed that he was taken with the idea, and I admit I rather liked it also. But before I could say so his expression turned blank and he said, "Nah, that'd never work."

"What wouldn't?"

"A true story about pimps. Nobody'd believe it."

"It must be tough being in a misunderstood profession," I said, making no effort to disguise my disgust.

But Motion, ignoring my sarcasm, nodded agreement.

"Even the people at the *Times* misunderstood the purpose of our ad," he lamented.

"What ad?"

"Our ad protesting the show that's gonna open on Forty-third Street in a couple of weeks. The one about them freaks."

"I know the show," I said. "But what about the ad? What about the *Times*?"

"They turned it down. They said—"

"Whose ad?"

"Ours. The Times Square pimps." He tightened the wide knot in his slender red tie.

He may have had the wit to be putting me on, yet what he said seemed too bizarre not to be true. "Are you saying you have a formal association?"

For the next ten minutes I scribbled notes furiously while Motion told me his improbable story, and at the end I allowed as how the *Free Press* just might accept the ad. Several days later we published my article, which had the city talking for days: an O. Henry-like story of how a group of Times Square pimps started discussing the Freak Show in a coffee shop one morning, and how all of them were disgusted by what they read about it in the handbills. When they finally saw the announcement on the electronic billboard above Broadway, one of them suggested they express their opposition in a newspaper ad.

"You were willing to identify yourselves as pimps in the ad?" I asked.

"That was our original plan. 'Course, we would use just our first names or nicknames."

"Of course."

"But then so many people wanted in after they heard about it. People like that fucked-up Celeste. A few of the old men and women who're always outside that hotel next to the Ko-rean market on Forty-third. A waitress and cook in the coffee shop. So many people wanted to sign it that we opened it up to everybody."

172

My astonishment encouraged him, and his enjoyment knew no bounds when he told me, "We even got 'bout twenty hookers to contribute. Voluntarily," he added, after seeing my skeptical glance. "Too bad we got to give it all back now."

My story was held a couple of days while our lawyer sought another opinion about whether it was libelous to refer to a self-described pimp as a pimp. Meanwhile, we ran other stories I wrote, including one about the high rate of arson in welfare hotels, another about the high infant mortality rate in the same hotels.

Although the threat from the *News* and *Post* never materialized, I worked as hard and as long as if both papers had dispatched swarms of reporters and photographers to Times Square. When not writing I was interviewing for future articles—"saving string," in the argot of journalism.

I spoke with a number of the neighborhood's street-corner preachers and with welfare mothers, some of them surprisingly articulate, who described in stark terms the crippling impact of drugs and violence on their children. For an article I hoped to do soon on deinstitutionalization, the policy under which patients are discharged from mental institutions only to find themselves homeless and adrift on city streets, I talked with enough doctors, social workers, and civil liberties lawyers to conclude that the principal victims were the drifters.

When my article about the pimps ran, on what Dick Suft told me tongue in cheek "must be a real slow news day," it led the paper. It did little to inspire confidence in the separation of *Free Press* news and advertising that in the same edition as my article there appeared the full-page protest of the Freak Show sponsored by the "Times Square Ad Hoc Civic Association," many of whose members had colorful first names and vague occupations.

The story was picked up by every television and radio station in town, as well as by the wire services, all of whose truncated accounts omitted any mention of my article. Nevertheless, for the better part of a day I bathed in that special warmth that comprises so large a part of a reporter's psychic income, the satisfaction that comes from one's colleagues stopping by to congratulate you on a job well done.

Even Parks made a pilgrimage to my desk, although I could not shake the feeling that his praise was related at least partly to the paid ad.

The piece also inspired unexpected loyalty: when a *Post* reporter attempted to write a catch-up story the next day, Celeste refused to discuss it. "It's all in the ad," he said, holding forth at his usual outpost between the hotel and the delicatessen.

When the reporter's repeated protests proved unavailing, he muttered something about Celeste being "a fuckin' fag." Celeste had been his usual polite self until that moment, according to Raymond Nelson's eyewitness account, but he erupted at that remark. Before the reporter could retreat more than a step, Celeste grabbed him by the wrist, twisted his arm behind his back, and pushed sharply upward until he was on his tiptoes, writhing in pain. "It isn't nice to call people names," Celeste hissed, maintaining the pressure until the reporter seemed on the verge of collapse. When he loosed his grip, the reporter slunk away clutching his shoulder in pain.

I finally accepted the envelope from Motion with the stipulation that I turn it over to Willis Robeson to give to Iris Ruiz, if he saw fit, with whatever explanation he deemed appropriate.

I was afraid that if the minister knew where it came from he would insist that I return it. But that wouldn't have helped Iris, who surely had earned for Motion many times over the thousand dollars he gave her on this occasion. And it was a thousand dollars more than Iris was likely ever to earn again.

When I handed the envelope to Reverend Robeson he

looked puzzled. "Who is it from, Alex?" he asked, in a voice that made me wonder if he suspected me of illegal activities. I was mute for a moment, but finally muttered something about having promised the donor anonymity. If it troubled him in any way, I added, I would ask Dingo to give it to her or I would do so myself.

"But she does not need money yet," he said. "Dingo takes good care of her."

"Dingo?" I couldn't imagine him taking care of anyone except himself.

"He has been helping her right along," he said. "Last week he told me he would soon have enough money to buy a bicycle. Yesterday when I asked if he had decided what kind of bicycle, he told me he had given the money to his mother. He said he would buy his bike once she got better."

There was almost no way that drug-addicted, possibly AIDS-infected Iris Ruiz could ever get better, of course. But Dingo did not know that, and his was a noble gesture.

"You know what that boy went and did, Alex?" the minister asked.

"I'm afraid to guess."

He tried to suppress an embarrassed smile. "No, nothing like that," he chuckled. "He asked could he go to church with me and pray."

It crossed my mind that Dingo's motive had been to find a new audience for his flame-thrower routine, but mostly I was pleased by the news. Both reports, in fact, gave Jill and me enormous satisfaction. "Reverend Robeson," I said finally, "do you really believe there's hope for a child like Dingo?"

He looked at me the way he must have looked at countless parents during his Tennessee ministry. "There is hope for every child, Alex," he replied soothingly. "*Especially* for children. 'Except ye be converted, and become as little children, ye shall not enter into the kingdom of heaven.' Matthew eighteen three."

The light of faith shone so brightly in his eyes that at that moment I too had not the slightest doubt about Dingo's future. Later that night I even managed to allay any doubts Jill still had, a task made considerably easier by her eagerness to believe the best about the boy.

But some of my enthusiasm cooled the next day when, after emerging from the subway, I decided to browse in the newsstand in the Grace Building. There in Grace Plaza stood Dingo, spouting flames before a larger audience than usual.

Seeing him there disappointed and alarmed me, but I had only seconds to think about the dangers before Dingo suddenly bolted across the Avenue of the Americas and dashed toward Forty-second Street, weaving in and out of traffic like a broken field runner.

Then I saw why. On the far side of the Avenue, the side Dingo had just come from, Officer Savage impatiently waited for the light to change so he could take up the pursuit. But unless his partner Buckholtz had posted himself farther up Forty-second Street, they would not get their hands on the boy this morning. Yet how much longer could he elude them, I wondered? And if he continued to elude them, how much longer could he survive in Times Square?

M y stories about the Freak Show, which ran on four consecutive days, generated a lot of comment and even increased street sales—largely, I regret to say, because they were wrapped in a package that bordered on sensationalism. Beneath the headline, *'Freak Show' Denounced By Canadians as Exploitative,* the first article, the so-called "curtain raiser," set the tone for the entire series by recounting the torrent of criticism the production had stirred up in cities from Quebec to Calgary.

Although Parks turned down Haines's suggestion that the *Free Press* send me to Canada, claiming that the news department was running way over budget, I managed to piece the stories together from dozens of telephone interviews, some of them lengthy enough to give our bookkeepers anxiety attacks. In the first article I quoted from a review in a Montreal newspaper that said the show lacked even a single redeeming quality, and from another in an Edmonton newspaper describing it as "pornography masquerading as drama, but even worse, pornography that is grotesque beyond imagining."

In subsequent articles I quoted Canadian constitutional lawyers, artists, social workers, and writers, almost all of whom denounced the play as exploitive or obscene. I even spoke to the dean of the drama department at a college in Winnipeg, who, after viewing part of the show, suggested a boycott.

The boycott failed because the Freak Show, although beset by controversy and denounced by politicians and the press in city after city as it made its way across Canada, soon became an "event" rather than a show in the conventional sense. A number of people walked out of every performance, including some rumored to have been put up to it by the show's operators, and many who remained complained to interviewers of the show's prurient exploitation of human deformity.

Despite that, or possibly because of it, long lines of curiosity seekers formed at the box offices, and overflow crowds jammed the Canadian theaters and auditoriums.

I would gladly have paid to have seen the expressions

on the faces of the editors of the *Daily News* and *Post* when they read my series. Parks also ran a line in agate beneath my byline that said the articles were copyrighted, and that essentially meaningless but impressive-looking act resulted in even the rip-'n-read television and radio reporters grudgingly acknowledging the source of their material. One network affiliate interviewed me for its six-o'clock evening news, during which I did little more than summarize my articles, and one of the independent stations asked to interview me for a Sunday evening talk show.

That interview turned out to be an unscheduled debate with none other than Donald H. Driggs III, who on the day the first of my articles appeared had delivered himself of one of his electronic homilies, his peroration to the effect that some (unnamed) newspapers and (unnamed) reporters were getting all worked up without yet having seen the play. "For all any New York reporters know," he concluded from his bully television pulpit, "the Freak Show may be no more shocking than any other avant-garde forms of expression, the best of which force us to alter and sometimes break out of our narrow aesthetic constraints."

When I met Driggs at the television studio he seemed to have lost little of his stuffiness since I had encountered him last, but this time he deigned to shake hands when we were introduced before the show.

Only then did I begin to have reservations—not about being overwhelmed by Driggs's logic, but about appearing to align myself with a position that might even remotely suggest I was calling for censorship. I had serious reservations about the Freak Show, all the more so after having spoken with so many Canadians, but I had the typical journalist's fear of censorship and suspicion of those who advocated it.

When the talk show started, the moderator, a natty

178

television type with a red and white polka dot bow tie and an insincere smile, asked me to summarize my articles. Then he asked Driggs why he disagreed with me that the show should be barred from New York.

I watched his lips moving, eager to begin his sermon, and I saw that familiar semi-smile of superiority. But before he could utter a word I interrupted. "I didn't say the show should be barred."

The moderator turned the color of the red in his bow tie and he stammered and stuttered, while Driggs looked as if he had been stripped of his First Amendment rights. When he finally regained his composure, the moderator said, "But all four of your articles were highly critical, were they not? And did they not suggest that New York would be well advised to ban the show?"

"It's fair to say they were critical," I replied. "But I *reported* the criticism, I didn't *express* it. And—"

"But you're the one who selected the quotes and gave direction to the story," he insisted.

"Sure. But the quotes reflect what my sources told me, not necessarily what I wanted to hear. And the combined reaction of those people is what gave direction to the story."

I was tempted to ask him whether television reported the news differently—by selecting quotes to fit a predetermined point of view, for example. But I let it pass, perhaps out of residual respect for Ann, my ex-wife.

"Your professional detachment is commendable," I heard the moderator saying, not meaning a word of it, "but surely you must have arrived at your own conclusions. I wonder if you would mind sharing your thoughts with our viewers."

Driggs cleared his throat several times and even bounced his eyebrows, possibly in involuntary imitation of Kenneth Parks, across from whom he sometimes sat at

Sardi's. But since the question had been directed at me, all he could do was bide his time.

"Not at all," I replied, hoping I looked as confident on the television screen as I sounded in that studio. "My first thought is that whether or not the Freak Show opens on Broadway for a week is much less important than what's been happening in and around Broadway for some years now—the sexual exploitation of teenagers, the degradation of kids, even infants, who have to live in welfare hotels overrun with criminals, drug dealers, arsonists, prostitutes, and pimps. I think—"

"I can appreciate your concern about that matter, Mr. Shaw," the moderator interrupted, his eyes now as hard as flints. "Perhaps we can devote a future show to the broader problem of Times Square. But right now let's try to stick to the subject at hand, namely the Freak Show, which is scheduled to open in less than three weeks. I'm sure you agree it's an important topic, since you just wrote four lengthy articles on it in the *Free Press*."

With dramatic flair, he held the appropriate issues of the newspaper in front of the camera and flipped slowly through them.

"Yes, it's important," I said, "because a lot of people are upset about a show that exploits our fellow human beings who have physical defects."

I stared directly at the moderator, remembering to move my head and my hands the way Ann taught me. "But I've written almost a dozen stories about the kids who are being exploited in Times Square by middle-class businessmen and by a callous city bureaucracy," I said, "and they haven't caused much more than a ripple. Do you want to know why?"

The question had been addressed to the moderator, but Donald H. Driggs III answered. "I'd like to know," he said.

"The reason why," I said, wondering why Driggs would

ever admit to not knowing *anything*, "is that these kids are mostly black and Hispanic. If they were white kids, especially middle-class white kids, the public outcry would shake the city's very foundations. But who cares about poor kids already born with two strikes on them?"

The several times I had touched on that theme in my articles, Parks had suggested that I stick to reporting and "leave the editorializing to the Deep Thinkers upstairs."

I had expected the usual platitudes from Driggs, but he surprised me.

"There's a good deal to what you say," he replied with apparent sincerity. "It's a classic example of what Walter Lippmann described as the 'politics of invisibility,' not only the failure to remedy but the refusal even to acknowledge obvious social or political defects."

"But what about you, Mr. Driggs? As I understand it, you favor allowing the Freak Show on Broadway," the moderator said, trying to steer the conversation back on course. "Is that right?"

Again he cleared his throat, then took a drink of water. "I favor it in theory," he said. "That is, I take the traditional civil liberties position that it is dangerous to ban plays or books, no matter how distasteful they are. However, I also take the position that one has no obligation to support plays or books that are exploitive."

"But how would one know they are exploitive unless one saw or read them?" The moderator beamed with self-satisfaction.

"Ordinarily one wouldn't, which is why it is usually dangerous to join boycotts. I wouldn't advocate banning the Freak Show in New York, but Mr. Shaw's articles convinced me that it is exploitive and therefore not worthy of my patronage.

"And his comments tonight are also to the point," he added, pausing several times to try to light his pipe. "If these were *our* children, the children of middle-class

181

white America, we would have the Peace Corps, Legal Aid lawyers, paramedics, and maybe the United States Marines in there tomorrow to rescue them. But it's still true, I'm afraid, that even in our society, some are more equal than others."

To this day I have not been able to find where Walter Lippmann, or anyone other than Driggs, ever talked about the politics of invisibility, but after the show I learned a good many other things over drinks at a bar outside the studio on Fifty-second Street.

I learned, to my surprise, that Driggs was a fundamentally shy person whose Midwestern reserve often came across as arrogance. I also learned that his interest in Jill, whatever it may have been in his subconscious, was professional and correct. When he told me he had offered her a job at CBS, and had spent several lunch hours vainly trying to talk her into it, I could have kissed him—mustache and all—for his explanation.

My attitude toward Jill, though, was somewhat more ambivalent at that moment. I could have kissed her too, for not leaving the *Free Press*, and thereafter possibly drifting away from me, but I was also annoyed at all she had put me through. Only later did I realize I had put myself through it. When I mentioned my conversation with Driggs to her that night, after we had taken Dingo and Reverend Robeson on a twilight boat cruise around Manhattan, she seemed upset that I knew. When I pressed her on it, she finally said she was afraid I might not have liked it.

"Not liked it?" How could she think I would be displeased that she had a chance to work for a news organization that was not constantly teetering on a precarious financial ledge.

"But you're the one who really deserves it, Alex," she said when later I brought up the subject. "And knowing how you feel about TV 'journalists' . . ."

I finally managed to convince her that her solicitude was appreciated but unnecessary, because I was no more temperamentally suited to be a radio or TV reporter than I was to be a city editor. Besides, at that moment I was riding about as high as a *Free Press* writer was likely to get. My articles were still the talk of New York, as was my television appearance—less for my own role in it, perhaps, than for Donald Driggs's uncharacteristic performance. "Whatever got into that guy?" Gilbert Shipley asked me as soon as I arrived at the office the next day.

It wasn't until Dick Suft told me that Parks had ordered our "media reporter," Jay Lavine, to write an article about the program, presumably to show readers that a *Free Press* reporter had held his own with the big boys of CBS, that I remembered that the *Freep* had some of the same tendencies toward boosterism as newspapers I had worked for out in the boondocks.

I said as much to Irwin Haines in hopes that he would talk Parks out of the idea, but Haines was his usual philosophical self. "It's not the kind of thing they award Pulitzers for," he agreed, "and the Columbia Journalism School probably won't hold it up as a model—"

"Except as a bad model!"

He smiled indulgently, unclasping his hands from behind his back. "We're facing big odds just trying to survive," he said, snapping his suspenders, "and bragging a little about one of our own is a harmless enough way to try building readership and reader loyalty."

"What's the difference between that and those phony promos for TV news that Lavine and the rest of us always criticize?" I protested. "The ones showing the anchormen out walking through neighborhoods they wouldn't dream of visiting off camera? Besides," I said, hoping to accomplish with humor what I had failed to accomplish with indignation, "didn't some of my readers show how loyal they are with their full-page ad?"

"'The Great Pimp Protest,'" Haines laughed. "The advertising department tells me it's getting a big response."

I would have felt better if the big response had been to my articles about the lost and abandoned neighborhood kids, but as far as I could tell that part of the Times Square problem didn't even register "1" on our readers' Richter scale.

But the bartender at the café where Driggs and I bent an elbow after the talk show recognized us from our television appearance. "You think lots of people are gonna go see that freak show?" he asked.

"I wouldn't be surprised," I said. "What about you, are you going to see it?"

"I been thinking about it," he replied, blushing slightly.

"What about the homeless kids, or the ones living in the welfare hotels? You think the city's going to do something about them?"

The questions elicited only a blank look. Somehow that part of the talk show had little impact on him, as it had little impact on most of my friends and co-workers. Jill was one of my few colleagues who had more than an abstract interest in the problem, although Dick Suft sometimes expressed anger about the situation. Jill also shared my concern that the area's inexorable development, punctuated at every turn by a "Lullaby of Broadway" played to the accompaniment of jackhammers, cement trucks, and bulldozers, would enrich mostly a few developers, builders, and crime families, while leaving the fundamental social problems untouched.

Partly at my suggestion, Raymond Nelson had presented Edmundo Burke with poignant photographs of abandoned kids in Times Square, and Burke had promptly fashioned from them a two-page photographic essay to which I supplied the text.

A day later Willis Robeson turned in a column on the same subject, describing how almost every day during his search for Noah he ran into children as young as six or seven who had already been initiated into crime and sex. To illustrate that column, Burke chose a Nelson photograph showing two youngsters huddled under the marquee of a Times Square porno theater, smoking crack and staring at the photographer with eyes that managed to be simultaneously frightened and frightening.

Neither the minister's column nor Nelson's photo display had any palpable impact on the mayor, who meanwile resumed his attack on the Freak Show. In a television interview he explained that a preliminary legal opinion concluded that while the city could not bar a show just because it was sexually explicit, the city council could bar a live performance deemed offensive to public morals.

The *Free Press* published two editorials on the subject, a flaccid one cautioning the mayor to follow established procedures in deciding whether to bar the play, the other suggesting that the city adopt an emergency program to ensure that each youngster in Times Square be assured proper adult supervision, proper nutrition, and, once the school year started, adequate educational opportunity.

A few days later a clerk in the editorial department told me they had received a few letters agreeing with the first editorial, but none about the one on the youngsters.

That night Jill and I tried to console each other about public indifference to human tragedy, or this human tragedy, at any rate. "If the people putting on the Freak Show had been smart enough to cast it entirely with black and Hispanic kids," I said, "it could probably open on Broadway and remain there for years without city hall or the tabloids uttering a word of criticism."

As I groped for the ringing telephone, all I could think of was that the call was from Dingo—or, worse, from someone calling about him. So I was surprised when a familiar voice said, "I hope I did not awaken you, Alex."

"No problem," I replied, trying to sound wide awake although I imagined we had been asleep several hours. As I hurriedly tried to clear my foggy brain, I couldn't be sure if the time on the illuminated clock was twelve-fifteen or three A.M. "What's the matter?" I asked apprehensively. "Is Dingo in trouble?"

Reverend Robeson chuckled. "Dingo is right here alongside me, and no, the boy is in no trouble, thanks be to God," he said.

Only then did my anxiety subside. "Amen," I replied.

"I am phoning because I hope it is not too late for the Honorable Leonardo Ruiz and Reverend Willis Robeson to request the pleasure of the Honorable Alex Shaw and Jill Leigh at lunch later today at a restaurant of your choice."

Jill and I actually had plans to eat lunch together this day, for lately our schedules had allowed us precious few minutes for each other, except late at night when we were both exhausted. But the clergyman never would have telephoned at this hour—it turned out to be 12:15 A.M.— unless he felt it was urgent.

"We'll be there. How about Riazzi's?" I asked, naming

an Italian restaurant near the *Freep* that was both decent and generally affordable.

"I was thinking about that hotel you took me to, the beautiful one with the linen napkins and the fresh flowers," he said.

"The Algonquin?"

Surprise must have registered in my voice, for he said, "That is the one. Is there something wrong with it?"

"No, it's fine," I replied, thinking of him going into shock when they presented the bill. "But Riazzi's isn't as crowded at lunch, and Dingo loves their pizza and Jill loves their pizza and heroes."

He chuckled. "That Jill, she loves every kind of food," he said.

"The more the better," I agreed, looking at her in the semidarkness, surprised to see her lying on her back, listening to my end of the conversation.

When I hung up, after confirming the time we would meet, I told Jill as much as I knew. "Is it possible he's found Noah?" she asked.

"I don't think so, otherwise he'd be shouting it from the housetops, not waiting to break the news over lunch."

"Maybe he hit the lottery," she said, alluding to the Algonquin's prices—for that matter, to the prices of every first-class New York restaurant.

I crawled back into bed and snuggled up to her. "We'll have lunch by ourselves another day," I said, resting my hand on her bare shoulder and feeling suddenly energized. As she cuddled her head to my chest I moved my hand slowly down her back, along her spine, and onto her firm buttocks. I was breathing faster and harder.

"Don't you think you better stop?" she asked.

I knew she was trying to get a rise out of me—some kind of rise at least—so I said, "Why? Do you have something better to do?"

"Not at the moment. But if you keep it up, a man of

187

your advanced years, I'm afraid you won't recover in time for lunch."

I recovered fine, as it turned out, and when we arrived at the restaurant at the appointed hour, Reverend Robeson and Dingo were waiting. The minister was dressed in the suit he had worn on his bus ride North, although it was several sizes too big now that he had lost so much weight in New York. To my great relief, Dingo wore patched but clean jeans, running shoes, and a maroon T-shirt adorned with I LUV NEW YORK, the first slogan I had ever seen on him that was not crude or scatological. His hair was freshly combed, although his cowlick still stood on edge, and his hands and face were spotless.

After hugs all around, we slid into the booth across from them and I asked what was the occasion.

"In due time, in due time," the Reverend said. "Order a drink first. What will you have, champagne? Wine? Something harder?"

"Why Reverend Robeson, I thought you were against alcohol," a perplexed Jill said.

"Oh, I am, for myself. But this is a special occasion, and I would be honored to buy you a drink."

He started to order champagne but we assured him we preferred chianti. He ordered another soda for Dingo, who fidgeted in his seat but was otherwise well behaved. I smiled at the boy, overjoyed to see him looking so well, and when he returned the smile his eyes sparkled with a clarity I had not seen in several weeks.

The minister was drinking bottled water with a twist of lime, and after our wine arrived he cleared his throat twice and said, "Dear Jill and Alex. We invited Raymond, but he had to work at this hour. But he knows all about it. He knows we have asked you here to join us in celebrating a miracle that could have been made only with the help of our Heavenly Father." Then, gazing upon Dingo

188

with pride and love, he raised his glass in celebration. "It is my great pleasure to inform you," he added, "that Leonardo—"

"I'm goin' back home with Reverend Robeson," Dingo interrupted excitedly.

Jill and I looked at him, looked at the two of them, then looked at each other. Although we could scarcely believe our ears, we were overjoyed. "How long are you going for?" I asked after we offered our congratulations. For reasons not altogether clear to me, I hoped they would be away during the Freak Show.

"At least until Leonardo finishes high school," the minister replied.

I thought maybe he was joking, but he was perfectly serious. "You mean you're going to adopt him?" Jill asked. "What about his mother?"

"I am going to raise him, not adopt him," the minister replied, putting his arm around the boy and patting him affectionately. "I am much too old to adopt a child, I am sorry to say, but I am not too old to share my house with Leonardo. And my congregation will make him feel at home."

"He's gonna give me Noah's bicycle," Dingo exclaimed. "I get to ride it wherever I want, to school and everywhere." He began squirming, and I realized that what I earlier took to be impatience was excitement.

"Is it okay with Iris?" I asked, overcoming my reluctance to mention her name around Dingo.

"She could not be happier," the clergyman said. "She promised she will sign all the necessary documents."

For a moment I didn't know what to think, but I soon concluded that if Reverend Robeson had the physical strength to cope with a handful like Dingo, the weight of his abiding moral strength stood at least an outside chance of transforming him into a law-abiding citizen.

That transformation, in fact, had already gotten underway, albeit slowly. In addition to giving money to his mother, Dingo had even attended church with Reverend Robeson on a few occasions. And he seemed to enjoy having the minister read aloud such stories from the Bible as Jonah and the whale, David and Goliath, Daniel in the lion's den, and the parting of the Red Sea.

Raymond Nelson also attested to that transformation by reporting that Dingo, although he disdained washing dishes because it was "girl's work," sometimes swept or dusted the apartment.

"What about Noah?" Jill finally asked.

The minister's expression turned grave. "I do not know where he has gone," he said, "but I have come to the conclusion that he is not here. Not after the newspaper stories, the billboard, the days and nights traipsing the streets and sidewalks." He lowered his eyes. "I pray the Almighty Father will bring him back safely, but I have done all I can do here, and now I must return home." Glancing lovingly at the boy, he said, "And I must return soon, for Leonardo's sake."

Dingo talked excitedly about living in a big house with a room of his own and a big bed. "I'm even gonna have my own bike to ride 'round," he said again. "An' I'm gonna help Reverend Robeson deliver messages and packages, I'm gonna help him 'round the church. I might even ride a horse, ain't that what you said?"

The minister had indeed said that, and apparently much more, as his thoughts turned increasingly toward his Tennessee home. Over the next couple of days he told us several times how he could not bear to think of returning home without Noah knowing that he had left Dingo (or Leonardo, as he now insisted on calling him) in such a squalid environment. "I am already an old man," he said, "but two such failures would have hastened my death."

It was then that he began thinking about the possibility of taking Dingo back home, at first for a visit, then for the school year, and finally for good. He telephoned several members of his congregation to learn their reaction to his plan and they encouraged him to bring the boy for as long as he wanted.

Dingo, I'm certain, was won over by the promise of the bicycle, but maybe he also finally wanted to escape his surroundings. And Iris had no difficulty being won over simply by the clergyman's promise to provide her son with food, shelter, education, and a religious environment—in short, everything he lacked now.

I was deeply moved when I learned of Iris's approval, for he was her only child, and Times Square, as bad as it was, was still her home and work place. So even though she was acting in what she regarded as Dingo's long-term interest, approval still meant relinquishing the only thing of value in her otherwise squalid life. Her only stipulation, Reverend Robeson told me, was that after she straightened herself out, she be allowed to come visit Dingo.

"I'll miss him, almost as much as you will," Jill said to me that evening. We were in a deli on Fifty-first Street, but our thoughts were so focused on Dingo that I had barely touched my coffee and Jill had eaten only half of her slice of cheesecake.

"I'll miss them both a lot, also, that's for sure," I said, idly stirring my coffee. "But it's almost too good to be true that he's escaping Times Square with a person as fine as Willis Robeson, that he's going to a place with sunshine and grass and trees and clean air. I sometimes think there isn't a neighborhood anywhere that doesn't smell of urine."

"Or where there isn't crime on every street corner," Jill added.

"And," interjected the waitress, who had overheard part of our conversation, "where hookers and pushers don't proposition you in broad daylight."

Jill and I laughed as the waitress darted to another table. "In spite of all that, I wonder why he agreed to go?" Jill asked. "Don't you remember how frantic he was, that time at your apartment, until he set foot again on Times Square concrete?"

I nodded. "Sure do. But I think it was a combination of things. The vision of the bicycle, which has assumed an importance out of all proportion. Love for Reverend Robeson. The daily fear of being stabbed, shot, or arrested. Besides, dodging both the cops and Che's gang would finally have worn down anybody."

"What's so depressing," Jill said, pausing with the fork in her hand, "is that we're talking about a boy who is already physically and mentally burned out at fourteen."

I nodded despairingly. "Don't be surprised if I use that theme for an article the day they leave," I said.

"What are you going to title it: 'Farewell to Arms'?"

"That's a thought. Or maybe, 'Escape From Devil's Island.'"

"Better yet," Jill said, bringing the title search to a satisfactory conclusion, "how about 'Survivors of the Lost World'?"

Jill and Raymond Nelson came up with the idea of a going-away party for Reverend Robeson and Dingo, and by next afternoon practically everyone I met knew about it.

Outside the doughnut shop I ran into Celeste, who made me promise to let him know the time and place.

Maria, looking more pregnant but no older than ever, begged to be allowed to attend. Even the dour, scar-faced owner of the deli across from the *Free Press*, in whose store a drenched and shivering Dingo had once threatened me with a cup of hot coffee, asked if I would bring the boy around before he left so he could give him cigarettes.

About the only person who knew Dingo but did not ask about him was Martha Liston, with whom I exchanged civilities in the elevator a few mornings after the lunch at Riazzi's. But even she was touched by Reverend Robeson's column explaining his decision to leave, expressing his love for New Yorkers, and describing his sorrow at failing to find Noah and of his joy at finding Leonardo. For that very day Liston sent an aspiring young reporter to the Hotel Miami, outside of which she was solicited by drug dealers and a pimp, to ask the clergyman to come to the publisher's office.

When he arrived, Liston offered him a generous one-year contract to continue his column, focusing on Dingo's adjustment to his new surroundings. And she asked the newspaper's lawyer to take care of any legal obstacles to Dingo's departure and his enrollment in school in Tennessee.

"Is Dingo going to make it?" asked Howard Eisenhart, stopping by my desk at mid-morning while I was writing the latest installment of the Freak Show saga. This piece was about the coalition of civic, religious, and labor leaders who were planning a protest march down Broadway in two weeks, culminating in a rally outside the King Theater.

"I think so," I replied, looking up at the young reporter. "I'm praying for him."

"Glad to hear it," said Ben Rocha, the religion writer, a reporter so protective of his journalistic turf that he undoubtedly regarded my reply as an invasion of his territory.

"He'll make it, don't worry about that," said Dick Suft. "He's one ballsy kid."

"Is ballsy anything like gutsy?" Jill asked in that ingenuous manner she reserved for just such occasions.

"No fair, you've been reading your *Roget's* again," Suft replied. He had seen Dingo only once, but since his journalistic credo consisted of hating publishers as a matter of principle, he delighted in the story of how Dingo shocked Martha Liston in the elevator.

I thought he would also love the idea of the parade and rally to protest the Freak Show, but he insisted he was outraged at the idea. "Battalions of young kids roam Times Square all day and night," he said, "but the crusaders don't care about that. They want to ban a sex show that's either a rip-off or the only way for some mistakes of nature to earn a living."

"They want to protect community standards," Jill said wryly, before biting into an overpriced cookie.

Suft looked at her with furrowed brow. "You should lay off the junk food," he said. "Too much of it's bad for the brain."

Jill and Raymond wanted the going-away party in Bryant Park, which stretches from behind the New York Public Library on Fifth Avenue to the Avenue of the Americas. I had reservations, since the park usually crawled with junkies and derelicts, and since five of its six entrances were narrow passageways that, despite the manned police sentry box in the northwest corner of the park, offered an open invitation to muggers and extortionists.

Dingo must have had similar reservations, because he vetoed the suggestion.

So Jill and Raymond settled on Grace Plaza, a pocket-sized park a block away. Junkies and derelicts often congregated there also, but they usually confined themselves to the stone benches along Forty-third Street, where squads of down-and-outers armed with squeegees waited for cars to stop at the traffic light.

Grace Plaza offered other advantages. It was close to the fast-food outlets that Dingo loved. Much of it was shaded by clusters of tall, angular locust trees. And its several broad rows of benches, which were rarely occupied by the street people, were ideal for a picnic or party of our size.

A day or so later I ran into officers Buckholtz and Savage on the street, and for a moment I was afraid we would have to cancel the party. They had heard about it, they said, but instead of threatening to arrest Dingo, they offered to provide protection.

"Protection?" I exclaimed.

"Don't worry," Savage said, as if reading my thoughts, "we don't necessarily want him in detention, we just want him out of our precinct."

"I don't want him in detention at all," said Buckholtz, almost in a whisper.

"Why the hell not?" Savage seemed slightly annoyed.

Before Buckholtz could reply, a heavy-set woman approached, her hands and arms tattooed like a yakuza, one of those Japanese gangsters. "Hey, officer," she hollered at Savage in a voice unsteady from drink and drugs, "where can a lady take a piss around here?"

"Can't you read? It says, 'Pissing Prohibited,'" the officer said, pointing to a traffic sign that said "Parking Prohibited."

The woman looked at the sign, looked once more at Savage, looked at the sign again, then shook her head. "This city gets more chickenshit every day," she mumbled, then took off down the block.

Buckholtz laughed along with us but soon became serious again. "I'm against detention except as a last resort," he explained, "because I was in detention when I was a kid, and I didn't see that it helped anybody."

"You were in detention? What—" Savage bit off his question with a shrug. Turning to me he asked, "When are he and the old man leaving?"

"Soon. A week at most."

He nodded approvingly. "I wish them both well, but I can't say I'm sorry that kid's going."

"Oh my God," Buckholtz said in disgust, placing a hand on his hip. "Would you look at that."

Fifty yards down the block a half-dozen youngsters were laughing and pointing at a figure squatting alongside the entrance to a decrepit bar and grill. A moment later the figure struggled to its feet, all the while cursing the taunting children. It was the tattooed woman.

"Son of a *bitch*," Savage said through clenched teeth. "I hate it when people use our streets and sidewalks as toilets."

"It's even more unbelievable that we can't run them in," Buckholtz grumbled.

"Isn't it against the law?" I asked.

"Sure it's against the law. So is playing your radio or tape machine too loud. So is public drunkenness . . . and profanity . . . and sleeping in doorways . . . and soliciting on street corners. There are laws against all of them. But with so many more serious crimes," Buckholtz added as his partner nodded vigorous assent, "try bringing somebody in for cursing in public, or for pissing in public, and see what kind of reception you get at the precinct."

"They call them 'quality of life offenses,' and we just don't have time or manpower to do anything about them," Savage added. "So we ignore them—first in Times Square, then before long people are pissing on the sidewalk on Fifth Avenue and Madison Avenue. Much of Grand Central, Penn Station and the bus terminal already smell like one big toilet."

196

Their plaints were intended for Alex Shaw the journalist, of course, rather than Alex Shaw the civilian. Still, few people were in a better position to catalog the extent of the city's growing squalor. And despite Parks's repeated admonition not to play sociologist, I made a mental note to ask some of my friends in academia whether public behavior had in fact deteriorated, and if so why.

Savage was not the only one who would feel relieved when Dingo departed for Tennessee. As I passed Nathan's later that day, my attention drawn to the large flock of pigeons circling high above the junction of Broadway and Seventh Avenue, the security guard who had ordered Dingo to stay away called to me. "We finally gonna get rid of that troublemakin' friend of yours, huh?" he said with a smirk.

Rather than give him the satisfaction of confirming the rumor, I replied, "Hell no. In fact, he just got a job here, so he'll soon be seeing you every day." His jaw seemed to drop a foot, but I was out of earshot before he regained his power of profanity.

Jill and I spent the next few lunch hours buying farewell gifts, including a canvas bag like the bicycle messengers used, and an illustrated volume of Grimms' fairy tales that Reverend Robeson could read to him.

If it had been in my power, I would have given Dingo a guarantee that he would find happiness and contentment in Tennessee. As it was, I did not know what to expect. Could a young kid who had already been involved with drugs and sex avoid further temptations when he grew bored or restless? Could he, would he, avoid falling in with the wrong crowd? Again, I didn't know. But deep in my soul I felt that Reverend Robeson's invitation represented not only an opportunity to exchange a crippling environment for one that held out hope and promise, but represented Dingo's last chance.

We would miss them, because we had come to love

197

both of them, but love had not blinded us to Dingo's shortcomings, including how exasperating he could be. Jill summed up that exasperation when, while discussing his impending move, she said, "Now when the phone rings in the middle of the night, I'll be at a loss to know who's calling."

I arrived at the party about ten minutes late, held up at the last minute because I had to confirm a rumor that the governor and the mayor were setting aside their mutual antagonism long enough to join the march against the Freak Show. The Manhattan borough president, the comptroller, and any number of aspiring officeholders had also joined what was now a virtual stampede to align themselves on the side of virtue. About the only organization not yet supporting the march was the ASPCA, and I expected its formal pledge any moment.

When I arrived at Grace Plaza, they were gathered along the cement benches against the face of the building, away from the usual midday crowd. A smiling and voluble Dingo, wearing his "I Luv New York" T-shirt, was surrounded by a group of well-wishers, including several people I did not recognize. But I did recognize Celeste, resplendant in a low-cut red dress; Maria, her hair in pigtails tied by white ribbons and her belly looking to be in the last hours of pregnancy; and Raymond, who was busy snapping photos for a layout in the *Freep*.

Jill was there, of course, having left the *Free Press*

building when I told her I would be at least twenty more minutes on the telephone. I was especially pleased to see Irwin Haines, Howard Eisenhart, Edmundo Burke, and Gilbert Shipley, all there to pay respects to Reverend Robeson, their newest colleague. I was even pleased to see Donald H. Driggs III, who said he had to leave shortly but also wanted to pay his respects.

I had been there only a minute before Iris showed up, walking unsteadily with the help of Motion and looking more wasted than ever. Dingo's smile turned to unalloyed hatred when he saw his mother's longtime procurer, and probably only the fact that he was the guest of honor— and that Motion prudently remained well off to the side— restrained him from some sort of outburst.

Iris approached Dingo to embrace him, but had to settle for an impersonal "hi" from the embarrassed boy. I wondered whether it was Dingo's age, his mother's profession, or the presence of Motion that accounted for his restraint. I was still mulling it over when Reverend Robeson came up and embraced Iris. "I am so glad you were able to be here," he said. "I did not tell Leonardo you would come, in case you could not make it. I know he is very happy."

The boy did indeed seem happy, smiling even when the minister asked us to bow our heads while he said grace. Thanking all who had helped him, Reverend Robeson called upon the Lord to bless Leonardo and him as they embarked on what he called their "new venture." When he finished, a wino on the fringes of our crowd hollered, "Amen, brother."

Afterwards, Dingo stuffed himself with fried chicken, cheeseburgers, pizza, and ice cream. Between mouthfuls he talked animatedly with Maria, and before long he and Iris seemed to be sharing confidences.

Jill and I had just finished talking with Maria, who drifted off in search of more food, when Dingo came up and squeezed onto the bench between us. "Are you gonna visit me?" he asked, looking at each of us in turn.

Her mouth full at that moment, Jill only nodded, while I stammered, "Sure, Dingo, we'll try to visit."

"Don't try, do it," he commanded. Displeasure clouded his face. "Else I don't wanna go."

"We will," Jill assured him, swallowing her last bit whole. "But you have to promise to do well in school."

The boy turned up his nose at the reminder that Tennessee would not be all fun and games. "I still don't see why I need to go to no school," he groused, his cowlick semi-erect.

"So you can get a good job and make lots of money." I hoped that by caricaturing the value of an education, I could make it sound appealing.

He lit a cigarette, squinting from the smoke that burned his eyes. From a distance, several unsavory characters eyed us and our food, but the presence of Celeste and Raymond Nelson discouraged them from edging closer.

"I can make lots more money workin' than in school," the boy declared. I shuddered and looked at Jill, who rolled her eyes heavenward. Already doubts were beginning to form like distant rain clouds.

I reiterated Jill's and my pledge to visit him. I added that we would take him and Reverend Robeson to the Grand Ole Opry in Nashville, and after I explained what it was he seemed interested.

"I'll miss you," Dingo told us, suddenly kissing Jill on the cheek, the first kiss—in fact, the first real sign of affection—we had ever seen from him. He blushed, although he looked quite pleased with himself.

We assured him that we would miss him also, promising to write and phone regularly. Although we expected to see him every day until their departure, I clapped him on the back. "It won't be the same here without you,

Dingo," I said, feeling great sadness rising within me. "Do your best to watch over Reverend Robeson for us." Some drug peddlers wandered toward us, but each time a few soft-spoken words from Celeste or Raymond Nelson—who was dressed all in white this day, but still as menacing-looking as when he wore his usual black—was enough to make them peddle their wares elsewhere.

During a pause between shooting roll after roll of film, Raymond proudly informed us that he had been approached by *New York* magazine and *Sports Illustrated* about possible photo assignments. It had taken years but now his talent was finally being recognized, and I was pleased at the *Free Press*'s part in his discovery.

"I know that preacher man is gonna take real good care of my son," Iris said to me, just seconds after Raymond persuaded a bedraggled drunk to practice his ranting elsewhere.

When I added my reassurances, Iris said, "I'm gonna visit him one of these days. Next year I 'spect to have enough money to make the trip." I must have looked doubtful, because she quickly added, "I've given up the life, this time for good."

"The life" was street talk for prostitution, and just in case I had any doubts about either her rectitude or financial future, she declared, "Motion gonna set me up in a new business. I'm gonna be a baby sitter."

To prove it, she summoned her pimp to our section of the lengthy bench. Although Dingo was talking and laughing with Celeste and Maria, far down the other end of the bench, he followed Motion's movements with undisguised loathing.

The pimp verified Iris's claim, and she explained that she was going to baby-sit for the sons and daughters of prostitutes from the Southland Hotel, the Midtown Arms, and other nearby hotels. "Me and Motion figured it up, there must be seven or eight workin' girls with babies,"

she said, using another of her euphemisms. "Instead of
taking them 'cross town to a baby sitter 'fore they go to
work each day, or leavin' them 'lone in a room, they can
drop 'em off with me."

"Iris loves kids," Motion said, evoking a matronly blush
from Dingo's mother.

"That's a fact," she agreed. "I always wanted five or six
kids, but the Good Lord only sent me but one."

At that moment a noisy argument broke out on Sixth
Avenue, where two husky bicycle messengers were berat-
ing and threatening a rotund taxi driver who they claimed
had run them off the road two blocks earlier. While Iris
and Motion hurried over to see the commotion, which
quickly attracted a crowd, I thought of how implausible
her story was. In the tabloids, and probably in the *Free
Press* as well, it would read like this:

A woman perhaps not yet thirty years old, although she looked like she was in her fifties, had
spent her entire adult life as a prostitute. Unable
to have more than one child, and now so unattrac-
tive she could not sell her body even in Times
Square, she decided to baby-sit for the children of
other prostitutes. And her business partner was
none other than her longtime pimp, a schizo-
phrenic who lavished affection on her one minute
and brutally beat her the next. Then there were
those rumors about her dying of AIDS . . .

The moment Dingo heard the angry curbside exchange
he sprinted toward the commotion and forced his way
through the crowd, seeking an unobstructed view. Just
when a physical confrontation seemed inevitable, someone yelled "Police!" prompting the messengers to re-
mount their bikes and peddle away, trailing a stream of
profanity after them.

"Goddam it!" Dingo said, punching his fist into the palm of his other hand. "There woulda been a good fight if that cop car hadn't came along."

"It is fortunate it came along," Reverend Robeson said, clasping Dingo's shoulder. "'Put away violence and oppression, and execute justice and righteousness.'"

You could see Dingo trying to formulate a reply, for in his experience fighting and force were the answer to most disputes. But something about the minister's words and expression caused him to remain silent. Jill and I looked at one another, tacitly acknowledging the significance of what we had just witnessed. One of the rain clouds, at least, had disappeared.

Shipley took orders for ice cream, which he bought from the sidewalk vendors. And after dessert, Dingo and Reverend Robeson opened their presents, gifts that included twenty dollars for each of them from Celeste and airline tickets to Nashville from Jill and me.

"But we are planning to take the bus home," the minister said. "It is not that far away, and besides, I arrived in New York by bus."

"Then make other plans," Jill said with a pleased smile. "You arrived in New York in despair and now you are returning home in triumph—a columnist, a celebrity, a savior to a young boy . . ."

"I am returning home with everything except what I came for," Reverend Robeson said, his face still etched with concern although no longer with sadness. "But I have faith that God Almighty will still return Noah safely. And meanwhile," he said, putting his arms around Dingo and Iris, "I have been given the honor of raising Leonardo under my own roof."

Iris was beaming with parental pride, her frail body stretched to its full height as if she were in the spotlight. "He is a wonderful boy, my Leonardo," she said, gazing on her son with loving eyes. "Sometimes he worry you half to death with his comin's and goin's, but he is a good boy—not like lots of other kids around here who are shootin' up and smokin' crack."

Dingo squirmed, but otherwise managed to suffer his mother's praise with a semblance of good grace. Then he slipped away while the rest of us talked among ourselves. Five minutes later he was back with a kid in tow, a stocky street kid named Hector, about fifteen years old. I recognized him as a crack addict, who I knew financed his addiction by mugging, chain snatching, robbery, and working as a "mule"—that is, by transporting crack and coke from supply houses in Harlem to the open-air retail outlets in Times Square. He was carrying the type of gym bag favored by the street peddlers and scam artists, into which they stashed their goods at the first sign of a policeman, and this day he looked more spaced out than usual.

"We gonna have a contest," Dingo declared.

I didn't like the idea of Dingo having anything to do with Hector, but with his mother and Reverend Robeson on hand, I had nothing to say about it.

"What kind of contest?" the clergyman asked.

"We gonna see who's the best flame thrower," Dingo replied.

Iris let out a gasp that attracted the attention of several loungers who were basking in the midday sun, and Reverend Robeson shook his head vigorously. "Oh, no," he said. I also warned Dingo that it was dangerous to him and to those around him, and reminded him he would be arrested if the police saw him.

But he waved aside our objections as Hector proceeded to wrap a rag around a bent coat hanger. "We're gonna do three throws each," he said, as if he were talking about playing baseball at some suburban ball field. "I'll be careful. Besides, I wanna do it once more before I move away, 'cause I know I won't be able to do it in Tennessee."

The suggestion that he planned to be on his best behavior in his new environment had the effect of defusing some of Iris's and the minister's opposition. And his mother also found it hard to refuse his last request, even for something so dangerous, when he was about to leave her and the only surroundings he ever knew.

Hector, meanwhile, set the rag on fire with a lighter, then filled his mouth with liquid from a metal container he had been carrying in his gym bag. Walking purposefully toward the vertical portion of the Grace building, some distance from where we were gathered, he stopped about ten yards from the gleaming travertine wall, took a deep breath, and vigorously blew the liquid onto the rag. At once the flames shot forward, as if propelled from a flame thrower, and burst against the side of the building.

As much as what they were doing repelled me—I later read that the kerosene or diesel fuel used by the *tragafuegos*, or fire-eaters, frequently caused neurological damage—I was fascinated in spite of myself by the orange-red flames leaping in a rainbow-like arch, exploding against the wall, then scattering in hundreds of shards of light reminiscent of Proust's fountain.

Without hesitation, Dingo took a swig from Hector's container, then with his cheeks puffed out and carrying the flaming coat hanger, he walked to the same spot as his rival. After a brief dramatic pause he took one step backward toward Forty-third Street, then spat out the liquid with all his might. Once again the flame arched forward, exploding in a burst of color against the side of the building.

Haines, Eisenhart, Burke, and Shipley had read my story about *tragafuegos* but they had not seen any in action. Now they too were transfixed by this live demonstration. So were many passersby, for a big crowd quickly gathered. When I could take my eyes off the human dragons, I scanned the park for policemen and undercover cops, afraid they might swoop down and cart Dingo off to jail. But no one interfered, and the two street kids went at it like youthful gunslingers, sizing one another up from a respectful distance.

Instead of moving back a step or two in hopes of exceeding Dingo's distance, Hector, for his second shot, sent the flame in a high, looping arch, bringing it to another explosive finish at the base of the wall. Several spectators clapped and a stoned youth with a customized "blaster box" on his shoulder exclaimed "Awwww-riiiight." Hector smiled and pumped his arms in the symbol of triumph adopted by so many athletes.

I saw the initial bewilderment on Dingo's face, then watched it give way to a look of determination. His eyes searched the crowd until they met mine, then he flashed me a smile as if to say he had things under control.

"Fifty dollahs says he don't outdo Hector on this one," a voice said. I looked up and saw Motion, who had pushed his way to the front of the semicircle with Iris.

I had no intention even of talking with Motion, but there he stood, his cocky bearing and the cut of his off-white suit loudly proclaiming his occupation, his oversized Afro and his gold crowns glistening in the midday sun, and five yards away stood the kid whose life he had helped make so miserable.

"You're on," I heard myself saying. A second later I added, "But I'll have to pay you tomorrow, in the unlikely event I lose."

Motion laughed, producing a sort of scoffing sound meant to underscore his financial superiority. But I concentrated on Dingo as he stared at that blank wall, not saying a word as more people crowded around to watch, pressing in and tightening the semicircle.

Dingo moved back yet another step, stepping it off somewhat ostentatiously, I thought, lest anyone fail to appreciate that this shot would be longer and harder. He stood there holding the hanger with the charred rag wrapped around it, then picked up the container of liquid. In the midst of his concentration he walked slowly over to me and said, "After I take a swig, light the rag for me, will you Alex, then hand it to me?"

I didn't know why he couldn't do it himself, but I thought, what the hell. "Sure, but only if you turn the other way." I was not anxious to have a ringside seat at his immolation.

He shrugged, said okay, handed me the hanger and a pack of matches, then turned to face the wall. When I returned the lighted rag to him, he kept it at arm's length and walked unhurriedly back to his spot. Then, after coming to rest for a few seconds, he sent a burst of flame in a straight line toward the wall. The instant it landed, he spat another burst of flame, which seconds later also crashed into the wall, and also extinguished itself on the travertine floor.

J ill and I joined in the cheers and applause, and I even saw a glimpse of pride on the face of Reverend Robeson.

"Pay up, you fool," Iris demanded of Motion, elbowing him sharply in the ribs. "That'll teach you to bet 'gainst my son."

"Whose son?" the pimp demanded, raising his eyebrows and grinning at me. With a sly smile he reached into his pocket and produced a wad of bills, from which he grandly peeled off a fifty. I pocketed it without a word, wondering how often this portrait of Ulysses S. Grant had gotten high from its various owners sniffing cocaine out of it.

"Want to do it again?" I asked the pimp, suddenly eager to take even more of his ill-gotten money. "If I lose this time," I said when he accepted the bet, "you won't have to wait to collect."

He gave me a sideways glance, then turned back to the main event. Jill nudged me and smiled her congratulations. Hector was standing about where he stood last time, only now he started weaving back and forth, either to psych himself up or to stop the wall from moving. I noticed his hands and arms were badly scarred from knife cuts, and I made another of my mental notes to contact him in a few days to see if he would tell me how he managed to survive on the streets as long as he had.

Dingo stood off to the side near Reverend Robeson, intently studying his opponent. Hector paced back and forth, all the while continuing to weave unsteadily. For a moment he scanned the crowd, probably looking out for the police. Then he took a big swig of liquid, lighted the rag, and blew with all his might. The fire hurtled through the air, but crashed onto the pavement two feet before the wall.

A few spectators groaned while Hector stared in disbelief, wondering what had gone wrong.

Except for Motion, who hid behind a mask of stoicism, the rest of us were happy for Dingo. Iris wore a grin almost from ear to ear and Celeste, who had also tried to talk Dingo out of flame throwing, was positively beaming. If we did not actually forget the dangers, in our euphoria we managed not to think too hard about it. I also rationalized that winning even this reckless competition would help Dingo's confidence and self-esteem.

By now the crowd had grown to several hundred, including a few notorious drug dealers and some "squeegee men," who were taking a break from their extortionate labors. Any second I expected to see officers Buckholtz and Savage, accompanied by a paddy wagon; not until the next day did I learn they had responded at that hour to an "assist officer" call in Bryant Park, where a deranged panhandler had jammed a jagged bottle into the face of a patrolman. They had managed to subdue him, but not before another cop suffered a nasty cut on the forearm, which he threw up at the last second to protect his face.

Dingo's confidence seemed to be in no need of bolstering, at that moment at any rate. Now the crowd was shouting encouragement, no one louder than the usually mild-mannered Irwin Haines, and Dingo was playing to the gallery for all he was worth. He bummed a cigarette from a bicycle messenger who had stopped to watch, and after several exaggerated puffs he asked Celeste to hold it for him. Then he swaggered up to the puzzled Hector to reclaim the hanger, promptly turning his back once he had done so.

To a chorus of ooohs and aaahs, Dingo marked off a spot about eighteen inches farther than last time. After studying the faraway wall for almost a minute, he stepped back yet another ten to twelve inches, this time to even greater acclaim. Standing perfectly erect, his small body seemed to have added weight as well as height.

Again Dingo walked toward me, the picture of self-assurance. Again he asked me to light the hanger while he took a swig of liquid. This time he turned his back to me without having to be told, and in a moment I stuck the fiery hanger in his left hand. He took a step forward, holding it at arm's length like a flaming wand.

But before I knew what was happening, Dingo whirled, dashed several steps forward, and from a distance of no more than ten feet blew a stream of fire that seemed headed for my face. Instinctively, I threw a protective hand over my face and felt a rush of hot air. Then I heard a scream alongside me and saw the flame engulfing Motion's hair. An instant later another flame lashed out and caught him as he slumped to the hard calcite floor of the plaza, desperate to escape additional fiery blasts while struggling to beat out the fire that had turned his head into a flaming bush.

Some people in the crowd also started screaming, and I experienced again that momentary fright I had known as a reporter in a dozen dangerous situations. Iris was also screaming, bouncing up and down in confusion and panic. But the loudest screams continued to issue from Motion, who, after he had struggled to his hands and knees, suffered another blast from Dingo's blowtorch.

His face and hair wreathed in flame, the panic-stricken procurer lurched blindly toward the street, screaming and flailing at the fire. Still holding the flaming rag, Dingo brandished the container of fluid as he hollered something indecipherable to his crawling enemy.

Jill grabbed a towel from a nearby bench and I quickly placed it over Motion's head, before I was driven back by the flames. Raymond Nelson and Celeste, as stunned as the rest of us, managed to find a sweater and blanket to throw on Motion. Despite his agony, the pimp still struggled to rise.

Dingo's face was twisted with anger. Still holding the firebrand and the container of liquid, he moved close to the prostrate body and hollered something about ruining his mother. Iris continued screaming, and as Reverend Robeson rose from the bench to which he had slumped in horror, police sirens wailed above the bedlam. I prayed the cops would get there before the mood of the crowd—which knew nothing of the relationship between Dingo, Iris, and Motion—changed from shock to rage, and the mob would begin to direct its fury at the boy.

I started toward Dingo, to ask him to wait for the police with me, but Maria ran up to him shouting something I could not hear. Dingo looked warily about him, then, jettisoning his hanger and the container, he dashed through the stunned crowd toward Forty-third Street. I tried to follow but by the time I reached the sidewalk I heard the squeal of brakes at the intersection, followed by shouts and curses. I scurried atop a bench and saw several figures running toward Broadway.

I did not recognize Dingo among them, but I jumped down anyway and ran to the corner. As I waited for the traffic light to change, an Emergency Medical Service ambulance pulled up to the plaza along Sixth Avenue. Two attendants leaped out, ran up the five broad steps, and disappeared into the crowd, looking for Motion. At that moment, however, I was thinking more about the pain Reverend Robeson and Iris must be suffering.

When the light changed I threaded my way across the crowded intersection, and as I passed the liquor store on the corner I heard shouts coming from the direction of Broadway. In a moment Dingo came running as fast as he could toward me, pursued by Che and three of his henchmen, all of them shouting and cursing.

"Help me, Alex," Dingo shouted, his eyes filled with terror.

I signaled frantically for him to come to me. "Over here," I yelled, motioning for him to take refuge behind me, or in the liquor store, where I could try to bar the door. But Dingo's every instinct was to outrun and outmaneuver his enemies, not stop and confront them, so he kept right on going, dashing into the intersection again and again narrowly avoiding being hit by a vehicle, this time a bus.

By the time I could react Che shot by me also, but I slammed into the second pursuer, knocking him to the street with a body block that sent me sprawling also. Another of the gang stopped his pursuit long enough to run at me and aim a kick at my face. I managed to jerk back out of the way, and his boot landed flush on my collarbone.

I expected him to kick me again, but instead he resumed the chase. The kid I had knocked down, a lowlife I recognized as a lookout at three-card monte games, picked himself up and ran off with his buddy.

As soon as I pulled myself to my feet I too plunged headlong into the middle of Sixth Avenue, my mind more on my aching body than on the traffic. Luckily, the light was in my favor and in a few seconds I was bounding up the plaza stairs two at a time, my collarbone and bruised body throbbing with every step. I spotted Jill, Celeste, and Raymond running toward the back of the plaza, from where I heard several anguished screams. By the time I arrived, Dingo was slumped on the plaza floor and Che and his friends were brandishing their large, menacing knives.

"Stay the fuck away or you dead too," Che warned, ominously waving his knife back and forth as I started toward Dingo.

I did not doubt that any or all four of them would knife me in an instant, but I figured that right now, with the crowd closing in and a police car having just pulled up with its emergency lights flashing, their first thought was to get away.

"Try it!" I said, brushing past Che and making straight toward Dingo. Che took a hesitant step toward me, then apparently thought better of it. He yelled something in Spanish and the four of them started running, but they had gone only a few yards when Celeste stuck out his foot, high heels and all, and sent Che sprawling. The impact dislodged his knife, and before he could scramble over to it Celeste pulled him to his feet and began pummeling him.

The calcite beneath Dingo was coated with blood and the boy was breathing with great difficulty. I dropped beside him, lay my hand on his head, and bent close to assure him he would be okay, to tell him the ambulance was already here. I started to turn him over but when he screamed I decided to let him lie in that position until medical help arrived.

"I . . . hate it . . . that . . . Che got me, Alex," Dingo gasped. "I . . . got Motion . . . but . . . Che got . . . me." He sucked in his breath in pain.

A few seconds later he said, "I wanted . . . to go to Nashville, Alex. I . . . wanted . . . to have a bike. But . . ."

"You'll still go, Dingo," I said, fighting back tears as Jill dropped beside me and took the frightened boy's hand. "You'll still get the bicycle and a horse."

"Will you . . . and Jill . . . still come to see me?" he asked through clenched teeth.

"We will, I promise." But I'm not sure he heard me because of the loud commotion as a distraught Reverend Robeson and a distraught Iris pushed through the crowd. Jill and I withdrew to make room for them alongside the boy.

The clergyman lay his hands on Dingo's head and began praying softly, the sunlight glinting eerily off his cracked eyeglass lens, while Iris lifted her son's head into her lap. "Leonardo, Leonardo," she cried, soothing his cheek. "I love you, my little boy, I love you."

"Where are those paramedics?" Raymond Nelson roared, finally stomping off in search of them.

Breathing heavily, Dingo groped for his mother's hand. "I . . . done it . . . for . . . you," he gasped. "'Cause of . . . all he did to you."

"I know, Leonardo, I know," she said. She pressed her head alongside her son's, then turned and kissed his cheek as tears streamed from her eyes. Jill and Reverend Robeson were also crying unashamedly, and tears blurred my own vision. I didn't want Dingo to see me, although

213

under the circumstances it would have made little difference.

Buckholtz and Savage pushed their way through the mob toward us, and soon the plaza was crowded with policemen. There were clusters of people around Motion and Che, but the largest number of spectators had gathered around Dingo. Whatever hostility the crowd felt toward the boy just minutes earlier had already been supplanted by sympathy and concern.

Seeing Iris and the minister kneeling alongside Dingo, and seeing the lights flashing on the waiting ambulance, Buckholtz and Savage stayed at the edge of the crowd. Catching my eye, Savage jerked his head slightly upward, signaling that he wanted to know Dingo's condition. When I flashed thumbs down, he shook his head slowly and lowered his eyes.

"They're coming, clear a path, here come the medics," Raymond Nelson announced. A moment later two other Emergency Medical Service attendants appeared with a stretcher and asked Iris and Reverend Robeson to move aside.

Clinging to her dying son, Iris motioned them away with her free hand, raising her index finger to indicate she wanted another minute with her son. Reverend Robeson's hands were clasped in prayer. Through his own tears, Raymond Nelson shot several photographs of the tragic vigil before he could no longer bring himself to photograph Iris's and the minister's private agony.

Jill and I kept a respectful distance, but at one point Dingo looked toward us and seemed to smile through his pain and shock.

The paramedics, fearing they would be blamed if they did not get the boy to the hospital in time, were becoming impatient. "Somebody done a job on him," one of them whispered to his partner. But before either could say another word, Dingo whispered something to his mother and Reverend Robeson, then lay perfectly still.

214

Iris shook her son, gently at first, then with increasing force. Then she let out a loud, mournful scream, a scream that seemed to be as much a lament for herself as for her dead son. It took several seconds before Officer Buckholtz could persuade her to let the paramedics place Dingo's body in the ambulance, and he succeeded only because he promised she could go with them.

We watched the paramedics turn Dingo's lifeless body on his back. Jill almost fainted at the sight of the knife wounds, which had left his "I Luv New York" T-shirt in shreds. Before the paramedics covered him with a blanket I noticed his cowlick, as predominant and as unruly as ever, and it reminded me of the first time I had seen him, not more than a couple of months earlier.

The policemen helped Iris and Reverend Robeson into the back of the ambulance. When I learned it was on its way to Bellevue I told the minister that Jill and I would hail a taxi and be there shortly.

The ambulance pulled slowly away from the crowded curb, its flashing orange lights clearing a path as it moved up the Avenue of the Americas. I spotted Irwin Haines, who also was in a state of shock, and told him not to expect me back that day. Only then did I realize that Motion and Che had also been taken away.

Dingo's blood was not yet dry on the plaza floor but already life was returning to normal, or to what passed for normal in and around Times Square. The drug dealers were biding their time waiting for the cops to leave, some of the men with squeegees had converged on the cars stopped in traffic, and several three-card monte games were in progress down the street, far enough away from the cops for the dealers to get a running start.

"You tried," Jill said, her voice choked with tears, as she slipped her arm through mine.

I nodded, blinking to hold back my own tears. "*We* tried," I replied, signaling to several cabs that sped by without slowing. "But we tried too late. You have to get them the minute they hit the street."

"Or better yet," she added, "you have to prevent them from ever landing on the street, or from being sentenced to those . . . welfare hotels." Again she broke into tears, and I was powerless to comfort her beyond putting my arm around her shoulder and hugging her.

I went through the motions of flagging down a cab, trying to ignore my aching body and especially my aching collarbone. All I could think of was Dingo stretched out on that bloodstained floor, a victim of "doggers" who were far more numerous and much more vicious than those in Australia.

Two more taxis rattled by before an empty Checker pulled up. Jill hopped in first and I followed, locking the door just before a panhandler began yanking on the handle. Unable to open the door he kicked angrily at the fender and shouted at us as we pulled away, but I was too grief-stricken to understand what he was yelling.

"Where to?" the driver asked in heavily accented English.

I told him Bellevue, but then immediately corrected myself. "First drive us to the Crossroads of the World," I said.

Jill looked at me with a puzzled expression, wondering why I was being cryptic at this moment and with a taxi driver who almost certainly would have no idea what I was talking about. Sure enough, after lurching the cab to a halt for a light at Forty-fourth Street, the driver again asked our destination.

"The Crossroads of the World," I said, again without elaboration.

"The Great White Way," Jill chimed in, signifying that now she understood.

"Where's that?" he asked, pronouncing it, "Vere's dot."

As heartbroken as I was, I remembered that the Harvard Club and the Bar Association building were just up the street, in front of each of which stood those saplings that were struggling for maturity. I made a wish that the iron bars surrounding them would continue providing the protection necessary in this neighborhood to sustain life—protection that was vital not only for little-leaf linden trees but for Leonardo "Dingo" Ruiz, Noah Robeson, Maria, and thousands of unfortunate children like them.

Just as the light changed I told the bewildered driver, "Forget it, take us directly to Bellevue."

His face broke into a relaxed smile and the cab shot forward, turning east on Forty-fourth and sending a jay-walker scrambling for safety. This time the driver did not need to ask directions. This time he was headed for an address with which he was well familiar.